"I couldn't wai[...]r. I utterly love her company. [...] well educated! More, more, m[...]

Praise for *Miss Blaine's Prefect and the Golden Samovar*:

"A delightful addition to the ranks of comic crime, mixing sharp observation with a lightness of touch." LAURA WILSON, *Guardian*

"A hefty dose of Jane Austen stylings and Stella Gibbons satirical wit." *The Scotsman*

"Every bit as light-hearted, level-headed, inventive, hilarious, and altogether enchanting as its heroine, who richly deserves another jaunt through time and space." *Kirkus*, STARRED REVIEW

"Marvellous… [a] laugh-out-loud farce… Readers will appreciate the skill with which Wojtas mirrors Spark's style." *Publishers Weekly*, STARRED REVIEW

"I loved this book. Shona is a unique sleuth whose mission made for most entertaining reading." ALEX GRAY

"Knowing, original and very funny." SIMON BRETT

"A carefully and delightfully constructed romp in the tradition of Gogol and of Wodehouse." NORTHWORDS NOW

"Anna Karenina written by P.G. Wodehouse." LINDA CRACKNELL

"A thrilling and fast-paced tale … written with verve, lightness of touch and joie de vivre … unadulterated fun." ALISTAIR BRAID-WOOD, SCOTS WHAY HAE

"The crème de la crème of crime fiction debuts." ALLAN GUTHRIE

"Clever, witty, and brain-tickling." RAVEN CRIME READS

"Laugh-out-loud funny and a real charmer of a book." LIVE AND DEADLY

Also by Olga Wojtas:

Miss Blaine's Prefect and the Golden Samovar

MISS BLAINE'S PREFECT
and the

Vampire Menace

Olga Wojtas

CONTRABAND ◖

Published by Contraband
An imprint of Saraband,
Digital World Centre, 1 Lowry Plaza
The Quays, Salford, M50 3UB

and

Suite 202, 98 Woodlands Road
Glasgow, G3 6HB
www.saraband.net

ISBN: 9781912235506
ISBNe: 9781912235513

10 9 8 7 6 5 4 3 2 1

Printed and bound in Great Britain by Clays Ltd, Elcograf S.p.A

For Lesley

One

I was in the dark, literally and metaphorically. What would happen if I moved? I might plunge to my doom or step in something unsavoury. A risk not worth taking. I stood stock-still, pretty difficult considering I was still suffering the severe abdominal pain that is a side effect of time travel.

It was pitch-black and there wasn't a breath of air. I must be inside. But inside what? The belly of a whale? An Ethiopian underground church? A salt mine?

In the distance I could make out a faint, metallic sound, like the dragging of heavy chains, and keys turning in padlocks. I inadvertently shifted in that direction: a serious mistake. My lower calf hit something and I toppled backwards.

I fell into some sort of a receptacle. It felt very snug. Too snug. I was stuck fast. My arms were jammed down by my sides, but I could wiggle my hands. Gingerly, I began a fingertip search of my surroundings.

I was encased in wood. The sides were some eighteen inches high. It felt as though there were pieces of earth and gravel at the edges. With difficulty, and a lot of breathing exercises, I eased them up and out.

My stomach was still sore, and my head ached as though there was a tight band across my forehead. I reached up to massage it and discovered there was a tight band across my forehead. I was wearing a head torch. I definitely hadn't been wearing a head torch a moment ago. In Morningside Library.

With a struggle, I managed to wriggle my shoulders free, lean my elbows on the wooden sides of whatever I was in, and propel myself semi-upright. I switched on the head torch and almost fell back into the container as light burst all around me, and I saw myself reflected hundreds, thousands of times, to infinity and beyond.

It was a hall of mirrors. No, it was *the* Hall of Mirrors. In the Palace of Versailles. Squinting and blinking, I recognised the seventeen arches, each containing twenty-one mirrors, separated by marble columns, and gloriously gilded.

But something was wrong. The endless reflections meant the mirrors were being mirrored, rather than facing a wall of windows. And either the Hall of Mirrors had shrunk, or I had grown. I'd always envied Alice in Wonderland with her "Eat Me" cake that made her bigger. Just the thing to intimidate Heriot's boys. But I hadn't eaten a cake, or even a Bourbon biscuit.

I put my hands on the rough edges of the wooden container and eased myself out, my eyes still adjusting to the head torch's reflected brilliance. But I could see now it definitely wasn't Versailles. I was in a large windowless hall, its two longer walls replicating the palace's mirrors. Hanging from the ceiling were chandeliers holding pristine beeswax candles. At the far end was a wooden stage, with stacks of wooden folding chairs leaning against it. The wall at the back of the stage was disappointingly plain, without a scrap of gilt or glass. Its only ornament was a large shield with a series of black upside-down Vs on a grey background.

There was an upright piano by the steps up to the stage. I went over to check it out, and found it was made by the distinguished French company Érard – not top-grade but pretty good. I was about to play a few notes but stopped. I wasn't here to enjoy myself, and there would be time for the school song on the successful completion of my mission.

That mission might not yet be clear, but success was essential. My recent encounter with Marcia Blaine, the eponymous founder of my alma mater, the Marcia Blaine School for Girls, had been extremely unpleasant and I had to succeed, both for the honour of the school and to restore my own credibility.

The sight of the mirrored hall made me forget the container I had recently vacated. Now, as I walked to the other end of the room – another drearily plain wall punctuated by a large wooden door – I had a clear view of it. It was a coffin. A coffin with a note in it. I lifted out the piece of paper and read the few words written on it in French: *"Souviens-toi, tu dois mourir."*

In my head, the English was snappier: "Remember you must die."

I wondered if the note qualified as a tautology. After all, there's nothing like a coffin for reminding you that you must die. I ran my hand over the rest of the base but there were no other clues, apart from the small bits of earth. I decided to investigate further, licking my finger, pressing it on the earth, and licking it again. It tasted quite Scottish – like the mineral gleys you find all over the country. This surprised me, since the note, and the make of piano, not to mention the Hall of Mirrors, pointed to somewhere Francophone. But French isn't exactly unknown in Scotland, ever since we joined forces in 1295 to resist the ruthless expansionism of the Auld Enemy.

Perhaps I would get a clue as to where and when I was if I found out what I was wearing.

I walked up to one of the mirrors. My head was obliterated by the reflection, but I could see a russet-coloured two-piece suit: a close-fitting jacket nipped in at the waist, over a high-necked frilled and pleated white blouse, and a long tulip-bell skirt that just skimmed my ankles. I stuck out my foot and was relieved to see that I still had on my trusty Doc Martens. You never know what you're going to meet on a mission, and sturdy, comfortable footwear is essential.

My attention was caught by another noise away in the distance, like the howl of a wolf. I closed my eyes and listened. I could faintly hear voices. It was as though someone had left a radio on somewhere and it was broadcasting a play. The howling and the clanking must have been sound effects. But it was too indistinct to hear the dialogue and work out the language. By now, I had a sore head, a sore stomach and a slight tingling sensation in my extremities. I felt a brisk walk would do me good.

As I turned, I nearly tripped over something. The endless reflections from my head torch were so confusing that I had failed to see what was on the floor, lying beside the open coffin. A small suitcase, leather over a wooden frame, with brass caps on the corners. It was new, and the style suggested it dated from the late nineteenth century, when suitcases first came into fashion, superseding unwieldy travel trunks. There was a name stencilled on it: S. A. McMonagle. I was pretty sure it was mine, since I'm Shona Aurora McMonagle, and Miss Blaine assured me on a previous occasion that she would be responsible for the practicalities when I was sent on a mission.

I picked it up. It was heavy, but my weight-training stood me in good stead. You start losing muscle mass when you're in your thirties, up to five per cent each decade, unless you do regular resistance exercise.

I made my way down the mirrored hall to the double doors; there was a serious-looking lock, but they were just on a latch. I opened them and stepped outside into the fresh air. High mountains loomed over everything, craggy and oppressive. It must be either dawn or dusk, the sun newly set or about to rise, but I could get no sense of which, because the mountains blocked out the sun, wherever it might be. This definitely wasn't Scotland – these sharp peaks were well over the height of Ben Nevis.

I switched off the head torch and studied my immediate surroundings. I was looking down a slope on to an Alpine village, perched precariously on a high mountain valley. Half-timbered chalets with stone-built ground floors and white plastered walls were separated by narrow, roughly cobbled lanes. The ground floors were clearly storage areas, as wooden steps led to doors at the first-floor level. From my vantage point, I saw that most of the chalets had a sizeable back garden, practically a pasture.

I looked round at the building I had just left. It was only a single storey, built entirely of wood, but it was larger and more imposing than everything else round about. In fact, it seemed

4

even larger now than when I was inside, a sort of reverse Tardis. It didn't seem to have had any other rooms leading off the central hall as there were no other doors – or any windows. If they were round the back, that wasn't very practical, since the town hall backed on to, or rather into, a mixed coniferous forest that looked positively impenetrable.

A red, white and blue tricolour flag fluttered from the sharply slanting roof, and above the double doors was a carved sign that read *Mairie de Sans-Soleil*. The Town Hall of Sunless. A very unprepossessing name for a village. But perhaps that was just my own prejudice – I pride myself on my sunny disposition, which always inclines me to look on the bright side. And I was particularly delighted by this confirmation that I was in France, where I knew the locals would welcome a citizen from the other side of the Auld Alliance. Plus, my French is pretty nifty

Narrow stone steps led down the slope to the village. As I descended and made my way through the maze of lanes, the strong scent of pine from the forests around the valley gave way to the occasional whiff of something quite unpleasant. A smell of decay. But the chalets I passed were neat and well-maintained.

I found myself in the village square. In the middle was a stone plinth with the statue of a monk on it, his hands raised heavenwards: in one hand, a bottle, and in the other, what looked very like a truckle of cheese. He must be the village's venerated patron saint.

A road sign pointing down a lane in the opposite direction to the town hall read "Paris 562km". All of the buildings round the square seemed residential apart from one, smaller and shabbier than the others. Smoke filtered out of its chimney, and a dilapidated sign hung outside: *Chez Maman*.

Since I didn't know what part of France I was in, it wasn't clear whether I should call it a café or an estaminet. Better to use the Scottish name: a howff. The door was open – when I walked in, I discovered this was to get rid of the thick fug of smoke. The windows were covered in grime and looked as though they hadn't

5

been opened in decades.

I seemed to be spending my initial hours in Sans-Soleil adjusting my eyes to different light levels. The howff was tiny, just a few round tables and a scattering of old wooden chairs. But what concerned me more was the clientele. A group of men, all wearing dark three-piece suits, which seemed respectable enough, but in the murk their pale faces looked sinister. One man was surrounded by four others, and I sensed that he was about to get, as the Glaswegians so picturesquely put it, "a doing".

I believe violence is never the answer. There are other ways to deal with difficult situations. Take Morningside, for example. People shape up pretty fast when they find nobody in the fish queue nodding to them.

I quickly weighed up which of my martial arts skills would be best for taking on four potential assailants in an enclosed space, surrounded by glass bottles. But suddenly the man at the heart of the group shook himself free of their grasp and stepped forward to greet me, hand outstretched. He was young, probably late thirties. He had the look of a wide boy, and clearly fancied himself, but I had to concede he had a certain louche charm.

"A visitor to our little village! Let me welcome you – I am the mayor of Sans-Soleil." He shook my hand warmly, dodged round so that he was safely between me and the door, and gestured towards the others. "May I present some of our most distinguished citizens? Our judge and teacher and police officer and undertaker and cheesemonger."

All in one breath without a comma in sight. I peered into the darkness at the disgruntled group. "Sorry," I said in perfect French, "I can see only four gentlemen, not five."

"That's right," said the mayor. He gestured towards them again. "Our judge. Our teacher. Our police officer. Our undertaker and cheesemonger."

The switch from the absence of commas to the presence of full stops clarified the situation. The mayor hadn't said which was which, but even though none of them was wearing any sort of badge of office, it was obvious. I shook hands with the distinguished middle-aged man with the long beard. "Your Honour."

I moved on to the tall, severe-looking man with the bushy side whiskers. "Professor."

I greeted the young, muscular, moustachioed man with the piercing stare. "Officer."

And finally, the chubby, florid young man who was clearly more cheesemonger than undertaker. "Sir."

They looked puzzled. "I'm the judge," said the chubby, florid young man.

"I'm the teacher," said the young, muscular, moustachioed man with the piercing stare.

"I'm the police officer," said the tall, severe-looking man with the bushy side whiskers.

"And I'm the undertaker and cheesemonger," said the distinguished middle-aged man with the long beard.

So I had to go through it all again, "Your Honour", "Professor", "Officer", "Sir".

"And you are?" asked the mayor.

I thought of doing that bit in *Educating Rita*, where Michael Caine says to Julie Walters, "And you are?" and she says, "Am I what?", but I realised there was little chance they would have seen it, so I just said, "Madame McMonagle".

"What a very strange name," said the middle-aged, distinguished undertaker and cheesemonger.

This irked me. We East Coast McMonagles are very proud of the French root of our name, *mon aigle*, my eagle, which goes back to the earliest days of the Auld Alliance.

"Say again?" said the chubby, florid young judge.

Our name might have a French root, but it's been Scotticised, and I wasn't going to reFrancophone it.

"Madame McMonagle," I repeated.

He shook his head. I was going to have to break it down for them.

"Anyone know about art?" I asked, looking at the muscular,

moustachioed teacher. He gave a Gallic shrug, which I always find a wee bit irritating.

"I know a bit," said the tall, bewhiskered police officer.

"OK," I said, "what do you call a small model of a sculpture?"

"Is it a maquette?" he asked.

"Yes, very good. Now just say the first syllable."

"Maque," he said.

I took a slight gamble on my next question, but a calculated one. I ran into a bit of difficulty on my previous mission when I wasn't entirely clear what date it was. I hadn't yet found out the date here, but I knew the person I was thinking of had been born long before the invention of the suitcase.

"Now, an Impressionist painter–"

"Renoir!" shouted out the muscular, moustachioed teacher.

I gave him the look I used as a prefect when the second years were playing up. "I haven't finished yet," I said. "An Impressionist painter–"

"Cézanne!" said the middle-aged, distinguished undertaker and cheesemonger.

"No, he's Post-Impressionist. Will you all wait until I've finished the question? I'm looking for a founder of the Impressionist movement, very keen on haystacks."

There was a long silence. Then the mayor said hesitantly, "Monet?"

"Exactly. So, Maque-Monet. And now, last question: what's the word for an animal's face?"

Since we were talking in French, they didn't have to ponder words like "snout" or "muzzle".

"*Gueule*," they all chorused.

"Put them together, and what have you got?"

"Maque. Monet. Gueule," they all said.

"That's my name. Don't wear it out."

"But please, do sit down, madame," said the mayor, carefully not wearing out my name, although you could see him savouring it in his head: *Madame Maque. Monet. Gueule.*

"Perhaps something to drink?"

"That would be lovely. A wee cup of tea."

An ancient cracked voice came from the corner. "Tea? What sort of an establishment do you think this is?"

I looked over, and now that my eyes were getting accustomed to the howff's gloom, I could see that there was a bar at the back and behind it was a withered crone, her head just visible above the wooden counter. Her face looked very white against the blackness of her surroundings. She had been smoking a pipe, which she was now jabbing in my direction. This was presumably Maman, chez whom we were, and I didn't much like the look of her.

"You Parisians with your fancy names and your fancy ways!" she went on, her wrinkled face wrinkling even more in disgust. I couldn't help beaming; I was delighted to be mistaken for a Parisian.

"You can have beer, or red wine, or absinthe, or cognac," she snapped.

I would never drink on a mission.

"Don't you have anything else?" I asked and a definite frisson went through the assembled gathering.

"No," growled the crone. "Nothing else."

"Oh, come now," said the mayor. "There must be something else you can offer our visitor?"

The undertaker and cheesemonger took a step towards him with a barely suppressed growl and the mayor backed away, raising his hands in an appeasing gesture.

"I meant coffee," he said. "Without milk, obviously."

It wasn't obvious at all. It was quite impertinent of him to decide unilaterally how I took my coffee.

"Tea is all I require," I said firmly. "I'm sure it won't be too much trouble for you to boil a kettle. Perhaps a croissant if you have one. And just to let you know, I'm not from Paris, I'm from Scotland."

"Where?" asked the muscular, moustachioed teacher, which made me doubt the quality of his teaching.

"Scotland," I said. "Linked to you for…" (I did a quick

9

calculation. Since they knew about Monet, this was clearly round about the late nineteenth century.) "...six hundred years." It was a pity I couldn't mention General de Gaulle describing it as the oldest alliance in the world, but they were already looking confused enough. "The bonds between our two nations are deep and unbreakable. You must remember Mary, Queen of Scots, who was also queen consort of France. And, of course, her mum, Marie de Guise, who was married to our King James V until he died of grief after Henry VIII unfairly beat us at the Battle of Solway Moss. Then Marie became Scotland's queen regent."

They exchanged bemused glances.

"Scotland," I persisted. "Big island just across the Channel from you, top half, Scotland."

The young judge's face cleared. He turned to the others. "Ah, she's English."

The crone spat on the floorboards, her pale wrinkled face wrinkling even more in disgust. "Foreigners."

I was so taken aback that, for a moment, I couldn't speak. Eventually I managed to gasp, "I'm not English! I'm your ally."

"But," said the middle-aged, distinguished undertaker and cheesemonger, "you said you came from the island across the Channel. That's England."

"That's Great Britain," I said. "Made up of Scotland, Wales and England, with the Kingdom of Great Britain created in 1707 by the Acts of Union between the parliaments of Scotland and England. Although our own Scottish parliament was reconvened in..."

I tailed off, in case they thought I was a lunatic. But they were already looking at me as though I was a lunatic, and I saw the tall, bewhiskered police officer mouth, "English!" at the others. I decided to leave it for the moment. You have to choose your battles, and sometimes it's just not worth it. The Battle of Solway Moss, for example.

The young, moustachioed teacher fixed me with his piercing stare. "Why are you here? Are you from the authorities?"

He started advancing on me in quite a threatening manner. I

was preparing to go into a Tae Kwon-Do spinning kick when the chubby judge caught him by the sleeve.

"How can she be from the authorities? She's a woman," he said.

"She's not got much of a figure," said the teacher. "She might be a man pretending to be a woman."

I really didn't know which to tackle first, the sexism or the poor grasp of gender diversity. But before I could try to put them right, the middle-aged, distinguished undertaker and cheesemonger said, "Have you come to visit the English milord?"

I still didn't quite know what my mission was, but I was pretty sure it wasn't to visit an English milord. If he had any problems that needed sorting out, they could be sorted out by the former pupil of an English school, rather than misusing the resources of Marcia Blaine.

I glanced around for inspiration, and my gaze fell on a newspaper on the neighbouring table, looking as fresh as if the English milord's butler had just ironed it for him. It must be that day's edition. My eyesight is excellent, so I was able to make out the date: 9 July 1900. Five days before Bastille Day. With the quick thinking for which we Blainers are known, I said, "I'm here for your celebrations on the fourteenth."

They started boggling again. "You know about our celebrations?" said the chubby, young judge.

They were conflating me with the English again, an insular people who know little of other cultures. Whereas we Scots are cosmopolitan and internationalist, as evidenced by the tens of millions of people of Scottish origin around the globe.

"Of course," I said. "I've travelled a considerable distance to get here specially."

The young, muscular teacher frowned. "I never heard that the cart had been booked. How did you get here?"

That was a difficult one to answer. "I imagine cosmic strings and transversable wormholes had something to do with it" would have been true but unhelpful. I decided it was wiser to say, "I didn't book the cart. I made other arrangements."

The attractively louche mayor rubbed his hands in glee. "Of course!" he said. "Of course! It is scarcely surprising that cosmopolitan visitors make other arrangements to attend our celebrations. This proves how successful I have been in promoting our beloved Sans-Soleil. Would you not agree, gentlemen?"

The judge, the teacher, the police officer, and the undertaker and cheesemonger muttered a bit at this. There was some underlying tension that I didn't yet understand. If it was relevant to my mission, I would get to the bottom of it; if it wasn't, I would leave them to sort themselves out.

I realised suddenly that they had all gone quiet, to the extent that they were scarcely breathing. All five of them, the mayor included, were gazing at the doorway, their eyes saucer-like in their pale faces.

At last the muscular, moustachioed teacher sighed, "La Madeleine!"

Two

I turned to see a young woman silhouetted against the dusk outside.

The teacher presumably wouldn't make any non-PC criticisms of her figure, which was what one would describe as "hour-glass", with a tiny cinched-in waist. She wore a thin cotton dress that reached just below her calves, the backlight turning her into that image of Princess Diana, displaying her spectacularly long legs. The dress had a V-neck, and the gold crucifix she was wearing round her neck drew attention to her impressive décolletage. She wore a headscarf, but it was arranged in such a way that stray curls enhanced her fine bone structure. She obviously cared a lot about her appearance. She was, in short, the sort of woman I find it a challenge to like on sight.

She waited for her eyes to adjust to the howff's darkness, and when they had, she marched straight up to the tall, bewhiskered police officer.

"Is there any news?" she demanded. Now that she was indoors, I could see that she had a deep tan compared to the pallor of the howff's other occupants.

The officer took a step back. "News?" he stuttered. "What sort of news?"

She looked as though she was about to punch him so he took another step back, colliding with the table and sending it clattering across the floorboards. I began to think very slightly better of her.

"You know what news," she snapped. "News of my husband, my beloved Sylvain. Have you found him?"

The middle-aged, distinguished undertaker and cheesemonger came up to her and took her gently by the arm.

"You know where he is," he said, his voice soothing. "He's dead and buried in the graveyard. You know that, Madeleine. You were at the funeral."

Impatiently, she shook her arm free. "Oh yes, I was at the funeral. But my husband wasn't, since he's not dead."

"I can assure you he is," said the undertaker and cheesemonger. "You know why we couldn't let you see the body – it would have been too dreadful for you. But he is in his grave."

"He is not dead," said Madeleine distinctly. "You fools! Don't talk to me about bodies and graves. If he were dead, I would feel it here." She clasped her hands to her bosom in such a way as to give it quite a lot of uplift. There was another collective sigh from the men.

She jabbed a finger at the mayor. "It should be up to you, as a civil officer of the state and overseer of the local constabulary, to find out what has happened. But we all know you're so obsessed with the celebrations that you can't think of anything else." She turned back to the policeman, who was trying to hide behind the judge. "So, it has to be up to you, as an officer of the law, temporary replacement for my husband, who is not dead, to find him. I'm sure these other gentlemen will be pleased to help you."

They all looked at their feet and shuffled a bit. I was almost impressed, and thought, again, very slightly better of her. When I came in initially, the gang of four had definitely been intimidating the mayor, if not preparing to do him serious damage. And now they were being put in their place by what I thought of, from my fifty-something perspective, as a wee lassie.

The mayor stepped forward. "Madeleine, you're in the middle of the grieving process. It's a difficult time, we all understand that. You need something to occupy you. I have the very thing. Madame Maque-Monet-Gueule."

"What?" she said impatiently. "Maque-Monet-Gueule? What sort of a name is that?"

"Mine," I said. "Don't wear it out."

She turned and stared at me. It was a decidedly unfriendly stare, even worse than the teacher's piercing one. I stopped being

14

almost impressed and thinking very slightly better of her.

"Madame Maque is a distinguished English visitor who is here to participate in our celebrations," the mayor said.

"No, I'm not," I protested. "That is, yes, I'm here to participate in your celebrations, but I'm not English." Then I thought that made it sound as though I accepted that I was distinguished, which really wasn't for me to say.

While I was pondering whether or not to argue about that as well, the mayor went on, "We thought she was here to visit the English milord, but she isn't. Since she needs accommodation, obviously she should stay with you."

"No," I said, just as Madeleine said, "No."

At least we agreed on one thing. Two things. We didn't want to share accommodation, and we heartily disliked one another.

"I'll just stay in a *pension*," I said

"But there is no *pension* in Sans-Soleil," said the mayor. "Nobody ever comes here. Apart from you and the English milord."

"I came here," said Madeleine. "I came here to be with my beloved Sylvain."

"So you did," said the mayor equably. "And now, tragically, he's dead, and you're rattling around in your chalet all by yourself. What you need is a nice companion, like this English lady."

"I'm not–" I began, but Madeleine was already talking over my protest.

"The only companion I want is my life's companion, my beloved Sylvain. See to it." And with that, she stormed out and disappeared from sight.

"Newly widowed," said the mayor. "You have to make allowances. She'll love having you to stay."

The foursome seemed to be heading slowly towards him in quite a menacing way.

"Gentlemen! What will our English visitor think of you hanging around Chez Maman when you should be at work?" the mayor asked.

Nobody was paying attention when I said, "–not English." They had all stopped where they were and turned to look at the old crone behind the bar. Grumbling, she got down off her seat, her pipe still clamped between her jaws, and went over to the far wall. From a series of coat hooks, she retrieved a long black gown, a white jabot and a black cylindrical hat, which she gave to the judge; a wing collar and tie for the teacher; a dark blue cape and kepi for the police officer; and a long white apron covered in bloodstains for the undertaker and cheesemonger. I hadn't known that undertakers did post-mortems, but presumably in a small village you had to turn your hand to whatever was necessary.

"Sans-Soleil is ready for another day," said the mayor, taking a white sash out of his pocket, and draping it over his chest. "To our posts, gentlemen."

"I wonder if there will be anything of interest waiting for you in the town hall," sneered the young, moustachioed teacher, taking an unfiltered cigarette out of his pocket and lighting it.

"Wait until the day of our celebrations, and there will be something of interest for the whole village," said the mayor, sounding smug. "In the meantime, I shall escort our esteemed visitor to her new home."

He reached for my suitcase and had barely lifted it off the ground before he dropped it back down, wheezing.

I said, "Let me get it," and picked it up: the trick is to engage the lats and the abs. And of course, to keep up the strength training.

It was as well to be civil to everyone; so far, I had no idea who were the goodies and who were the baddies.

"Gentlemen," I said, nodding to the foursome who were now dressed in their work clothes. "Madame Maman." The crone, now back behind the bar, grunted and blew a smoke ring in my direction. I wasn't sure whether that was supposed to indicate cordiality or disdain, but it struck me that I'd never got my cup of tea.

The mayor and I went out of the howff into the street. He was talking about them starting work, which suggested that this was morning rather than evening. I thought back to my first glimpse of daylight when I stepped through the town hall's double doors, light so dim that I thought it must be dawn or dusk. A July morning should be bright and luminous, but the light was just as dim as it had been earlier.

"Do you never see the sun here?" I asked jocularly.

He gave me a bit of a strange look. "Of course not. That's why the village is called Sans-Soleil."

I studied my surroundings. I had been looking at the dark, pine-covered slopes before. Now I looked more closely, the sky above the sharp peaks was clear blue. There must be sunshine up there, but the topography of mountains encircling the high valley meant that the village was in constant shade. It wasn't surprising that people here were a bit gloomy and bad-tempered.

"That explains the design of your village shield," I said. "Those black upside-down Vs on a grey background. A very clever artistic representation."

He stopped. "You've been in the town hall? But the town hall is nowhere near the road into the village."

I stopped as well. I could scarcely say that was where I had arrived via time travel. And even though the door hadn't been locked, perhaps I shouldn't have been there. Having a coffin lying around was quite odd, and he might be trying to keep it private.

"I was in the vicinity of the town hall," I said. It's always wise to stick relatively close to the truth, especially as someone might have seen me. "I came up the Paris road into the village and had a wee wander round just to orientate myself. Since it's such a lovely day. Well, it's mild at any rate."

"But our village shield," he said. "How did you see that? It's inside the town hall."

"Your village shield is famous, didn't you know?" I said. "I saw it in…" I gave a faint shudder. "…the International Exhibition of Science, Art and Industry. In Glasgow. In 1888." He wasn't to know there was no way anyone from Edinburgh would go to an exhibition in Glasgow. "There was a competition for shields from around the world, and yours won third prize. Did you never get the prize money? Oh dear, I'm afraid that's Glasgow for you. Someone will have nicked it and gone off to buy electric soup."

"Electric soup?" he said. "I've heard there is electric street lighting in Paris, but I've never heard of electric soup."

"It's a Glasgow thing," I said. "You wouldn't understand. I certainly don't. Anyway, that's how I know all about your artistic shield. Is the original in the town hall? I must come in and see it some time."

"Of course," he said. He didn't seem alarmed by the prospect. "I've organised a grand concert for our celebrations, with a proper singer coming all the way from Paris. If that doesn't consolidate my position as mayor, I don't know what will."

"No indeed," I agreed, although I thought bringing in electric street lighting would be even more popular.

As we rounded a corner, I could see Madeleine at the far end of the street. She didn't so much walk as sashay, her hips undulating from side to side. Since she was wearing wooden sabots, this would have been impressive had I not decided to be unimpressed by her.

All along the street, pale men standing at their chalet doors peered after her lasciviously, while white-faced women clipped them round the ear. It was depressingly heteronormative.

"Footloose and fancy free, is she, now that she's a widow?" I asked, trying not to sound judgemental.

"Oh no," said the mayor. "She has no interest in anyone except her husband Sylvain. Despite the fact that he's dead."

I reflected that denial could be the first reaction to bereavement. It was obviously taking her time to accept her loss.

We continued down the street, past one of the narrow lanes where a woman was rubbing down a rickety two-wheeled cart. Her brawny physique suggested she did an impressive amount of resistance exercise. She stared at me.

"Who's this?" she called.

The mayor gestured towards me as though he was showing off a prize exhibit. "This is Madame Maque, an international visitor who has come here specially for our celebrations. Isn't that wonderful news? Sans-Soleil is now firmly on the map – we'll be inundated with visitors before you know it."

"How did she get here?" Cart Woman demanded.

The mayor's enthusiasm evaporated. "She made other arrangements," he mumbled.

"And how's that wonderful news, inundations of visitors who make other arrangements? As if things aren't already bad enough with you ruining my business." She smacked her hand against the side of the cart. "I might as well chop this thing up for firewood."

"Nonsense," said the mayor. "I'll be putting more work your way any moment. Things aren't entirely under my control just now."

"Well, get them under your control. You're the mayor, aren't you?"

"For the moment," said the mayor, his voice so low that Cart Woman didn't even hear him.

"And I hope there's no problem with the celebrations," she went on. "My girl's all excited about being in the choir, hasn't talked about anything else for weeks."

The mayor roused himself to give a feeble laugh. "I said these would be the best celebrations yet, didn't I? That's why Madame Maque is here. If you'll excuse us, we must get on."

He hustled me down some more streets until we reached a small chalet that had a more cheerful look than the others. Its door and window frames were painted blue and there were red geraniums on the windowsills.

The mayor led me up the stairs to the first floor and pushed open the front door, staying on the doorstep.

"Now then, Madeleine–" he said, and ducked as a plate came whizzing by him. It looked as though the widow had progressed from denial to anger. Instinctively, I raised the suitcase to protect myself, and the plate shattered against it.

"Madeleine, you'll have no crockery left at this rate," the mayor said, stepping over the threshold. "And without Sylvain's salary, I don't see how you're going to buy more."

Her shrug was quintessentially Gallic. "I'll buy it with the rent

I get from my new lodger."

The mayor beamed. "I knew you'd see sense. Right, I'll get off to work and let you two girls get better acquainted."

"I'm not a girl," I called after him as he headed down the stairs. "I mean, I'm cisgender," I explained to Madeleine who was eyeing me suspiciously. "But once someone's over eighteen, it's inappropriate to call them a girl. It's used by men to demean and infantilise, and we must call it out whenever it occurs." She didn't need to know I thought of her as a wee lassie. That was quite different.

"I have no idea what you're talking about," she said.

I hoped that by the end of my mission, I would have raised her consciousness sufficiently not to allow any man to call her a girl. But standing on the doorstep with smashed crockery round me wasn't the place to start. I stepped over the threshold into a small hallway and put down my case. If Miss Blaine's time-travelling rules and regulations remained the same, and I had no reason to think otherwise, I was allowed one calendar week to compete my mission.

"I'll be staying for a week," I said.

"Staying for a week?"

"At the most."

"At the most?"

"Perhaps less."

"Perhaps less?"

Madeleine repeating everything was really quite irritating. And then I remembered how I had been accused of doing exactly the same, very recently.

I was sitting at my computer in Morningside Library, checking the reservation requests, when a borrower appeared and said, "*Bonjour.*"

Having had the finest education in the world, I'm fluent in a great many foreign languages, and slip easily from one to another. I didn't even notice that I had been addressed in French, but simply responded automatically, "*Bonjour, Madame.*"

"*Que veut dire cette conduite?*"

Since my conduct is at all times exemplary, I merely asked, "*Conduite, Madame*?"

I looked up to see Miss Blaine glaring down at me, just as her marble statue glared down on everyone in the school assembly hall.

"*Tu es perroquet*?" she demanded. Being accused of being a parrot was bad enough, but "tu" is the word used to address children. Given that I was an adult, and wasn't related to the Founder, this was quite offensive. On the other hand, since Miss Blaine was at least two hundred years old, my being fifty-something no doubt qualified as childhood in her eyes.

However, I still didn't understand. "*Je ne comprends pas.*"

She waved a yellow-covered book in my face. "*Ce n'est que trop evident!*" she hissed. "*Tu ne comprends presque rien. Tu n'as pas vu ce… ce… bouquin qui vient de reparaître avec sa héroïne détestable? Il risque de réintroduire cette harpie à de nouvelles lectrices. C'est abominable.*"

It was very difficult to work out what she was on about. She was obviously completely fluent in French, but she had retained her thick Morningside accent, which made it tricky to follow. She was also agitated, one might even say enraged, which didn't help her comprehensibility. But I tried to piece it together. Why hadn't I seen some book that had a detestable heroine. I wondered what book it might be. Reading literature is very subjective: one person's detestable heroine is another person's role model. Anyway, Miss Blaine was worried that new readers would be introduced to this awful woman.

But before I could seek further clarification, she slammed the book down on the desk in front of me.

I can't say my blood froze, because blood only starts to freeze at minus two degrees Celsius and we like to keep the temperature in the library at twenty degrees Celsius, despite council cuts. But I did feel a distinct chill.

"Oh, lovely," said Dorothy as she passed. "Dame Muriel's wonderful book in the marvellous new Polygon edition, with all their colourful covers."

She leaned over confidentially to Miss Blaine. "I feel so privileged to work in Morningside Library. When Dame Muriel was a wee girl, she came in here twice a week. I really think we should celebrate that in some way. A plaque would be nice, don't you think? Shona, could you maybe draft a petition and we can collect signatures? We'd have hundreds in the blink of an eye. And in the meantime, we could get the Marcia Blaine pupils to put on a wee exhibition, just to show how grateful they are to Dame Muriel for writing *The Prime of Miss Jean Brodie* about their school."

Miss Blaine made a choking noise.

"Oh, sorry, here's me prattling on when you're wanting to take a book out," said Dorothy, taking the yellow-covered volume off my desk. "Do you want me to help you with that, dear? These machines are very confusing when we're that wee bit older, aren't they?"

There's a lot of dangerous things you can do in this world. Swim in shark-infested waters. Scale the Empire State Building without a safety harness. Visit Glasgow. But by far the most dangerous thing you can do is address Marcia Blaine as "dear". The Founder, her face puce, was staring at the ground, but if she turned her gaze on Dorothy, I was sure my colleague would be turned to stone.

I snatched back That Book. "Thank you, Dorothy, I'm already helping this lady."

Dorothy wandered off humming Rod McKuen's "Jean", no doubt thinking of plaques, exhibitions, kittens and rainbows.

"Miss Blaine," I said urgently, since the Founder looked as though she was about to tear apart the nearby shelves with her bare hands, "let me take you upstairs and get you a wee cup of tea. That's always good for shock."

She growled a bit but she followed me up to the small meeting room. I brought her the tea and some Bourbon biscuits as quickly as I could, but she had picked up That Book, which I had left on the table, and was riffling through it with an expression of revulsion.

"*Dame* Muriel, forsooth!" she exclaimed. "These pages are an offence to right-minded people. The mockery of the team spirit! Outrageous! We are as nothing without cooperation and competition." She flung it back down and glared at the cover, which read under the author's name, "Introduced by Alan Taylor".

"And who, pray, is this Mr Taylor who insists on introducing unwary readers to Mrs Spark's scribblings?"

"I believe he used to be a librarian," I said.

Miss Blaine looked heavenward. "I remember a time when librarianship was an honourable profession," she said.

She crunched her way through a Bourbon biscuit much as I imagined a tiger would crunch through human bone. "The name of my school is paraded throughout these pages. One can no longer rely on readers in these end times. Many will take it as fact, not fiction. And those who take it as fiction will see it as a *roman à clef.*"

She picked up another biscuit and studied me over the top of it.

"I wonder," she said, "which character the readers would think was based on *you.*"

I thought. Although I am now fifty-something, it would be likely, since I am a Former Pupil, that a reader would conflate me with one of the girls rather than a teacher, suggesting that I would be one of the so-called Brodie set. I had a number of characters to choose from: Monica Douglas, famous for her mathematical abilities; Eunice Gardiner, famous for her gymnastics and swimming prowess; Jenny Gray, who spoke beautifully and was a stalwart of the Dramatic Society.

"I believe," said Miss Blaine, "they would think you to be one of two."

I wondered which of Monica, Eunice and Jenny was to be jettisoned.

"First, Mary Macgregor, a character of the utmost stupidity who is always to blame."

I felt myself flinch, not least because I remembered that Mary Macgregor died by fire in Chapter Two.

"Or, and indeed more likely, Sandy Stranger, a character so repugnant that even the author detested her. A character who claims to be dependable, but who outrageously betrays the trust placed in her."

I was close to tears. "Miss Blaine," I whispered, "how can you say such a thing?"

"Because!" Her hand crashed down on the wretched yellow book.

"I'm so sorry!" I burst out. "I've been running a community choir – singing is very beneficial both for strengthening the immune system and reducing stress levels – and after a sell-out performance, we went out for a celebration. I had a wee half of shandy. I remember feeling very sleepy the next day, which must have been when..." I dropped my voice, "...that Book sneaked in. But you must know even Homer nods."

"I do," she snapped. "I think it shame when worthy Homer nods. And he nods off for only a couple of minutes – you, girl, are a positive Rip Van Winkle. You have one simple job to do – one! – to ensure that this flawed and outrageous narrative is not read. And yet I find it not only on the shelves but positively displayed. You surely cannot have failed to notice that 2018 was the centenary of Mrs Spark's birth."

I had noticed it, but I didn't dwell on it. The year 2018 was notable for a number of anniversaries: 1,175 years after King Kenneth MacAlpin united the Picts and the Scots; two hundred years after the first human blood transfusion; one hundred and fifty years after the first Trades Union Congress; a hundred years after women over thirty getting the vote, Stonehenge being donated to the nation, the death of Debussy, and the end of World War One.

Miss Blaine picked up another Bourbon and virtually swallowed it whole. Then she drained her teacup in a oner. She rose. "I am disappointed in you."

Her words cut me to the quick. I am a Blainer, I am the crème de la crème, and it is my duty to make the world a better place. Now, through the sin of omission, I had made it worse. At that moment, I vowed never to drink again.

The Founder moved towards the door.

"Please," I begged, "give me another chance. You won't regret it."

"You have been guilty of a gross dereliction of duty," she said, disappearing into the corridor. "Nevertheless…"

It was shortly after that that the abdominal pains began.

And now, here I was in fin de siècle France, having time travelled back more than a century, trying to sort out my accommodation with a very uncooperative young woman.

"If you have a room to rent, I should like to book it for a period of up to a week," I said slowly and distinctly.

"A week's rent is the minimum," she said.

"Are those your usual terms?" I asked.

"They are now. I've never let out a room before. And it's rent in advance."

"I'd like to see the room first."

We glared at each other for a while, and then she picked up my weighty suitcase as though it was a bag of marshmallows, leading the way up a narrow wooden staircase to a tiny room nestled under the chalet's sloping roof. It wasn't the Ritz, but it was perfectly adequate, with a single bed, dresser and chair. The small window had a view over dense forest and the ubiquitous mountains.

"I'll take it," I said.

She gave a sardonic smile. "Well, there's a surprise. Do I get the rent from you or the mayor?"

It struck me that Sans-Soleil would get a lot more visitors if people thought the mayor would pay for their accommodation. But I was on a mission, and I was sure Miss Blaine would be prepared to support the local economy.

"From me. Just give me a moment to unpack," I said and Madeleine went back downstairs.

I opened the suitcase. There was a small reticule with a purse in it. A long-skirted suit just like the one I was wearing, except in dark grey, and another frilly white blouse. Proper M&S underwear rather than anything Victorian, with an ordinary balcony bra, not the multiway ones I had been given to accommodate the revealing ballgowns on my previous mission.

Beneath the clothes were a few other things that would presumably also come in useful, although I couldn't immediately see how. I stowed them neatly in the dresser along with the underwear, and hung the spare suit and blouse over the chair.

As I smoothed down the clothes, I looked at my hands. My skin colour was midway between Madeleine's deep tan and the pallor of the other inhabitants of Sans-Soleil. I wondered whether she frequented a beauty salon or perhaps self-medicated. Spray tan wouldn't have been invented, but I knew that by the turn of the century, the Glasgow firm of Paterson & Sons had been producing Camp Coffee for over twenty years. I supposed you could have a bath in it and rub it in.

I picked up the reticule and went downstairs. Madeleine, her curly brown hair spectacularly wild now that she had taken off her headscarf, was busying herself in the small kitchen, preparing to peel vegetables. I held out my purse to her. "Just take whatever you think is suitable for a week's rent."

She opened it and gave a gasp. "Where did you get all this money?"

"From my employer," I said. Strictly speaking, Miss Blaine wasn't my employer, since I was working pro bono, albeit with expenses. But I felt that was the easiest way to put it.

Her lips tightened. "I see. Your employer must expect a lot of you." She rummaged in my purse and extracted a couple of coins.

"Are you sure that's right?" I asked.

"Are you accusing me of overcharging?" She held out her hand to show me what she had taken. "Don't you think this is reasonable for a respectable home?"

I judged her to be irritable but honest. "You misunderstand. I was worried you might be undercharging."

"Really?" Her tone was acid.

"Really. Apply some logic, please. If I thought you were on the take, I wouldn't have handed you my purse."

"You might have been trying to trap me."

"Believe me, if I was trying to trap you, I'd be much more

subtle than that."

"Really?"

"Really."

We stared at one another. She was the first to look away.

"I suppose you'd like something to drink?" she muttered.

"Yes, please. A cup of tea would be lovely."

"We have no tea. You can have coffee or water. Or cognac." The distaste in her tone at the last offering would have done credit to Miss Blaine.

"Thank you, no, I don't touch alcohol when I'm on a mission," I said with dignity.

"And what's your mission? To comfort the poor widow?"

I felt terrible. I had momentarily forgotten all about her being a widow, what with the undulating and the bosom and the irritability. She was obviously in a very volatile emotional state if she couldn't even accept that her husband was dead. She deserved to be treated with kindness and understanding, whatever she looked like.

"If there's any help I can give you, of course," I said.

"So, you'll be with me every moment of the day?"

This was awkward. "Well … if you want me around, I'll do my best. But I've got one or two things to do while I'm here."

I wasn't entirely sure what they were. A good start would be to find out who I was supposed to help. I really felt Miss Blaine should provide written instructions. But it had all happened so quickly that perhaps she didn't have time. One moment she was saying, "Nevertheless…" and the next I was suffering severe abdominal pain.

Madeleine looked a bit nonplussed at my answer, before becoming sardonic all over again. "I see. You go your way and I go mine, and then by a strange coincidence, we meet en route."

"I suppose it would be a strange coincidence if we went our separate ways and then met en route," I agreed. I was going to have to be really nice to her to make up for being cranky earlier.

"What can I get you to drink?" she repeated.

"Just a glass of water, please."

27

She poured me out a glass from a large jug. As she handed it over, her hand brushed against mine, and I thought I felt a mild tingling. Tingling was what alerted me to the subject of my mission. But I wasn't sure whether I had felt it or not. And I couldn't exactly say, "I think I tingled when our hands touched. Can we do it again?" because that could be misinterpreted.

Instead, I said, "Sorry, I've changed my mind. Could I have a coffee after all?"

She looked grumpy, but she got up and started to make it. I'm always a bit dubious about coffee. The studies have come up with conflicting results, some saying it prolongs your life, others saying it kills you, while a few insist it doesn't do anything at all. And the NHS website doesn't adjudicate. It just says: "Cohort studies can't show cause and effect, so aren't able to prove that drinking coffee decreases or increases likelihood of death. A randomised controlled trial where people are put into groups to either drink coffee or not drink coffee until they died would be needed to prove this, something that wouldn't be feasible." It sounds perfectly feasible to me. I'd be happy to volunteer.

Madeleine placed two bowls on the table for us to drink out of, before bringing over the jug of coffee. I picked up one of the bowls and tried to manoeuvre my hand so that it would touch hers. I was obviously behaving perfectly appropriately under the terms of my mission, but I could just imagine what the Royal High boys would have said about it. So juvenile.

I managed to jog her arm as she was pouring, and coffee splattered onto the wooden table. She gave a sigh and fetched a cloth.

"I'm terribly sorry," I said, fetching another cloth and making sure that as we cleaned the table, I made contact with her several times. There was definitely a slight tingle, but the tingle was definitely slight. She wasn't the person I was here to help, but she must be a link in some way. I would have to be on the alert the whole time to work out who it was.

The coffee was black.

"I wonder, could I have a drop of milk?" I asked.

Madeleine gave me exactly the same look that you would get in an Edinburgh chip shop if you asked for vinegar instead of brown sauce.

"No," she said. "I don't have any."

"Don't worry, this is fine," I said, although I didn't fancy it at all. She was observing me over the rim of the bowl.

"Was your husband a soldier?" she asked.

I found the question offensive, attempting to categorise me by a man's status. I was reminded of an appalling newspaper headline: "Schoolteacher's Wife Wins *Mastermind.*" We Blainers retain our own identity whatever our marital status.

"I'm not married," I said stiffly.

"Excuse me." There was something of an edge to her voice. "I should have realised you were someone who disregards convention. Was your lover a soldier?"

This definitely wasn't the sort of conversation one had in Morningside. And another thing… "What's with the 'was'?" I demanded.

She gestured towards my DMs.

"I presume he is dead since you are wearing his boots."

"These are my boots," I said. "Bought with my own money. Money I earned through gainful employment."

She looked at my DMs again. "You have very big feet."

"Better than having a big mouth" came to mind, but I contented myself with saying, "Where I come from, they're very fashionable." The make is now sixty years old, slightly older than myself, born of the happy union between the Northamptonshire boot-making company Griggs and Dr Klaus Märtens, whose broken foot inspired him to create an air-cushioned sole. DMs started off as workwear, but thanks to Pete Townshend, music festivals and female customisation, they have been transformed, as the brand itself proclaims, into creations for authentic individuals with a sense of self-expression.

"You must find us very unsophisticated here," she said, smoothing down her cotton frock in such a way as to emphasise her curves. "I suppose your hat is the latest thing."

"I'm not wearing a…" I began, putting my hand up to my head and discovering I was still wearing the head torch, "…hat." I continued, "We call this a fascinator."

I took it off and laid it on the table.

She sniffed. "And you're wearing a bustle. Nobody here in the country does that."

"I'm not wearing a bustle," I said with much greater confidence.

She shot me a sceptical look.

I stood up and turned round. "See?"

"Yes. I see your bustle."

"I'm not wearing a bustle," I repeated. "These are my glutes."

She looked blank.

"Gluteus maximus. The strongest muscle in the body. The muscle that lets us walk upright. Crucial for running, jumping, climbing. I do lunges, stretches and barbell exercises to keep it in shape."

She looked almost admiring. "And you save yourself the cost of a bustle."

We seemed to be bonding.

"And can I ask you something?" I said.

Shrug.

I wanted to find out how natural that tan was. "Do you use Fake Bake?"

"How dare you!" she flared. "I bake everything from scratch – baguettes, pain de campagne, brioches, beignets, croissants. But I shouldn't be surprised by your question, since I know you English can't cook."

"I'm not English," I said. "I can prove it. The English say plate. We say ashet, from assiette. The English say cup. We say tassie, from tasse. And I can cook. My sauce Béarnaise is the best in Morningside."

"What does your Morningside know of sauce Béarnaise?" she sneered.

"It knows of *my* sauce Béarnaise, which is delicious. Perhaps it's time Sans-Soleil got to know it as well. Have you got any chervil?"

She gave a gasp of outrage. "You think I'm going to let you use my kitchen?"

"Oh, right, you're going to cook for me all the time I'm staying with you? That's very kind. I'll be glad to give you my opinion of your sauce Béarnaise."

I thought for a moment she was going to pick up the heaviest saucepan available and whack me over the head with it. But the fight seemed to go out of her, just like that.

"Of course, you're welcome to share my meals," she said.

I preferred her feisty.

She even rejected my offer to wash up the coffee bowls, claiming that my rent covered all that.

"Thanks," I said, "but you can't do everything. I'll wash up after tea."

"I told you, there is no tea," she said.

Foreigners can be almost as slow as the English at understanding what one says. "The evening meal," I explained. "In the meantime, if you can manage without me, I'll go for a wee walk and have a look round."

Madeleine's eyes narrowed. "You're leaving?"

"Not for long," I said. "Any messages you want brought back?"

"Who from?" she snapped. "Your friend the mayor? Tell him that anything he has to say to me, he can say to my face. No, tell him I don't want to hear from him at all unless it's to say my Sylvain is returning."

"Sorry," I said. "My meaning was lost in translation. I mean is there any shopping I can get for you? Since you haven't got any milk, I could pick up a pint or two. Anything else? Butter, cheese?"

She laughed out loud, but it wasn't the sort of laugh that suggests amusement. "You can get me all these things?"

"Of course," I said. Even though I was paying rent, I was sure my expenses would allow a certain amount of foodstuffs under the heading of subsistence. "Just tell me where I can get them."

"I don't think I need to tell you anything."

I was pleased that she recognised I had enough nous to work things out without instructions. I went out and realised the first thing I should do was gather up all the bits of smashed crockery on the doorstep. I put them in a neat pile on the top landing and went down to street level step by step, making sure I got it all. When I reached the bottom, I found a small girl who was apparently waiting for me.

"May I help you?" I asked.

She gave a little bob. "Not you, madame. There was no room for me to get past you on the stairs. I'm here for the cow."

"There's no call for that sort of language," I said severely. "I know she's very bad-tempered, but you have to allow for the emotional turmoil. And in any case, you should show proper respect to your elders."

But even before I had finished, the child had scampered past me up the steps to tap on the door.

Madeleine opened it. "Oh no, you're here to milk the cow," she sighed. "I've had a dreadful morning – I haven't even let the poor beast out. Come in, come in."

She suddenly caught sight of me. "Are you going for a walk, or do you prefer eavesdropping?"

I added the final couple of plate shards to my collection and clumped up the wooden stairs to add them to the pile at the doorstep.

"Yours, I believe," I said. "Now I can go for my walk."

I set off, trying to work out how she didn't have any milk when she had a cow. She might be lactose intolerant. That could explain why she had reacted so peculiarly when I suggested getting cheese and butter. I had been insensitive. Perhaps she was vegan – but no, if she was, she would have told me already.

Then I thought, you need milk to make beignets, and butter for brioches, croissants and sauce Béarnaise. Perhaps she had only just developed her intolerance, and that was why she had to get someone else to milk the cow. With someone else, I would simply ask, but my most innocuous questions made Madeleine snappier than an alligator with temporomandibular disorder.

But pondering the enigma that was Madeleine wasn't helping

me to investigate my new surroundings. Time to get to work. I've perfected the art of being unobtrusive. I don't mean I can be the Invisible Woman, but in ordinary situations, when I'm not the focus of attention, I can merge into the background.

That's what I did now, as I set off round Sans-Soleil. The village was full of activity, people shopping, gossiping, mending things, playing boules. As I watched, a small boy who looked slightly older than the moppet visiting Madeleine trudged up the stairs to a chalet. He wore an ill-fitting jacket over too-short trousers, and unlaced boots on the wrong feet. He hesitated for a moment before knocking on the door.

The householder opened it and began berating the child for being late.

"And take those filthy boots off!"

"But … the field?" the small boy ventured.

"Are you stupid? You put them on again before going into the field. But I'm not having you tramping mud through my nice clean house."

I crossed the road and edged round the side of the chalet to find the child being shoved out of the back door into the pasture, where a cow was placidly grazing. I could easily see what was happening through the fencing. The small boy, who had now acquired a bucket and three-legged stool, sat down beside the cow and began milking it. He seemed very nervous, and he was very tiny compared to the cow, but he was doing pretty well. Until the cow took a step forward to reach a particularly succulent bit of grass and the bucket went flying.

The householder raced out to grab the unfortunate child.

"You come with me right now and explain to the policeman what you did!" she yelled. "I'm not getting blamed for this."

"I didn't do anything!" the small boy wailed. "It was your cow's fault."

"None of your cheek," snapped the householder, dragging the child back through the chalet, boots and all. I edged round to the front and followed them up the street at a discreet distance.

The tall, severe-looking man with the bushy side whiskers, wearing his kepi and dark-blue cape, was progressing majestically along, studying each chalet carefully as he went. The householder bustled up to him, still grimly clutching the small boy.

"Officer, this wretched child spilled all the milk – it was nothing to do with me."

The policeman looked down at the boy. "Is this true?"

The boy went even paler than the usual Sans-Soleil skin tone. "No," he stammered. "The cow knocked the bucket over while I was milking her."

"He was in charge of the cow. It's his fault," said the house-keeper. "And he tramped mud all through my nice clean house."

"The law does not concern itself with the latter," said the policeman. "But as far as losing the milk is concerned, such care-lessness cannot go unpunished. Since this boy has jeopardised our celebrations, he will not be permitted to attend them."

The child slumped in abject misery.

"And you, madame, think yourself lucky that I'm not holding you responsible for letting such an incompetent lad near your cow," the policeman said to the householder. "I trust you will be more circumspect in future."

For an instant, the householder looked as though she was inclined to argue. Then she let go of the small boy and flounced back to her chalet.

The child stood there, quivering.

"Stop wasting time," snapped the policeman. "Be off with you before I arrest you for loitering."

The child fled, but from my vantage point, I saw that he had just run round the corner, and was huddled against the wall, trying not to cry. I wasn't impressed by the policeman's behaviour. He was being mean to the poor wee scone in a thoroughly unjustified way. Police cannot operate properly in a democracy without the consent of the citizens, and being unjustifiably mean to them is no way to keep them onside.

As the policeman headed off in the opposite direction, I

unobtrusively crossed the road and went over to the wee scone.

"Cheer up," I said. "No point in crying over spilled milk."

He quickly rubbed his eyes with the heel of his hand and stood up straight.

"Sorry, madame."

"You've got nothing apologise for," I said.

"Sorry, madame."

I tried a conversational gambit that wouldn't lead to an apology. "How old are you?"

"Seven, madame."

That was peculiar. He didn't look like a truant, and yet...

"Why aren't you in school?" I asked.

"This is our practical biology lesson, madame, milking cows." Tears welled up in his eyes once more. "But I'm not very good at it."

"Never mind, we can't be good at everything," I said, although I reflected that in my own case, that wasn't strictly true. "Just do your best, and try to remember what you've been taught about milking cows."

He bit his lip. "We haven't been taught anything about milking cows, madame. We were just told to get on with it."

"Come now," I said. "Even if this is your first hands-on experience, you must have had theoretical training through lectures, diagrams or scale models."

He shook his head.

I was appalled. Having had the finest education in the world, I know the importance of properly prepared lessons. A teacher must have a clear idea of the aims of a course, and the desired learning outcomes. Sending a child off to do something in a state of ignorance isn't education, it's criminal negligence. Almost as bad as the time the council sent us off on that team-building exercise, which involved building not only teams but also pontoons. My team was fine, because I made sure the buoyancy containers couldn't float apart. But Dorothy's team nearly drowned.

"The police officer can't know you've been sent out with no training," I mused aloud.

"Yes, madame, he does," the wee scone assured me. "He's told us to get on with it as well. So has the judge. And, of course, the cheesemonger and undertaker."

There was no "of course" about it. This was getting more outrageous by the moment. The teacher clearly wasn't carrying out his duties correctly, but there's nothing worse than interference in the school system from non-educationists.

"Please, madame," he pleaded, "the policeman told me to stop wasting time. May I go?"

"You may go in a moment," I said. "Just two things. First, next time you try to milk a cow, make sure she's secured in some way so that she can't wander off. And second..." I fished in my reticule and found a bulging paper bag, which I handed over, "... these should help improve matters."

The wee boy peeped into the bag. His eyes widened. "Are these...?"

"Yes," I said. "Violettes de Toulouse. Crystallised flowers, made with real violets and a great deal of sugar. Remember to brush your teeth properly afterwards."

"Thank you, madame!" He sped off with a beaming smile.

"And thank you, Miss Blaine," I murmured. The Founder was a marvel at providing what was needed at just the right time. I only wished she would be specific about what my mission was. I wondered why I had been selected for this particular one. My language skills were a plus, and my acumen, but that meant I was suitable for almost any mission. How many missionaries did she have? On my debut time-travelling outing, she had implied that this was a new venture. Perhaps I was the Founder's founder member.

But my musings wouldn't buy the bairn a new pair of breeks. Like the wee scone, I must stop wasting time. I continued on my peregrination through the village.

A hanging shingle at the end of a street announced the site of the cheese shop. I made my way to it. Even if Madeleine was lactose intolerant, I could do with some cheese and butter for myself, not to mention some milk for the coffee.

But when I reached the shop, it was closed. I peered in through the large window, which obviously hadn't been cleaned for ages. The shelves were completely empty apart from a few scrapings of rind. The counter was covered in dust. This was disappointing.

I walked on and turned left. Now I was in the rue de la Justice, a short street largely taken up by a large building that turned out to be the court. It was wooden, but rather than being in the style of an Alpine chalet, it was a ligneous Greek temple. Grand columns in front of the entrance supported a triangular pediment carved with the image of the goddess of justice, blindfolded to show impartiality, holding scales to weigh the merits of the case, and waving a sword to warn you that if you lost, you were in real trouble.

I walked up the steps to find the huge doors firmly closed with absolutely no sign of life inside. I shouldn't be surprised – Sans-Soleil was obviously calm and crime free. The judge must have virtually nothing to do, apart from the occasional boundary dispute over the fencing-off of cows. I could understand why he spent most of his time in the howff.

Beyond the rue de la Justice, I found the rue des Écoles, and there was the school, its playground and classrooms empty. But the young, muscular teacher was no longer in the howff with his judicial friend. He was sitting on the playground wall, his tie askew under the wing collar. He could have passed for a member of the PE staff had he not been puffing on a cigarette.

He gave me a piercing stare.

"Hello," I said. "I believe the pupils are out on a practical biology lesson."

"Are you from the inspectorate?" he demanded.

"No, I'm from Scotland," I said, hoping that this fact would sink in through repetition. It was odd, the way he always seemed to think I was here to check up on things. "But I'd be very interested to know how you've set the benchmark in terms of assessing how well the course is meeting its purpose."

"You *are* from the inspectorate," he snarled.

"I'm not," I said. "I'm simply interested in pedagogy. In fact, while I'm here, how do you feel about me taking a class? I'm TEFL-qualified – that's Teaching English as a Foreign Language."

He gave a mocking grin as though he had found me out. "I thought you said you weren't English."

"I'm not English, but I speak English."

"Why don't you speak Scotlandish?"

"Because there's no such language of that name," I burst out and his grin became even more mocking. I thought I heard him say, "And no such country," but I wasn't entirely sure, so I had to let it pass.

"Can we fix a time for me to come in and take a lesson with the kids?" I asked.

That Gallic shrug. "I don't think so. Their timetable's already full."

I surveyed the empty playground and school. "They're not even here."

"They're working," he snapped. "And that's what they'll continue to do while I'm in charge."

No wonder he was worried about the school inspectors. He had completely skewed the curriculum. Work experience is all very well, but this was ridiculous.

"Of course one appreciates the need for good-quality vocational education for the type of children who would benefit from it, but one really mustn't lose sight of the beauty of academic success, must one?" I said. "If there are some pupils you genuinely feel are not suited to the classroom environment, then perhaps your strategy is appropriate, but I would welcome the opportunity to help the rest develop the sort of skills that have stood me in good stead."

His piercing stare became more piercing. "What sort of skills?"

I could offer to prepare a lesson plan for him to review, but I had a feeling he was so obsessed with on-the-job training that he would disapprove of my more scholarly approach. I considered explaining that the word "education" came from Latin, "to lead out", and that I would be drawing out each pupil's intrinsic abilities. But I doubted he would understand my aim of achieving this through progressive, interactive techniques, since the approach to education in the 1900s was quite draconian.

He might also be suspicious of a passing stranger seeking access to the school: it was important to reassure him.

"I should explain that the police know all about me," I said. "Not here, of course, but back home."

His eyes flickered. "They do?"

"Oh yes. Disclosure Scotland is most insistent on carrying out criminal record checks. So, in light of that, can I take it you're fine with me coming in for an hour or so?"

"I told you. The pupils are currently very busy," he muttered.

"I'm sure you can find space somewhere in the timetable," I said encouragingly. "I'll check back with you later."

He gave a non-committal grunt. He was young, and this was probably his first teaching post; it wasn't surprising that he might feel professionally threatened.

And then his attention shifted. "No, no, no, you've overfilled it again," he called to a wee girl who was staggering along with a bucket almost as big as herself. "Oh, here, I'll take it – you get on with the next one."

He rushed up to the child and grabbed the bucket. The next thing, there was more spilled milk, but the teacher strode off with what remained in the bucket. I was about to follow him when the policeman hove into view, his gaze sweeping from one side of the road to the other. He spotted the milk.

"Is this your fault?" he shouted at the wee girl, who was heading back the way she had come.

She held up both her hands and waggled her fingers. "Can't be, can it? Look, no bucket."

"How dare you use that tone to an officer of the law?" he bellowed.

"My mum says you're not a proper officer of the law," the wee girl retorted. "My mum says Officer Sylvain was a good policeman and now this place is going to hell in a handcart."

The officer advanced on her threateningly. "What's your mother's name, little girl?" He was obviously one of those blokes to whom one small child looks very much like another.

"Wouldn't you like to know?" she chortled, deftly sidestepping him and running off.

Further down the street, I could see a wee boy emerge from a chalet, hauling a bucket. The householder came out behind him and said something that I guessed was along the lines of "Oh look, a giraffe!" since the child whirled away from her and stared in the opposite direction. The householder quickly dipped a bowl in the bucket, and then concealed the filled bowl behind her back.

The small boy, continuing to gaze hopefully in the direction of the giraffe, set off down the stairs. The householder glanced round to see if anyone was watching. She didn't notice me, since I was still in unobtrusive mode, but she caught sight of the policeman and jumped, spilling all of the milk. She shot back into the chalet, closing the door behind her.

The policeman had given up trying to pursue the wee girl and was progressing down the street, looking from right to left. Any moment now, he would spot the milk dripping down the steps.

I have the greatest respect for the constabulary, but this man was a disgrace to his uniform, shouting at wee kids. I wasn't sure what was going on, but I was sure that in this particular instance, I wasn't on the side of the law.

I emerged from my unobtrusiveness. "Good day, officer," I said. "I wonder if you could tell me the time?"

He looked tetchy at being waylaid, but he stopped. Although he was wearing a gold fob-watch, he ignored it, peering instead at the mountain range ahead of us.

"Fourteen minutes past three," he announced.

He was about to proceed in a southerly direction, but I stepped in front of him. "That's amazing. How did you do that?"

"What, telling the time by the sun?" he asked. "It's obvious."

The sky above the jagged peaks might be blue, but the village was still in shadow.

"You can't even see the sun," I said.

He gave an impatient sigh. "But I know where it is."

"Goodness, that's amazing!" I marvelled, placing myself between him and the milk-covered steps. "So, could you show me how you would know it was, say, seventeen minutes to ten?"

He waved his hand at a particularly impressive crag. "Because the sun would be behind there."

I shook my head admiringly, moving slowly down the street in order to draw him away from the possible crime scene. "And twenty-two minutes past eight?"

He gestured elsewhere. I wasn't really paying attention to him, but simply getting him away from the chalet.

"Marvellous," I said. "I always knew being a police officer required special abilities, but this is remarkable. I suppose the exams you took are quite strenuous?"

He stopped dead and scowled at me. "That fool of a mayor may think you're something special, but I advise you to watch your step, Englishwoman."

I was so taken aback by this extraordinary response that I didn't even bother to correct him. He was the one who needed to watch his step or someone was going to complain about police harassment. But at least I had steered him beyond the danger point.

"Thanks for telling me the time," I said frostily. "I must be getting back to Madeleine."

"Ah, Madeleine," he sighed, a faraway look in his eyes, and I took the opportunity to head off.

I kept passing small children carrying buckets of milk. Some of them nodded politely, some gave a little curtsey, some scuttled past. The wee girl who had refused to be intimidated by the policeman was back with another bucket.

"Hello," I said.

"Good day, madame," she said, with a skilful curtsey that didn't risk spilling the milk.

"I see you're all working hard at your practical biology lesson," I said. "But where are you taking the milk?"

"To the cheesemonger, madame. For the celebrations." She

gave a gap-toothed grin. "These are going to be the best celebrations ever. I'm going to be singing in the choir."

But the children were going in completely the opposite direction from the cheese shop. Instead, they were converging on a wooden shed in the next street. I glanced up at the street name. Rue Morgue.

Three

As I returned to my lodgings, I could hear an excellent recording of Debussy's *Valse romantique* emerge from Madeleine's chalet.

I was really excited about seeing one of Edison's phonographs up close, with its wax cylinders and horn loudspeaker. It was such new technology – invented in 1877 – that I was surprised that it had reached somewhere so isolated as Sans-Soleil. The sound quality was amazing. I would have expected an early recording to be really crackly, but this was as good as a live performance.

The sound was coming from a room that I hadn't been in yet. I gently pushed the door open. I found Madeleine sitting at an upright piano, giving a live performance. She caught sight of me and instantly stopped playing, turning to greet me with a glare.

"Please go on," I said. "You play extremely well."

The piano was a fairly battered second-hand Gaveau, albeit made of carefully polished mahogany. I gave it a respectful pat. "What a lovely instrument."

"My Sylvain bought it for me. You know about music?"

"A bit," I said modestly, not wanting to intimidate her by telling her I had reached Grade 8 in the Associated Board piano exams. Even if she wasn't sure exactly what that was, she would realise I was serious competition. "And I'm very fond of Debussy."

She sniffed. "They say all the ladies are very fond of Debussy. Not me. I have my Sylvain. But I have a fondness for Monsieur Debussy's music."

"Do you fancy a wee duet?" I asked. "Perhaps his *Petite Suite*?"

"I prefer Monsieur Fauré's *Dolly Suite*."

She was obviously determined to be difficult. But I was as familiar with one as with the other, having played them both at school. I looked round the room, a neat little parlour with a treadle sewing machine in one corner, an upright wooden chair in front of it. I picked the chair up, and Madeleine indicated for me to put it on the right of the piano stool.

"You can be *primo* and I'll be *secondo*," she said.

It sounded polite, as though she were deferring to me as her guest. But she was actually nicking the more interesting part for herself. Most of the time I'd just be playing the tune while she got all the harmony.

She riffled through a large pile of sheet music to retrieve the Fauré, ostentatiously placing it on the music stand so that most of it was on my side.

I shoved it back. "I don't need the music, thanks. I know it quite well."

She snatched the music off the piano and threw it back on the pile. I massaged my fingers and positioned them over the keys.

The first movement, *Berceuse*, has been my favourite since I was wee because it's the *Listen with Mother* theme. I shifted until I was sitting comfortably and then I began. Madeleine began as well. She really was very good, and I found I was having to up my game. Until we reached the bit towards the end before the tune comes back.

"If we had the music in front of us, you would see it says *ritardando*," I said. "That means you have to slow down."

"I know perfectly well what it says, and what it means, and I have slowed down."

"Not enough."

"Quite enough."

And then we were both thumping out our parts in a way that would have woken every infant in a half-mile radius. We thudded to a halt, breathing heavily. Before we could get on to the second movement, Madeleine slammed down the piano lid, and I only just got my fingers out in time.

"You should have played slower," I said.

"You should have played faster."

It struck me that she had been trying to sabotage our duet. I looked down at her wooden sabots: they were perfectly named. A good translation would be "putting the boot in".

I reminded myself that she was recently widowed, so I didn't make the response she deserved. Instead, I walked round to the pile of music and began to look through it. She had pages and pages of all the latest stuff, Fauré and Satie and Debussy.

"You must have a very good music shop here," I said.

"The village wouldn't know what to do with such a thing. Sylvain bought these for me when he bought the piano, last year in Paris during our honeymoon."

"I'm so sorry," I said. "That's awful, being widowed so shortly after getting married."

"My Sylvain is not dead!" she shouted. "You think if you say it often enough that I'll start believing it? Is that why you're here? You think you can convince me? In that case, you may as well leave now." She flung open the parlour door.

I wasn't sure how easy it would be to find alternative accommodation.

"He lives on in your heart, of course," I said in as sympathetic a voice as I could muster.

Madeleine took three steps in her heavy wooden sabots to bring herself nose to nose with me. She gripped my shoulders so that I couldn't back away. "My. Sylvain. Is. Not. Dead."

"That must be a great comfort to you," I said cautiously. "So, where is he?"

She gave a harsh laugh. "You don't know?"

"I don't know," I agreed.

"Nor do I. But I shall find him, and you will not stop me."

"Here's the thing," I said. "I really don't want to stop you doing anything, except perhaps digging your nails into my shoulders."

She took the hint and let me go.

"I suppose you want something to eat?" she snapped.

"That would be nice, since I've only had a coffee since I arrived."
I was aware I didn't sound particularly gracious, but she was so definite that her husband was still alive that I no longer felt she merited the sympathy due to a grieving widow.

"In fact," I said, "why don't I make it, and you can go and put your feet up, or go and look for your Sylvain, or whatever you like."

She whirled round with an incredulous expression, and as her curls swept away from her face, I caught sight of something.

"You're wearing my head – fascinator," I said.

Her blush reached the roots of the curls. She ripped off the head torch and handed it to me.

"I was just trying it on," she muttered. "I've already made a vegetable tian. If you want something else, feel free."

"A tian's always better the day after it's made," I said, heading for the kitchen. It didn't look promising. First, it was dairy-free and secondly, fin de siècle France didn't have the range of ingredients you get in the Morningside Waitrose. But I had to make an impression. Madeleine was already sceptical about my culinary skills.

I decided to make one of my signature dishes, sweetcorn and chickpea burgers. Admittedly, there was no sweetcorn and no chickpeas. But there was potato, beetroot, garlic and French beans.

I needed herbs to add to the mix. Madeleine was busy accompanying herself in Debussy songs and was likely to get irritable if I disturbed her. The vegetable tian suggested she had a vegetable garden, in which case she might well have a herb garden. I went down the stairs at the back of the chalet, which took me into a ground-floor barn, obviously the cow's bedroom. I pushed open the door to Madeleine's back garden, and there was the cow itself, ruminating.

"Hello," I said. "I'm looking for herbs."

The cow tossed its head in a morose way, suggesting "Join the queue."

No herbs were to be found, and no vegetables. Now that I saw one of the village gardens close up, I realised the meadow grass might be a vivid green, but it was tufted and spiky and didn't look very palatable. Sans-Soleil was so lacking in sun that only the toughest plant life could flourish.

But I did find something useful. At the edge of the chalet, the stonework offered an easy way to climb over the garden fence, without being overlooked by any other building. A good alternative to leaving by the front door and walking down the street.

"Bye," I said to the cow. "Shame about the grass."

The cow gave a doleful moo.

I went back upstairs, and started cooking. Madeleine had been to Paris. Madeleine had got up-to-the-minute music from Paris. And here I was, stuck in a tiny village in the middle of nowhere. I was missing the Paris Exposition with its art nouveau, and Campbell's Soup winning a gold medal. I was missing the Paris Olympics with competitors vying in football, fencing and croquet. I was missing the inauguration in ten days' time of the first metro line. Although I would miss that anyway, since I would have to complete my mission well before 19 July.

But to be sent to Sans-Soleil when there must be thousands of worthy missions available in Paris at this very moment, Sans-Soleil where they wouldn't recognise a Belle Époque if it bit them on the ankle. I could have been a flâneuse, a boulevardière, strolling along the banks of the Seine before settling myself in the Café de la Paix to watch the world go by. The only possible conclusion was that Miss Blaine was punishing me.

I bridled at the injustice. I had made one mistake, one.

But it was a bad mistake. An impressionable reader could easily have picked the book up, intrigued to find it featuring a well-known local school, and think the shocking and squalid ongoings were an accurate depiction. I had pledged to keep Morningside Library a Brodie-free zone, and I had failed.

"I'm sorry, Miss Blaine," I murmured. "I shall carry out this mission with good grace and diligence, and I hope you will be able to be proud of me again."

I applied myself to the cooking with renewed vigour and eventually called Madeleine through to eat, the burgers sitting on a nest of lettuce and tomato between slices of baguette, flanked by home-made chips.

She got a fork and poked suspiciously at her burger.

"You lift it up with your hands," I explained. "It's basically a sandwich. Invented by the Earl of Sandwich during a card game. Avoiding the need for cutlery."

She picked up the burger and took a tentative bite.

"What do you think?" I asked.

She gave a non-committal grunt, which I felt was actually quite positive. She just couldn't bring herself to admit she liked it.

Mentioning the Earl of Sandwich led me to think of the English milord. I was certain he wasn't the subject of my mission, but he might still be relevant to it.

"Tell me," I said, "what do you know about the English milord?"

Shrug. "Nothing. I've never met him. I don't even know his name. I hear he's very seldom in the village. All I know is that he comes from a castle in an English town called Aberdeenshire."

If I got home without bursting a blood vessel, it would be a miracle. "Allow me to correct you. Aberdeenshire is an administrative county, not a town. Aberdeen is a city. And most important of all, both city and county are in Scotland, and the milord is therefore not English."

Her lack of interest in what I was saying couldn't have been more evident. But I was mollified by the way she was chomping her way through the burger, and eating more than her fair share of the chips.

"I don't suppose you know which castle?" I asked. "Fyvie? Muchalls? Cairnbulg? Balmoral? Slains?"

"Yes, I think that's the name. That last one you said."

I ran through the list of Scottish castle owners I had memorised. "1900, Slains Castle, property of Charles Gore Hay, twentieth Earl of Erroll, Lord High Constable of Scotland and chief of the Clan Hay," I murmured. I resolved to pay him a visit. It's always nice to meet a fellow Scot abroad, and he could well have useful information.

"I'd like to call on him," I said. "Can you tell me the best way to get there?"

She gave a short laugh. "The best way is through the forest. But, of course, you cannot go that way."

"Of course," I agreed. Then I asked, "Remind me why not?"

She positively sneered at me. "It's out of bounds. Because of the–"

For a moment, I couldn't remember the meaning of the French word she said. And then I got it. *Sangliers*. Wild boar. I could see it would be sensible to stay out of their way – those tusks are quite something. As far as I knew, they were nocturnal, so crossing the forest during the day shouldn't be a problem – but perhaps if you woke them up, they got quite cranky. I know I do.

"You'll have to go the long way round, but you'll never find it yourself," said Madeleine. "I'll have to take you."

I was about to explain that I would have no problem, since I was an experienced orienteer. But while the UK might already have a well-organised system of Ordnance Survey maps, I had no idea what the situation in France was. And I hadn't seen a compass in my luggage. I had a look in my reticule in case one had now materialised, but there were no new additions. I took out my handkerchief and blew my nose, pretending that was what I had been looking for all along.

"Sorry, I used up the last of the tomatoes," I said. "I'll get more tomorrow. But I didn't find the greengrocer's on my walk round the village. Where is it?"

"In the next village," she said acidly.

That didn't sound at all convenient.

"The cart takes our produce to them, and brings back what we need in return."

"Well, next time, could they maybe add milk, butter and cheese to the order? I went to the cheese shop, but it was closed."

Madeleine, who had been reaching for a chip, raised her eyebrows. "But the cart deliveries have been suspended. Surely your friend the mayor told you what was happening?"

I remembered Cart Woman complaining that her business was going down the tubes. And I noted that this was the second time Madeleine had referred to the mayor as my "friend".

"Your mayor seems perfectly pleasant, but I can't presume to describe him as a friend," I said. "I met him only a few minutes before I met you. And he hasn't told me anything about anything." I could have added, "except that you're a widow", but that always got her riled.

Madeleine ate the last two chips and sat back in her seat with a bland expression. "Tell me, madame, exactly how do you happen to be in our little village?"

This was seriously awkward. I couldn't see Madeleine falling for the line that Sans-Soleil had starred in Glasgow's International Exhibition. And she knew that despite the mayor's best efforts, the village didn't feature on any list of top French destinations. I would have to take refuge in the truth, albeit not necessarily the whole truth.

"I told you, I'm here on a mission."

"And may I ask the nature of your mission?"

She would have been great in a police procedural series, the young detective politely asking seemingly innocuous questions and then getting the villain bang to rights. Except I wasn't a villain.

"I'm here to help someone," I said.

"May I ask who?"

It would sound totally unprofessional to say, "I've no idea." Instead, I said, "I'm afraid I'm not at liberty to divulge that information."

She nodded. "Of course. I understand."

Her smile was so sickly, it would have curdled milk had there been any.

"Thank you for such an interesting supper," she went on. "Would you like some coffee?"

I couldn't face another milkless hot drink. "Thanks, but I don't drink coffee so late at night, stops me sleeping. Speaking of which, I think I'll go to bed, since I'm quite tired after my journey here."

"I didn't hear the cart this morning. How did you get here?"

The patrons of the howff had been much less inquisitive.

"I made other arrangements."

"Which were?"

I clamped a hand over my mouth to stifle a yawn. "I'm terribly sorry, I really must go to bed. We can chat more in the morning. I did most of the washing up as I went along, but maybe you won't mind doing the rest?"

"How can I mind? You're paying rent, aren't you?"

"Goodnight, then," I said, and retired to my room. It was dark now (or rather, a bit darker than it was during the day), but I wasn't ready to go to sleep. I would soon have been in Sans-Soleil for twenty-four hours and as yet, I had no idea why I was here. The clock was ticking: Miss Blaine had told me on a previous occasion that I had a week to complete a mission. What would happen if I failed had been left unspecified, but I was in no doubt that it wouldn't be good.

I waited until I was sure that Madeleine had gone to bed and was asleep. Taking care not to make a sound, I crept downstairs to the barn. I didn't put on my head torch in case I woke the cow, simply taking small exploratory steps in the direction of the outside door. And then I thudded into something. Not some-thing. Someone.

Four

Someone with a voluptuous bosom.

Madeleine made a sound that might have been "oof", but with such a chic inflection that the word itself radiated voluptuousness.

There was a scratching sound, the smell of sulphur, and the safety match she had lit illuminated the barn. The cow opened a sleepy eye, and closed it again.

"What are you doing here?" Madeleine demanded. She was wearing an ankle-length black cape with a hood.

"I thought I heard a noise outside. I was coming to investigate," I said. "What are you doing here?"

"Same reason," said Madeleine.

We stood there for a moment, both aware that we were lying to a person who was lying to us. Madeleine gave a gasp as the match burned down to her fingers. She let it fall to the stone floor, where it fizzled out harmlessly, and lit another.

"It all seems to be quiet now," she said.

"So it does," I agreed.

"I think I'll go back to bed," she said.

"Yes, I think I will as well."

She shook the match out, and we climbed the two flights of stairs to the bedrooms in the dark and in silence. She had been really sneaky. She had closed her door loudly when she pretended to go to bed, and hadn't made a sound when she crept back out.

"Good night," she said as she reached her room, and even though I couldn't see her, I knew she was glaring at me. I decided to have a good sleep and start my mission properly the next day.

We set off after a breakfast of milkless coffee and butterless bread, accompanied down the village streets by sighs of "Ah, Madeleine!"

"Pigs," she muttered. "I don't give them the slightest encouragement, and this is how they behave."

I felt like saying it would be a good idea if she stopped undulating quite so much. And then I felt thoroughly ashamed of myself. It was Madeleine's right to undulate as much as she wanted. She wasn't the problem, they were.

Perhaps it was precipitated by guilt at my less-than-sisterly reaction, but I found myself turning and yelling, "What do you think you're looking at? Sling your hooks, you bunch of schemies!"

In my exasperation, I translated directly from the Edinburgh, but my tone must have conveyed my meaning, since the men scarpered and Madeleine gave a small smile.

I'd had problems on my previous mission with a woman with a dangerous cleavage. The problems stemmed from her personality rather than her cleavage, so it was important not to conflate the two. Madeleine couldn't help having an hour-glass figure. For all I knew, she might be forced to undulate by her unfortunate structure.

We bypassed the road to Paris and reached the edge of the village without further disturbance. To our right was the vast, seemingly impenetrable forest, shadowy and sinister, which bounded the village and reached the back of the town hall.

"The milord lives at the other side of the forest, over there." Madeleine pointed. "But–"

"I know," I said. "I can read."

A hand-made notice was affixed to one of the trees: "*Keep Out. Authorised Personnel Only. By Order.*"

Madeleine looked at me in a doubtful way. "The other way is dangerous. There is no proper path, and we must negotiate narrow ledges and fast-flowing streams."

"Oh, for goodness' sake," I said. "I'm a Munro bagger."

She stared at me, and I realised that didn't make a lot of sense in French.

"I'm in the process of climbing all two hundred and eighty-two Scottish mountains over three thousand feet, which is nine hundred and fourteen metres," I told her. "I've done two hundred of them already, including the In Pinn. The Inaccessible Pinnacle."

I felt like adding that if she could manage the dangers with her sabots and her undulating, I could certainly manage them with my DMs and my core stability.

"Nobody knows this route," she warned as we set off.

I spotted a contradiction. "Then how do you know it?"

"Nobody has ever taken this route apart from my beloved Sylvain and myself," she amended as she led the way along a non-existent path with a sheer drop on one side, bounding along like a wee mountain goat. She was pretty good, I had to admit. I was pretty good as well, with a more measured pace like a bigger and more mature mountain goat.

"My Sylvain discovered it when he was on important police business. It led to my village, the only way from this valley to mine."

She gave a reminiscent sigh. "Nobody from Sans-Soleil had ever visited my village. I didn't know who he was, where he was from, but as soon as our eyes met, we knew – we had each found the one who would complete us."

I feared this was heading towards too much information. "That's nice," I said as we scrambled across some scree. "Is it far to the milord's place?"

"No," she said, swatting away the question as though it was an irritating fly. "We ran hand in hand to the town hall in my village and were married immediately."

"How is that possible?" I asked, as fragments of rock tumbled into the abyss below us. "Don't you have to wait?"

"We explained to the mayor that we couldn't wait," she said.

Definitely more than I needed to know. "So, when you say not far to the milord's place, are we talking ten minutes, half an hour?" I asked.

She crossed a fast-flowing stream by jumping effortlessly from rock to rock. "I can't say. Every step of the journey from my village to Sans-Soleil is imprinted on my heart. But time has no meaning when I am with my Sylvain – all that matters is to be with him."

I suspected she had been reading a lot of very trashy romances.

"I simply know that when I saw the milord's castle–"

"Castle?" I interrupted. "The milord lives in a castle?"

"Of course he lives in a castle – he's a milord," she said impatiently. "As I walked hand in hand with my beloved Sylvain to begin my new life with him, suddenly I saw the castle, strange and black in a sunless landscape. My beloved told me we were now very close to his village. And I felt a surge of joy to know that this was where I would live out the rest of my days with my dearest."

"Why couldn't Sylvain move to your village?" I asked.

"Because he is Sans-Soleil's police officer. He takes his duties seriously. He would never consider leaving the village."

I felt like saying he *had* left the village, and the village seemed to have found a replacement with no problem. I was also offended that his job seemed to take precedence over whatever she was doing.

"Do you work outside the home?" I asked.

"Of course," she said, reaching for a handhold on the rock face to balance herself on the vestigial track. "I look after the cow, I go to the shops, I clean the windows, I paint the window frames."

I grabbed at the same handhold and hauled myself along. "I mean work that isn't connected to the home."

She turned and frowned at me. "Whatever are you suggesting?"

"You play the piano very well," I said. "You could give concerts."

She turned to me with a snort. "Ridiculous. All I wish to do is look after my Sylvain." But just before that snort, I had spotted a flash of interest in her eyes.

"Of course," I said emolliently. "Looking after your husband is the number one priority."

I was impressed that I managed to say it without snorting myself. "And thankfully, as you keep saying, he's not dead. But if, heaven forbid, you were left a widow at some point, you'd need an income, and I hear that concert pianists are quite well paid."

Another flash of interest, and then she snapped, "I shall never be left a widow, for the instant that my Sylvain dies, my own heart will break in two."

And with that, she set off again, not so much undulating as flouncing.

"If nobody knows about this route except you and Sylvain, and the forest is out of bounds, how does the milord get to the village?" I asked.

Shrug. "I don't know. Milords are a law unto themselves."

We inched our way along a particularly treacherous outcrop and suddenly there was Lord Erroll's castle. It wasn't at all what I expected. I had been thinking of the chateaux of the Loire, elegant and landscaped. This could only be described as Gothic, turreted, dark and forbidding. I wouldn't have been surprised to see a bat fly out of one of the narrow, mullioned windows.

"I'm fine from here on in," I said. "I would invite you to come with me, but we'll be speaking English and you would only be bored."

In fact, I didn't want her there in case she overheard information germane to my mission. The French often pretend they don't know other languages when actually they do. It amuses them to see foreigners struggling to speak French. And it enables them to eavesdrop unsuspected.

"How will you find your way back?" she asked.

"I kept my eyes open on the way here," I responded tartly. "Don't worry about me."

"Of course I worry about the village's distinguished guest," she said. "I would hate anything to happen to you." The way she said it suggested the opposite.

"And I would hate to take up any more of your time," I said. "I accept full responsibility for getting myself home."

"Perhaps I'll go back through the forest," she said. It sounded like a challenge of some sort.

"You do what you like," I said. "But since the forest is out of bounds, I'll be going back the way we came."

She glowered at me, and turned on her heel.

I trudged along the stony path to the castle. The massive wooden door, studded with iron nails, had a Victorian brass bell pull beside it, which I tugged. I imagined a sonorous clang but it just tinkled in a feeble sort of way. I waited to hear heavy footsteps, and the drawing back of massive iron bolts. The drawing back of massive iron bolts happened, but after that, there was only a small nervous cough before the door swung open.

There stood a man about my height but of much flimsier build, dressed entirely in black, a black woollen muffler wrapped round the lower half of his face. He had longish dark hair, which was perhaps why what I could see of his face seemed Sans-Soleil white in contrast. He looked more forty-something than my fifty-something. A young family retainer rather than an old one.

"Hello, I'm here to see the owner," I said.

He said something through his muffler that I managed to interpret as "That's me."

Not the servant, but the master. He would no doubt expect to be addressed as "Lord Erroll", but I've never seen why someone should be given special treatment because of an accident of birth. He came from Aberdeenshire, so I would address him in the vernacular – I speak all of the Scottish languages and dialects apart from Glaswegian. That is, I know how to speak Glaswegian, but I prefer not to. I imagine my tongue would cleave to the roof of my mouth if I had to say "I have went" or "definATEly".

I gave Lord Erroll the traditional Doric greeting: "Aye aye, min. Fit like?"

His eyes widened above the black wool scarf.

He needn't think he was going to intimidate me into forelock-tugging or my-lording. "Foo's yir doos? Aye peckin? Fairly," I added.

"I beg your pardon?" he said, his voice quite muffled, on account of the muffler. Not a hint of an Aberdeenshire cadence. Pure Received Pronunciation. He hadn't been offended by what I had said; he just hadn't understood it.

I sighed and returned to my normal accent. "Hello. My name's Shona McMonagle. I'm visiting from Edinburgh. Can I come in?"

"Welcome to my house," he said. "Enter freely and of your own free will."

This was definitely a tautology. But I thanked him politely and followed him into the castle. The small, narrow windows didn't allow for much light, but there were blazing sconces all around the entrance hall. The huge stone staircase in front of us was lit by antique silver lamps. It looked as though everything would feel cold and smell fusty, but in fact it was pleasantly warm and there was a lovely smell of baking.

I followed Lord Erroll up the staircase and through a large hall into a small octagonal room that had absolutely no windows and only one lamp. It was crammed full of Victorian furniture, including several little tables and high-backed wing armchairs covered in ox-blood leather.

"Do sit down," he said. I was getting used to the muffling. "May I get you something? A cup of tea, perhaps?"

I tried not to sound overexcited. "That would be very nice, thank you." Then I got worried. Perhaps he didn't mean proper tea. "It's not fennel, or camomile, or anything weird?"

Now he looked worried. "Not camomile. *Camellia sinensis*. Will that be all right?"

"More than all right," I said. Proper tea. "Did you know *Camellia sinensis* was the first ever tea plant to be discovered, in China? And then the botanist Robert Fortune, who incidentally worked for some time in Edinburgh's Royal Botanic Garden, took some Chinese plants to India to start growing tea there."

"Yes," said Lord Erroll. "I knew that." He made it sound as though it was common knowledge, whereas most people I tell are quite surprised.

"And could I possibly have a wee splash of milk in it?" I added.

He darted a suspicious look at me. "Milk? You think I have milk?"

I tried not to show my disappointment. I had been really looking forward to a wee cup of tea with milk.

"If you don't have any, that's all right," I said with as much cheerfulness as I could muster, which wasn't a great deal. "I'll just take it black."

He was still watching me closely. "You really want milk in your tea?"

Foreigners rarely take milk in their tea, something I find very frustrating. But I didn't think someone from Aberdeenshire would find it so odd. I've had plenty of fly cups in the north-east, always with milk.

"That's how I prefer it," I said. "But if you don't have it, you don't have it."

There was a pause.

"I might have it," he said.

He seemed to be waiting for my reaction.

"Then that would be very nice. I like a drop of milk in my tea." I felt I had made the same point around four times, but I find the aristocracy can be quite thick, presumably because of the inbreeding.

"A drop of milk. Yes, I think I can manage that."

And off he went. A few moments later, I thought I heard a moo, but it turned out to be the earl singing "Daddy Wouldn't Buy Me a Bow Wow".

He returned with a proper teapot containing a full-bodied Assam. I would have to cultivate Lord Erroll as carefully as Robert Fortune had cultivated the stolen Chinese seedlings. He set down the tea tray and said, "Let me get you an occasional table."

"That always makes me laugh, an occasional table," I said. "I wonder what it is the rest of the time."

There was spluttering through the muffler, which turned out to be laughter. "That hadn't occurred to me. Most comical."

It wasn't that comical, but it was nice of him to make the effort. He brought over the table and set out a fine bone-china cup, and a little plate of shortbread. Joseph Walker had opened his Aberlour bakery in 1898, and bought a horse and cart to make deliveries outwith the area. I wondered how long it took a horse and cart to get from Aberlour to France.

"You get Walkers to send this over?" I asked.

"No, I made it myself," he said. "I do hope you like it." He sounded quite nervous.

I took a bite. "Delicious," I said. "Excellent flavour, nice crunch, all of the biscuits perfectly symmetrical. If ever there's a *Great Scottish Bake-Off*, you should go in for it."

Above the muffler, his eyes twinkled with pleasure.

"And do you prefer the milk in first?" he asked, bringing over the teapot, and scarcely more than a thimbleful of milk. You hear about the meanness of Aberdonians, but this was ridiculous. I was reminded of Chic Murray in a guesthouse, picking up one of those wee jars of honey and saying to the landlady, "I see you keep a bee."

"I see you keep a cow," I said.

He straightened up, his eyes widening above the muffler. "No, I don't," he said.

"It was a joke," I clarified.

He started spluttering again. "Ah, another joke! Most comical."

There was something quite touching about his eagerness to please.

I returned to his question. "Yes, I prefer the milk in first, thanks."

He poured the tiny trickle of milk, put a silver tea strainer over the cup and poured out the tea. I could have done with about three times more milk, but it still tasted wonderful after my hours of deprivation. I began to worry that I could be a milk addict.

Lord Erroll sat down on the ox-blood leather armchair opposite me, but with no tea or shortbread for himself.

"Are you not having any?" I asked.

He indicated the muffler.

"Toothache?" I asked sympathetically. "It's horrible, isn't it? And you're quite right, hot tea and a sugary biscuit would just make things worse. You know, a really good folk remedy is garlic."

He made a sort of gurgling noise. I thought he was complimenting me on another most comical joke, even though I hadn't actually made one, until I saw he was looking astounded rather than amused.

"Really," I assured him. "The ancient Greeks knew all about it. Cut a clove in two, and rub it on either side of the tooth or the gum, whichever's giving you the problem, for about ten minutes. And when the pain eases off, chew the garlic. I have to admit, it stings a bit, but stick with it – it's a really good antibiotic."

I took another sip of tea and raised the cup to him in salute. His wee eyes glowed in delight, looking positively red in the low light. Even though he was an aristocrat, he was very personable. But despite being a fellow countryman, he wasn't the person I was here to help. I hadn't remotely tingled on the doorstep, and when I touched his hand while taking the teacup, absolutely nothing.

Perhaps he could be helpful to me, though. I decided to find out more about him. In Edinburgh, the question to ask is "What school did you go to?" Once you have the answer to that, you can pretty well work out everything else: where they live, value of property, family income, football team, favourite television programmes, voting intentions. It's not so easy with other parts of the country, but it would still give me something of an insight.

"Did you go to Aberdeen Grammar School?" I asked.

He shook his head.

"Gordonstoun? Fettes? No? Not … south of the border? Eton? Harrow?"

"I was home-educated," he said. "By my mother."

That explained things. Lord Erroll's mother was Eliza Amelia Gore, who had been lady of the bedchamber to Queen Victoria. She had obviously picked up her strange ideas from the royals, who traditionally home-educated their offspring, rather than sending her kid to the local school in the Scottish manner.

But I mustn't let that colour my view of the earl. It wasn't his fault that he hadn't had a decent education.

"I just arrived yesterday," I said. "Have you been here long?"

"Two years," he said.

"And what decided you to move to France?"

"The weather," he said.

This was the sort of ignorant remark you would expect from

the English, but not from someone brought up in the north-east of Scotland. Aberdeen gets more sun annually than London.

But the tea and the shortbread were good, so I let it pass. I glanced round the ancient room. "Were you looking for a while before you found this place?"

"I had it built specially." Even through the muffler, I could detect the pride.

"Sorry? You mean you renovated it?"

"No, I found a suitable site and designed a castle to fit."

"Two years ago? But it looks ancient," I said.

He nodded. "It's been done well."

It would have been impossible for builders to carry masonry and everything else along the route by which Madeleine had brought me.

"How did the workforce get here?" I asked. "I thought the forest was out of bounds."

"So I believe," he said. "But that's recent, and doesn't affect me."

I wasn't sure whether he meant he didn't go through the forest, or whether he meant the ban didn't apply to him. The upper classes can have a sense of entitlement that is totally unjustified.

"It still must have been a very complicated undertaking," I said.

"I couldn't say. I took no part in the construction."

Just when I'd started think he was a good guy, he'd confirmed my view that the landed gentry expected simply to snap their fingers and have their whims fulfilled.

"This is my favourite room," he said. "It's exactly like the one I had at Slains."

It was an odd room to have as a favourite, with absolutely no daylight getting in. But the aristocracy are so inbred that they can turn quite odd. When the third Marquess of Queensberry fancied a snack, he roasted a servant boy on a spit, so in the great scheme of things, liking a windowless room was quite an acceptable quirk.

"I'm very fond of Aberdeenshire," I said. "Shortbread, rowies, the Turra Coo, the poor monkey."

"I beg your pardon?" he said.

These aristos are the limit. I'm not surprised the French got rid of theirs. Not the faintest idea what goes on outside their elite circle.

"Shortbread you already know," I said, gesturing to the plate. "Rowies, also known as butteries, Aberdeen breakfast rolls, great with butter and marmalade."

He looked at me blankly.

"The Turra Coo, a white dairy cow that starred in a protest in Turriff over the introduction of compulsory national insurance by Lloyd George." I suddenly realised that Lloyd George wouldn't become chancellor of the exchequer until 1910, and hastily went on to my final example.

"Over a hundred years ago, fishermen from Boddam went out to get salvage from a shipwreck, and found a monkey. They weren't entitled to salvage if any living thing was on board, so I'm afraid they hanged it. Hartlepool has nicked the story and claimed it was during the Napoleonic Wars, and they hanged the monkey because they thought it was a Frenchman." I was quite glad I was telling the story to a Scot rather than the villagers. "But the Aberdeenshire story was definitely first. There's even a song, 'The Boddamers Hanged the Monkey-O' – I can sing it for you if you like."

The muffler moved a bit and I was absolutely sure that the earl had just yawned.

"Not boring you, am I?" I asked a little acerbically.

"Please excuse me," he said. "I don't sleep well. That is, I used to sleep well until…"

He broke off and the eyes above the muffler looked suddenly wary.

"I'm dreadfully sorry," he said, "but would you mind awfully if I asked you to leave? I really feel very sleepy all of a sudden. Absolutely nothing to do with your fascinating disquisition on monkeys, I assure you."

Those were not the eyes of someone who felt sleepy. He was just trying to get rid of me. However, I couldn't see what else to do but comply. I wasn't going to get any more information out of him. I followed him back down the spiral staircase. He opened the front door and seemed to shrink back into the shadows.

"That was very nice tea, thank you," I said. "Perhaps I could come round again?"

"I might not be in," he said. "Or I might be asleep."

"I'll just have to keep trying, then," I said and his eyes flickered in unmistakeable apprehension.

I stepped over the threshold and immediately the door slammed behind me. And this time, there was the sound of rattling chains, the clanking of massive bolts, and iron keys turning in locks. He definitely didn't want me back.

I retraced the route Madeleine had taken me, avoiding the forest with its dangerous wild boar, and instead edging my way along cliff faces and navigating fast-flowing torrents.

I was clambering over a particularly tricky bit when a sudden dreadful realisation came to me, and I missed my footing. Had it not been for my excellent reactions, seizing hold of tiny crevices in the rock, and painfully hauling myself back up, I might have plummeted hundreds of feet to my doom.

I slithered along to safety and sat there, getting my breath back. It was so obvious. Why hadn't I thought of it, the minute I heard the words "Slains Castle"?

Vampires. Bram Stoker's *Dracula*. People think it was inspired by Whitby, but Stoker started writing the book when he was on his holidays in Port Erroll, just along from Slains. Lord Erroll had been so proud of his windowless octagonal room that he had copied it in France. He wasn't the only one to have copied it. Stoker must have seen it when he went round to take tea with his lordship, and featured it in Dracula's castle in Transylvania. I wondered if he had asked Lord Erroll's permission.

But back to my shocking realisation. Vampires. I had thought the villagers were oddly pale. Of course they were. They were all vampires. They couldn't abide sunlight, and that was why they had chosen to live in Sans-Soleil.

But Madeleine, with her healthy suntan, she wasn't from Sans-Soleil. She wasn't part of this diabolical set-up. No wonder she wore a crucifix. It wasn't just to accentuate her cleavage (although I was pretty sure that was a major motive); she was avoiding becoming one of the undead.

It seemed unlikely that she would develop a sudden passion for a vampire, although I seemed to remember quite a lot of sudden passion in the book. Perhaps Sylvain had gone out one day without a crucifix and been bitten. Perhaps Madeleine shouldn't be so keen on getting him back.

If the villagers were vampires, that explained how they had managed to build a castle in the middle of nowhere. From the book, I knew vampires were cunning and had all sorts of illicit ways and means of doing things. And they would just ignore a prohibition on going into the forest.

I wondered if I should go back and warn Lord Erroll that he could be in terrible danger. He was such a frail wee soul that he wouldn't stand a chance against a ruthless blood-sucker. But then, he had lived there for two years without any problems, and according to Madeleine, he was seldom in the village, so there was no point in scaring him unnecessarily. Also, this was a very hazardous path and I was probably about halfway to Sans-Soleil by now. As Macbeth said, "Returning were as tedious as go o'er", so I decided just to continue.

And although I was returning to an extremely risky situation, I really felt quite cheerful, having discovered the purpose of my mission at last. It was up to me to rid the village of vampires. That would be to the benefit of everyone who wasn't a vampire, and explained why I hadn't felt the tingling associated with the person I was there to help. I was helping all humanity, and the very slight tingling I felt from Madeleine was because she was human, but just one individual. I wondered why I hadn't felt a similar tingling from Lord Erroll, but there was sure to be some technical reason Miss Blaine hadn't had time to mention.

Miss Blaine. The Founder had once warned me that I must never assume. It seemed crystal-clear that the villagers were all vampires, but I should still double-check. Meticulousness and accuracy are the hallmarks of a Blainer.

I was pondering how to go about this as I arrived in the village, and the first person I met was the mayor, strutting around in his white sash of office.

He hailed me cheerfully. "Madame–" Then he remembered about not wearing my name out. "Madame Maque! Enjoying this fine day?" He gestured to indicate the greyness that enveloped us. His expression changed to one of unease. "I hope you haven't been wandering near the forest."

"No," I said, "Madeleine's explained all about the forest being out of bounds."

"Ah, Madeleine!" he breathed.

I was even less impressed than I had been the previous day. The men's tongues were hanging out because they wanted to sink their gnashers into her. And then I realised it had just been the men. The women didn't care for her at all. In Bram Stoker's book, Dracula went after females, and the female vampires went after Jonathan Harker. It was disappointing to see such traditional gender stereotyping, but I had to remember it was only 1900 and we still had a way to go.

"Yes, Madeleine. So, I went all the way round the forest to get to the castle."

"The castle?" He looked shifty. "You have seen the English milord?"

"No," I said, and he relaxed.

"I've seen the Scottish milord, the gentleman who lives in the castle," I told him.

He looked shifty again.

"We had a very nice chat over tea and shortbread," I said.

Now he was puzzled. "Short bread? You mean a small baguette?"

"A Scottish delicacy."

"So, you talked about food? Not … anything else?" He sounded uneasy.

"We talked about lots of things, including cows and monkeys." I wondered whether I should offer to sing the Boddam song.

"He didn't … he didn't complain about anything, did he?"

"He had terrible toothache, but he didn't really complain about it, although it was ruining his sleep."

"Good," said the mayor. "Good. I mean, not good that he had terrible toothache, but good that he wasn't complaining about it."

During all our conversation, he hadn't opened his mouth wide enough for me to see his teeth and confirm that he was a vampire. I was going to have to tell him a joke, a joke so funny that he would laugh out loud.

The funniest joke I know – it makes me laugh every time – goes like this:

Q: What's brown and sticky?

A: A stick!

But it probably wouldn't come over so well in translation. I tried to construct a French variant, using *marron* (brown) and *marrant* (funny), but it didn't really work.

"Are you all right?" asked the mayor.

"Fine," I said. "Just thinking."

My second favourite joke is:

Q: What do you call a man with a pile of leaves on his head?

A: Russell!

That didn't work in French either. There was only one thing to do. I lunged at the mayor, grabbing the sides of his face and thrusting my thumbs in his mouth.

He shrieked.

I shoved my thumbs upwards so that I could check for long, sharpened fangs, and the next thing, his teeth were flying through the air. The mayor clearly wasn't a vampire.

I let go of him and wiped my thumbs on my skirt. "Oh," I said. "Falsers? Sorry."

As I turned to see where his teeth had gone, there was a shout.

"She attacked the mayor! Help! Help! Police!"

A crowd was rapidly gathering.

"What? What happened?"

"I saw it all, he was just talking to her, and then – whump!"

"Whump?"

"What's going on?"

"The mayor's been attacked!"

"Police!"

"What sort of whump?"

"The Englishwoman punched the mayor in the mouth – knocked all his teeth out."

"I'm not English," I protested. "And I didn't punch him." My second refutation was lost as the clamour intensified.

"Police! Someone call the police!"

"Whump! Just like that, completely unprovoked."

"Terrible! We're not safe in our beds with these foreigners around."

"Grab her!"

"You must be joking. I'm not going anywhere near her. I might get punched."

I took a step forward, and they all took a step back, falling silent.

"I did not," I said, "punch the mayor. It was an unfortunate misunderstanding." I looked around and spotted the teeth lying in some mud. At least, I hoped it was mud. I went and picked them out, and handed them back to the mayor.

"Maybe better rinse them under the tap for a while before you pop them back in," I said.

I turned to the baleful throng, many of whom were baring their teeth, with not a fang in sight. I had been too hasty in my conclusion. "I was checking for vampires. You can never be too careful. I'd advise you to keep your windows and doors closed at night just to be sure. Anyway, the mayor's not a vampire, so nothing to worry about in terms of municipal administration. That's reassuring, isn't it?"

I smiled encouragingly but nobody smiled back.

"Really, I am very sorry," I said to the mayor who was clutching the dentures. "If your teeth have been damaged in any way, I'll naturally cover the cost of repairs." I hoped Miss Blaine would see this as a necessary expense. "All I can say is that it was an honest mistake, and I very much hope you'll be able to accept my apology."

"Now then, now then." A tall man with bushy side whiskers, the police officer who had been so objectionable to the children, was being ushered towards me by a bunch of villagers. I noted that he was simply wearing his dark suit, without his uniform of cape and kepi. "There had better be a good reason for disturbing me."

The clamour erupted again.

"She punched the mayor!"

"I saw everything!"

"It was an unprovoked assault!"

"Arrest her!"

He looked at me and looked at the mayor, who had slipped his teeth back in. I really hoped it was mud they had landed in.

"It's something out of nothing," I said. "We'll be laughing about it by teatime. Shake?"

I extended my hand towards the mayor, who recoiled.

"Arrest her," repeated a villager in quite a belligerent way, and others took up the cry. "Yes, arrest her! Arrest her!"

The policeman put up his hand as though he was directing traffic. "I arrest you," he announced.

He was a disgrace to the uniform that he wasn't wearing.

"You can't just say 'I arrest you,'" I said. "First, you have to identify yourself as the police, especially since you're not in uniform, then you have to tell me that I'm being arrested, then you have to tell me the crime you think I've committed, explain why it's necessary to arrest me, and then tell me that I don't need to say anything other than giving my name, address, date and place of birth and nationality. Which is Scottish, by the way."

I suddenly realised that if I gave my date of birth, it would cause all sorts of difficulties.

"Scrub all that," I said. "You probably can just say 'I arrest you'. Now what?"

The policeman looked uncertain.

"Take her to the judge," said a villager, and that was them all off again. "Yes, yes, the judge, take her to the judge!"

The press of the crowd carried us through the village, not to the courthouse but to Chez Maman. The policeman entered first.

"I've arrested the Englishwoman," he announced.

I gave a loud sigh, which was ignored. I could discern the tiny figure of Maman behind the bar thanks to occasional glimpses of grey – she was using a filthy dish towel to dry glasses.

"Why have you done that?" she croaked.

"Because she attacked the mayor. Now it's a matter for the judge."

Maman flapped the dishcloth towards the back of the howff, and a figure rose and came towards us, still clutching a glass of cloudy pastis. A chubby, florid young man. The judge.

Maman had meantime gone to the coat hooks and retrieved the policeman's cape and kepi, and the judge's gown, jabot and black cylindrical hat. The two men got into their outfits, and the judge sat down at the nearest table and took a swig of pastis. I had been shoved in front of the table by the crowd, as many of whom as possible were inside the howff, with the rest thronged at the door. Maman was already taking drinks orders.

I stood there for a while, but court-wise nothing was happening, apart from the chubby judge making inroads on his drink.

"Are we waiting for the prosecution and defence advocates?" I asked.

The judge looked at the policeman.

"I don't know," said the policeman. "Are we?"

"I don't think we have any," said a villager.

"If we have, I've never seen them," said another. "Hey, I'm next in the queue. Absinthe please, Maman."

I stood around for a while longer. Eventually I said to the judge, "Are you an examining magistrate?"

"Might be," he said cautiously.

"If you are, it's your job to question me, the suspect."

"All right," he said, and paused. "How do I do that?"

It's just as well that jurisprudence is one of my hobbies, along with international law, and that I was familiar with the French inquisitorial system.

"You can start by asking the police officer about his enquiries."

"What about your enquiries?" the judge asked the police officer.

"What about them?" the police officer said.

The judge looked at me helplessly.

"Have you made any enquiries?" I asked the police officer.

"I asked Maman if she had any cognac, but she didn't."

"Enquiries about this case."

"No."

There was a silence.

"Honestly," I said. "Do I have to do everything round here? Just tell us, in your own words, how you came to find me and the mayor."

His face cleared. "I was drinking in here when a bunch of people rushed in and grabbed me and said I was needed. As we were running along, they said you had attacked the mayor."

"Ah," said the judge. "That's important evidence. So now we know you attacked the mayor."

"That's not evidence," I snapped. "It's hearsay, and hence inadmissible."

"Oh," said the judge, looking disappointed.

"Go on," I said to the policeman.

"They brought me to where a large crowd was gathered, and they told me you'd punched the mayor in an unprovoked assault."

"Ah," said the judge. "Further evidence of your guilt."

"You're not listening to me," I said in the tone I used to recalcitrant first years. "Hearsay, inadmissible. Go on, officer."

The policeman puffed out breath from hamster cheeks. "That's it, I think. They told me to arrest you and bring you to the judge, so I did."

"Thank you. You may stand down," I said.

The policeman sat down and was handed a glass of beer, which he drained in a oner.

"Now we can hear from the alleged victim," I said. "His honour the mayor."

The mayor was shoved forward by the crowd. He seemed to be

running his tongue along his teeth in a tentative way. I worried about how they tasted.

"Mr Mayor," I said, "please tell the court in your own words what happened."

He took a deep breath. "It all happened so quickly. We were talking about the English milord–"

"The Scottish milord," I corrected.

There was puzzled muttering from the crowd.

"Anyway, we were talking, and you stopped. You were just standing there – you seemed to be lost in thought. And then you shoved your hands in my mouth and pulled my teeth out."

"Guilty!" cried the judge.

"Hold on for a second," I said. "You don't even know whether the mayor wants to press charges."

"Do you want to press charges?" asked the judge.

The mayor looked at me. "Do I?" he asked.

"That's a matter for you," I said. "But probably not. It's not going to do your tourist industry much good if your first international visitor ends up in the clink."

"Then I don't want to press charges."

Maman had emerged from behind the bar, the rancid grey cloth over her shoulder, and was whispering something to the judge.

"Charges must be pressed in the public interest," the judge intoned.

"And what are the charges?" I asked.

The judge swirled the remaining pastis round in his glass and drank it down. "Just a minute," he said. "I need another drink." He went over to the bar, followed by Maman, who poured another slug of alcohol into the glass, followed by a dribble of water. I could hear whispering, but even with my remarkably acute hearing, I couldn't make out what was being said.

The judge came back and sat down. "Assaulting an elected official," he said, which led to a lot of satisfied nodding. He crashed his glass down as though it was a gavel, sending a spray of pastis shooting out.

"Guilty," he declaimed as Maman arrived with her manky cloth to wipe up the spillage.

There were cheers from the villagers.

When the noise died down, I said, "You can't do that."

"Yes I can," said the judge. "I'm the judge."

"You have to interview me first," I told him.

"Do I?" said the judge.

"It's the law," I said. "I have to get an opportunity to explain myself."

"In that case, explain yourself." He sat back and folded his arms.

"You're all very pale here," I said. "Apart from Madeleine, of course."

There was a collective sigh from the men followed by dark muttering from the womenfolk.

"This led me to develop a research project," I explained. "I had a hypothesis, but I needed empirical evidence. It was essential to collect primary research data, and after a critical analysis of alternative methodologies, I implemented the research strategy that appeared to best meet my aims. I evaluated my findings and concluded that my hypothesis was not proved."

The judge turned to the policeman. "Do you have any idea what she's on about?"

The policeman shrugged.

"I thought you were all vampires," I said. "I was checking whether the mayor had fangs. I didn't know he had dentures. I've already apologised."

The judge crashed his glass down again and repeated, "Guilty." Then he said, "Now what?"

"Now the disposal," I said.

The judge leaned forward. "We can dispose of you?"

"In a number of ways," I said. "Since I am of unblemished character, it could be an absolute discharge. You might come to that conclusion if you also take into account that the mayor doesn't want to press charges. Or you could impose a fine. Or a custodial sentence."

"That one," said the judge. "A custodial sentence."

"That means putting me in prison," I said, just in case he didn't know.

"Yes," he said. "Putting you in prison. That's good."

"No," said the mayor. "That's bad. We want to build our reputation as a tourist-friendly destination, not one where tourists end up in prison."

The judge glowered at him. "Are you arguing with me? Do you want a custodial sentence as well?"

The mayor subsided.

"Right," said the judge. "Madame Maque-Monet-Gueule, I sentence you to a custodial sentence."

This place was full of tautology.

I spoke over the applause that had broken out. "You don't say it like that. You sentence me to a period of custody."

"All right," said the judge. "I sentence you to a period of custody."

He was the most useless investigating magistrate I had ever encountered.

"You have to say how long the period is," I explained.

"How long is it?"

"That's for you to decide." I was getting slightly exasperated. It was bad enough being in the dock without having to be prosecution and defence advocate, clerk of court and judge as well.

"Life," the judge determined.

I was obliged to intervene in my role as clerk of court. "That's not appropriate for a crime of this nature. It's far too long."

"What would you suggest?" the judge asked.

I considered this. "Maybe a week?"

The glass crashed down on the table for a third time. "I sentence you to a week in custody. Take her away."

As I was being dragged off by the policeman, it struck me I could have said "an hour". I hoped Miss Blaine wouldn't find out.

Accompanied by the crowd, we made our way to the police station, where the policeman halted.

"Keys?" he said querulously.

"You should have them on your belt, shouldn't you?" I said.

He fumbled at his waist, then felt in all his pockets. "Can't find them."

"When did you have them last?" I asked.

He looked uncomfortable. "I don't remember."

There was a jangling sound behind us, followed by a familiar collective sigh: "Ah, Madeleine!"

"Are these what you're looking for?" asked my landlady. "My Sylvain keeps them safely at home, but I'll let you borrow them until he comes back."

The crowd broke into sympathetic murmuring alongside furtive gestures suggesting that she wasn't in her right mind.

The policeman seized the bunch of keys and started trying them in the front-door keyhole to no effect until Madeleine retrieved them and used the right one. The three of us went inside and the crowd dispersed.

Madeleine tutted at the sight of the dust covering the surfaces. "The state of this place. It was spotless when my Sylvain was here."

The policeman tugged at his bushy side whiskers. "Sorry, Madeleine. I haven't been in much."

Madeleine shook the keys. "Obviously not. You'd better get it sorted before he comes back. Here, this is the key for the cell."

She opened the door to what appeared to be a broom cupboard, albeit free of brooms. There was no window as such, apart from a transom window to the main office.

"I'll leave you to it," she said. "And by the way, madame, you don't get a rent rebate."

And with that, she departed, letting the front door slam shut behind her. The policeman, gazing in the direction in which she had gone, gave a wistful sigh.

Then he gathered himself. "All right, in you go."

I peered into the cell. "I'm not going in there. It's too small, there isn't adequate ventilation, there's no seating or bedding – it's completely against my human rights. What was the point of the French Revolution if you're not going to uphold the Declaration of the Rights of Man and of the Citizen?"

"You, madame, are neither a man nor a citizen," said the police officer, shoving me in the direction of the cell.

I was going to argue about the definition of the word "man", but I suspected he wouldn't be receptive. I tilted back on my DMs to turn myself into an immoveable object. "Look, I can't be imprisoned for a week. I've got things to do, people to see." Most important of all, I had to work out what my mission was if it wasn't to rid the village of vampires.

The policeman looked thoughtful. "I'm sure we could come to some arrangement," he said, rubbing his thumb and forefinger together.

A bribe. He wanted a bribe. If this was going to free me to carry out my mission, it would surely be an allowable expense. I reached into my reticule and pulled out my purse. It wouldn't open. I tugged at it, wrenched at it, tried to creep up on it unawares, but there was nothing doing. It remained firmly closed. Miss Blaine was being tougher on expenses than I had expected.

"Sorry," I said. "Would you accept an IOU?"

With a low snarl, he shoved me straight into the cell and locked the door. I heard him cross the main office and leave, locking the front door behind him as well.

The cell was very dark. And very cramped. There was no way I would be able to do my yoga exercises. I experimented briefly. Eagle Pose was fine, and I could just manage Reverse Triangle Pose, but Salute to the Sun was out of the question.

I have huge respect for the rule of law, but it seemed to me that, even leaving out the impossibility of exercising, it was my duty to escape. I was already two days into my mission, and the level of tingling still hadn't alerted me to whom I was trying to help.

I attached the drawstrings of my reticule to my skirt's button fastenings to keep it safe, before going as far back in my cell as I could. I took two steps and a hop, and then, engaging my glutes and my abs, I sprang into the air, fingers closing over the sill of the transom window. Keeping my shoulders back, I performed a perfect pull-up, and nudged the window fully open with my forehead. The heavy skirt with its two petticoats was a bit problematic – I wished I was on a mission where I could wear trousers – but eventually I managed to wriggle one leg over to freedom, followed a while later by the other one. It was the matter of but a moment to drop down, landing neatly on the balls of my feet and rolling back onto my heels. Perhaps I should do a parachute jump for charity some time.

I dragged a chair over to the cell door and stood on it to pull the transom window closed, in order to conceal how I got out. And then I found that all I had done was exchange a small, dark prison for a larger, lighter one. There were bars on the windows that proved immoveable, and a securely locked door. On my previous mission, I had been provided with a certain amount of useful equipment. This time, my luggage contained a number of unexpected items, but they were in my room at Madeleine's, and, in any case, I couldn't see how they would help here. I wondered whether the contents of my reticule might provide the answer. I emptied it out on the desk. Nothing practical, although I noted that my purse now opened. I wondered if it would close again if I went to the howff and ordered a stiff drink. Miss Blaine certainly wasn't giving me any extra assistance. In fact, that seemed to be the crucial point. She had provided violettes de Toulouse for the small boy, but she wouldn't let me bribe or dig my way out of incarceration. It was as though she was happy to see me being punished.

I would have to rely on my own resources. I began searching for a spare set of keys. Nothing was hanging on the wall, so I went over to the plain wooden desk and started opening the drawers. The top one contained a pen, a bottle of ink, and some pencil stubs. The middle one contained a bar of carbolic soap, a small scrubbing brush and some dusters. I detected Madeleine's hand in this. The bottom drawer contained three folders, the first bulging, the second less full, and the third looking empty.

The first contained page after page of meticulous paperwork in a fine, bold hand, presumably Sylvain's, since they were all incident reports. And what incidents they were. The most exciting ones I found were the occasional missing cow, which was invariably found before the day was out. Some people might describe Sans-Soleil as douce (yet another Franco-Scots word), but a better description would be utterly boring.

One missing cow report in particular caught my eye – the animal wasn't named, but Sylvain must have been particularly fond of it, since the report was embellished with a large heart. He had set off in search of the missing animal, following hoof prints and reports of the sound of a cow bell. It had taken him many hours of travel, but he eventually tracked the beast down to the village of Sans-Saucisse, where it was causing havoc, eating the flowers in the municipal flowerbeds. He took charge of the animal, assured the town council that it would be fenced in appropriately in future, and promised a letter of apology from the mayor of Sans-Soleil.

The report ended: "The happiest day of my life – united with my beloved." I was quite shocked for a moment until it struck me that searching for the missing cow must be the important police business that had led him to Madeleine's village. I could imagine the excitement among the lassies of Sans-Saucisse when a devastatingly handsome stranger came to call. True, I hadn't actually seen Sylvain, but he would have to be devastatingly handsome to pull a babe like Madeleine. And there's something about a man in uniform, even if it's only a kepi and a cape.

I turned to the second folder. If the first one made policing sound non-eventful, this was of a different order. Its reports consisted entirely of assaults. As I read, it turned out that these were assaults perpetrated on villagers by Sylvain. All of the victims were male. And they had all been in the process of trying to chat up Madeleine. Every report ended in the same way: "[X] apologised to Madeleine. Warning given. No further action."

Sylvain seemed to think he was not only a guardian of the law but also a guardian of Madeleine. Not only completely inappropriate, but also entirely unnecessary, since everything I had seen of Madeleine suggested that she was more than capable of looking after herself.

I flicked open the third folder, expecting to find nothing. There was a page with one log entry, frustratingly undated: "Discovered on my desk this morning." And beside it was a single scrap of paper. A paper with words I had read once before. "*Souviens-toi, tu dois mourir.*"

Remember you must die.

Five

A clear warning, if not a clear threat. It looked as though Madeleine was a widow after all, and I really would have to be nice to her.

And then a terrible thought struck me. Was it the mayor who had sent Sylvain the threatening message? Was it the mayor who had killed him? I didn't want to think of the mayor as a murderer, but was that purely because of his louche attractiveness? I had had no problem thinking he was a vampire. But vampires weren't technically murderers – far from killing people, they turned them undead.

I searched in vain for any notes Sylvain might have made that would cast light on who had sent the message. I looked again at the previous folder. It suggested quite a lot of suspects: every bloke he had beaten up. Or perhaps, unlikely though it seemed, a wife who objected to her husband being beaten up. Or at least objected to him being beaten up by someone other than herself. Since fingerprinting was still in its infancy and lie detector tests wouldn't be invented for another twenty years, the best I could do would be to wave the scrap of paper in each villager's face, demanding, "Did you write this?"

But I couldn't do anything at all while I was stuck in the police station. I had an urge to hurl myself against the locked door, like a moth crashing into a lightbulb. That would simply result in a dislocated shoulder, but even so, my pulse raced and my muscles tensed in anticipation. This was no good – I was tiring myself out to absolutely no effect. It was time to be zen, focusing on the moment, letting go of what I couldn't control, and releasing myself from frustration and anger.

I shoved the note in my reticule and sat on the floor in the lotus position, which was quite difficult given that I was wearing my DMs. Thoughts flitted into my mind, but I didn't focus on them, and simply let them go. More thoughts. Let them go. More thoughts. Let them go. I started to hum songs from *Frozen*. Gradually, so gradually that I didn't notice, I fell asleep.

I was wakened by the sound of a key turning in the lock. What passed for daylight was streaming through the windows. Fortunately, I'm not one of those people who take a while to come to. I scrambled to my feet, and by the time the door opened, and the mayor and the police officer came in, I was busy dusting the desk.

"Good morning, gentlemen," I said. "How may I help you?"

The police officer gaped at me. He rushed over to the cell and tried the door, which was still locked.

I didn't pay much attention to him. My focus was on the mayor, a potential murderer. Admittedly, he didn't look much like a potential murderer. He looked perplexed, more attractive than louche. But if he thought that would put me off my guard, he was sadly mistaken.

The policeman gave up tugging at the cell door. "How did you get out?" he demanded.

"Get out?" I repeated vaguely. "Oh, that. That was easy. Remember what Lovelace says about stone walls and iron bars."

The policeman gave the mayor a questioning look. The mayor gave a Gallic shrug.

"Stone walls," I repeated. "They do not a prison make." I waved towards the windows. "Nor iron bars a cage. I would have left already, but the place is in such a state, I thought I should tidy up a bit first. Madeleine doesn't want Sylvain to come back to such a mess."

"Sylvain is dead," grated the policeman. "He will not come back. Ever."

The mayor didn't respond to this. He addressed me. "You say you were leaving anyway?" He confronted the policeman. "In that case, I want my money back."

"Certainly not," said the policeman. "If she had escaped, I would have rearrested her and you would still have had to pay the fine to get her out."

It was an interesting use of the word "fine". It would have been more accurate to say "backhander".

"If I had escaped, as you put it, I would have made sure I left the area as quickly as possible, and you would have had no chance of rearresting me," I said. There was no need to tell them I would have to remain in the village until I found out what my mission was in time to complete it.

"I beg you not to leave the area, Madame Maque…" said the mayor, stopping there so as not to wear out my name. "Please stay for our celebrations. As mayor of our little village, it is my honour to pay your fine. Officer, you confirm that Madame Maque is not at risk of rearrest?"

The policeman gave me a hard look. "Not unless she gets into any more trouble."

I sensed an underlying threat.

"I guarantee madame's good behaviour," said the mayor, ushering me out of the police station.

"My behaviour is a matter for me, and me alone," I said quite sharply.

"Of course," he murmured. "I was simply trying to ensure your exit from the police station without further delay. Now, I believe you wanted to see our village shield? I would be delighted to show you round the town hall."

This could be an attempt at kidnap.

"That's very kind," I said, "but I really should get back to Madeleine."

Once he had got his sigh over and done with, he said, "It's not far out of your way. I insist."

Kidnap or assassination. My toes tensed inside my DMs. He might find it easy enough to do away with policemen, but he would meet his match with a Blainer.

"Well, if you insist," I said, bestowing an artless smile on him to keep him off his guard.

We walked through the village, and every time we saw someone, the mayor gestured towards me like a horse owner whose filly had just won at Ascot.

"Madame Maque, our distinguished visitor, is coming to the town hall to see our village shield," he said. "She tells me it won third prize in an international exhibition."

The villagers observed me in a sullen sort of way, like Ascot racegoers who had been forbidden to enter the royal enclosure.

He certainly wasn't making any secret of the fact that we were together. Perhaps he was creating an alibi. I wasn't convinced that peering at mountain ranges to tell the time was completely accurate, and he might be able to create enough confusion over when I had last been seen to get away with it.

Eventually we reached the town hall. The mayor pulled the door open and politely stood back to let me go in first. I knew how dark it was in there.

"Don't you keep the door locked?" I asked at the threshold, stalling for time as I let my eyes adjust to the darkness inside.

"No, I no longer have – what I mean is, it's the people's hall," he said. "They must be able to come here whenever they want. Please, madame, do go in."

I stepped over the threshold, bracing myself in case of attack. "It's very dark," I said in a startled voice, concealing the fact that I could now see perfectly well. Even the dim daylight coming in the doorway had some effect, reflected over and over again, and I noted that the coffin was no longer there.

"Yes, I'm sorry. Let me remedy that." His voice was shaking. That was good. He was nervous, and would make mistakes.

He walked past me to the other end of the hall and retrieved a brass lamp that was lurking beside the stacked chairs. Squinting through the gloom, I could see him remove the globe, adjust the wick, light it with a match and set it on the stage. It was only the endless mirrors that made it remotely effective. The globe was smeared and grubby with soot and gave out virtually no light.

He turned, and I could see that he was trembling. "I brought you here under false pretences," he whispered. "I had to make sure nobody could hear us."

"Really? Why?" I sounded politely interested, but I kept my distance. I would react the instant he advanced on me. I could easily get to the door before him, but it might be better if I disabled him before I left.

He hung his head. "What I did was terrible."

His plan was obvious. He was going to confess to murder, in the expectation that I would be paralysed by shock, and then he would attack.

"Oh dear," I said. "What did you do?"

"It's not what I did, it's what I didn't do."

I realised he was one of those murderers who insists on playing psychological mind games with the prospective victim.

"Oh dear," I said. "What didn't you do?"

"I didn't ... I didn't ... "

His voice was so faint that I could scarcely hear it, but if he thought that was going to make me come closer to him, he had another think coming. I had a mission to be getting on with, and I really couldn't be bothered playing psychological mind games with a murderer.

And then I realised he was crying. Tears were rolling down his cheeks, and I was sure he wasn't just putting it on: Stanislavsky hadn't yet done the groundwork for method acting. No, he was a murderer who regretted his crime. I took a couple of steps closer to him, still maintaining a cautious distance.

"You didn't mean it?" I prompted gently.

He didn't seem to be listening to me. "I'm so ashamed," he whispered. "I'm so sorry."

He was definitely remorseful. That was good. Perhaps not good enough to save him from the guillotine, but still proof that he was a fundamentally decent person.

"Madame Maque, can you forgive me?"

This was unexpected.

"I don't think so," I said. "I'm not a priest."

He was crying even more now.

"It's all my fault. I should never have let them arrest you and jail you."

"Sorry?" I said

"Yes, bitterly. I shall regret my cowardice to the end of my days."

"That's what you're upset about, me being arrested?"

"Yes, I should have stood up to them, and to hell with the consequences. But I was too much of a coward."

It was scarcely cowardice to let the police and the judiciary do their job. He had stated on the record that he didn't want to press charges, and had been threatened with jail when he tried to argue against my imprisonment.

"You couldn't have done anything more," I said. "It wasn't like you had a choice."

He turned grateful eyes on me. "You understand? Thank you."

"So, this is why you brought me here?" I asked. "To say sorry to me?"

He shook his head. "No. I have something to ask you. Something you may find impossible to agree to."

I hadn't completely relaxed my guard, and now I was back on full alert. "Go on."

"I have no right to ask this, considering the disgraceful way you have been treated, but when you get back to Engl–" He saw my expression and rephrased, "when you get back to wherever it is you come from, please, I beg you, don't tell anybody you were arrested."

I could imagine the headlines in the *Evening News*: "Morningside Librarian Jailed for Vicious Assault on Council Chief."

"Don't you worry," I assured him. "I won't say a word."

"You really mean it?"

"I really do."

He came at me with his hand outstretched, and I was about to fell him with a rising elbow strike when I realised he only wanted to shake hands.

"And I've got something to ask you," I said. "What happened to Officer Sylvain?"

He dropped my hand as though his bones had suddenly crumbled into dust.

"I don't know," he said dully. "Truly, I don't know. I only know that he's dead and buried."

This man was no murderer. I like to keep an open mind, but there was no doubting his sincerity. What I doubted was my own unexpected reaction when he shook my hand. I had tingled. It wasn't a full tingle, just a very faint one, but it was still a tingle.

I felt my face get hot. The mayor clearly wasn't the subject of my mission, so I must simply be tingling at the touch of a louchely attractive Frenchman. I hoped Miss Blaine wouldn't find out.

To cover my embarrassment, I looked around the hall.

"The lighting isn't very good," I said.

The mayor waved up at the chandeliers. "When people are in, I light the candles. When it's just me, I manage with the oil lamp."

"It's not much use," I said. "You have to clean the globe. Soap and water. Let's take it to the kitchen and get it washed."

"There isn't a kitchen," he said.

"All right, the bathroom."

"There isn't a bathroom. There's just the hall, here."

I looked round. "It's strange," I said, "how it seems so much smaller on the inside than the outside." There was no point making Tardis analogies, although I do feel a certain kinship with the Time Lord.

"There's nothing strange about this building," he said in an agitated sort of way.

I realised he thought I was criticising it. "It's really sensible to have cavity-wall insulation at this altitude," I said. "You must get pretty cold winters. And it looks great. Is that the shield up there? Yes, it is – that's exciting to see the original, very striking design. And I love what you've done with the interior. All those mirrors, the Versailles look, so clever. Are you going to put mirrors on the wall behind the stage as well, and beside the door?"

"How can I?" he burst out. "Of course, that was my plan, to have a town hall so grand that people would come to our village from far and wide to see it. But now it just looks … ridiculous. Even the villagers laugh at it."

"What's gone wrong?" I asked. "Funding problems?"

He nodded.

"You know," I said, "early last century, we decided to build the National Monument of Scotland in Edinburgh to commemorate the soldiers and sailors who died in the Napoleonic Wars. No offence, by the way."

He looked confused rather than offended, so I continued, "It was supposed to look like the Parthenon, but we ran out of money before it was finished. So now it gets called things like Scotland's Disgrace and Edinburgh's Folly."

This didn't seem to be cheering him up. "The point is," I said, "it was a great idea. Just like yours. It's important to be aspirational. You should be very proud of yourself for having had the vision in the first place, and for achieving so much of it. Pat yourself on the back."

But instead of patting himself on the back, he slumped, his head in his hands. "It's all over. Everything was going so well. There was money, more than enough. And now…"

Despite his financial difficulties, he had personally bribed the policeman to get me out of jail. It was a kind and generous thing to do. I felt for my purse. It opened easily – Miss Blaine seemed happy enough to reimburse my rescuer.

I held the purse out to him. "You mustn't be out of pocket on my behalf. I insist you take what you're owed."

"You're very kind." He removed a couple of banknotes and was reaching for a third when the purse snapped shut. Miss Blaine also seemed to know down to the last centime how much he was owed.

"Money," he groaned. "That's the heart of the problem. I built this town hall at my own expense with my own hands."

I didn't like to say it might have been better if he'd brought in an architect who would have included office space and sanitary facilities.

"I knew it would be costly, the mirrors, the gilding – that's why I built it the way I did."

"Makes sense," I said, while thinking the exact opposite.

"And now, what can I do?"

"If you need more money, you could put the taxes up," I suggested.

"The people have no money, so how can I ask them for more?"

This was the most cheering policy statement I had ever heard. But although it must have been very popular among the villagers, the mayor gave a heartbreaking sigh.

"When I was first elected, I said I hoped I would have this job for life, to dedicate myself to advancing Sans-Soleil's interests. And that's what I shall do, however long – or short – my life may be."

It seemed a very morbid thing to say, but perhaps it wasn't surprising, if he kept a coffin in the town hall reminding him that he was going to die. The coffin was nowhere to be seen now. I was going to ask him where he had put it, if there were no other rooms in the building, when I remembered this was supposed to be the first time I'd been in the town hall.

I eyed him critically. Louche, but definitely attractive. "You look in pretty good shape," I said. "Just be sensible. For example, no more than fourteen units of alcohol a week, which is six pints of beer or ten small glasses of low-strength wine."

I caught his look of disbelief. "OK, try to cut down gradually," I said. "And don't go overboard on dairy products, not too much cheese."

He gave a strangled groan. "The cheese! The cheese is essential!"

"All right," I said. "One thing at a time. Start by watching your booze intake for the sake of your liver, and we'll worry about cholesterol later."

He sank back down to the ground, mumbling, "The cheese … the cheese…"

I patted him consolingly on the shoulder. "You're in a state of negative energy," I said. "What you need is to be a bit more zen. Let's sit on the floor. I'm going to go into the lotus position, but since you're a beginner, just lean against the stage with your legs crossed."

I took him through observing the breath for a while, and then we moved on to observing the mind, just letting the thoughts come in and go away. A random thought came in that made me chuckle.

"I'm terribly sorry," I said. "I didn't mean to disturb you. I was just thinking of the rue Morgue, and then of Edgar Allan Poe's short story, and I wondered if you'd had a lot of murders there."

The mayor gasped. Then in a voice so soft that I could barely hear him, he said, "The undertaker is not the undertaker."

I was impressed. For a beginner, it was a pretty good attempt at a zen sentence. I decided to give him a better example.

"The guardian of the law is not the guardian of the law," I said.

He stared hard at me. I could see he was concentrating. "The judge is not the judge."

A second later, it just came to me, a sentence so zen that we could meditate on it for hours. "The teacher is not the teacher."

The mayor's gaze was now one of total awe. "You know everything."

"Not everything," I said modestly. "But I know most things. I had the finest education in the world, thanks to the Marcia Blaine School for Girls in Edinburgh, Scotland." I placed heavy emphasis on the last word, in the hope that it would eventually get through.

"If I don't do what they say, they've threatened to get rid of me," the mayor said. "Every day I ask myself when it will come to an end."

It was, of course, the electorate's democratic right to vote him out, and I could see that if he did decide to put up taxes, he might not get re-elected. But at least he was safe until the end of his current term of office.

"How long have you got?" I asked.

He ran his fingers through his hair. His thick, lustrous hair. With an effort, I stopped myself imagining running my own fingers through his hair. I was on a work trip, besides which, he was rather on the young side.

"I don't know. They're getting impatient," he said bleakly.

"Impatient about this?" I asked, waving at the far wall, blank except for the shield. It was ridiculous, the villagers giving him a hard time about the lack of mirrors if the funding wasn't there. "But that's not fair. It's not their business."

"You're right," he said with sudden force. "It's not. It's my business."

"That's the spirit," I said. "Be proud of what you've achieved. Refuse to be pressurised. Stand up to them."

He stood up. "I will. I will." He strode across the hall, a myriad of dim reflections. And then, "I don't know whether I can."

"Now remember, we're being zen," I said. "We must try not to overreact to perceived difficulties. Let's focus on the positive. You've got the festivities coming up, and everybody's going to have a wonderful time."

My pep talk worked. "Yes, the festivities!" he said. "The day will be a triumph. It has to be. All of the preparations; these will be the greatest celebrations we have ever had."

"There you go," I said. The villagers would love it, and there would be no problem about his re-election. "You said you've booked a singer from Paris?"

"Indeed I have. And a man to play the piano."

"That's great," I said. "What's the singer going to sing?"

"Songs," he said vaguely. "But good ones."

"That sounds very sophisticated," I said. "I'm sure everyone will be really impressed. And absolutely any help I can give you, you only have to ask."

He considered this. "Can you do art?"

"I can indeed." My ceramic model of a black poodle was displayed in the headmistress's room for half a term, even though when it was fired it came out green instead of black.

"Could you make a poster for the concert?"

Miss Blaine knew full well that I had been making posters for concerts, plays and sporting events throughout my schooldays. That must be why she included a set of watercolour paints in my mission kit, for just this sort of eventuality.

"Give me the details and some paper, and I'll make several," I said.

He rummaged around the side of the stage and produced a few sizeable sheets that would be ideal.

"The concert's here, seven thirty on the fourteenth," he said. His brow furrowed. "I can't remember the singer's name. Marie something, I think. Yes, that's it, Marie Jardin, but she spells it all wrong."

"Showbiz types," I said. "No respect for conventional spelling. And then ordinary parents use the daft names for their children, and before you know where you are it's literal anarchy."

"Yes, it's really peculiar, the way she writes it," he said. "It's not Marie, it ends in a Y."

Not Marie, but Mary. Was it possible? I did a quick calculation. She had moved from Chicago to Paris in 1896. "Is her name Mary Garden?" I asked.

"That might have been it," he said. "You've heard of her?"

"Mr Mayor, I have. The whole world will hear of her. She'll be one of the most celebrated divas of the age, composers will write operas especially for her."

The mayor was looking at me quizzically.

"I imagine," I added hastily. "She's very good. And her performance here will ensure that Sans-Soleil's name is known across the land. Thanks to you."

The mayor beamed in delight.

"And what's more," I said, "she's Scottish."

His face fell. "Oh. Not French?"

I could see he was considering cancelling the whole thing. I thought fast. "What better proof could there be that Sans-Soleil is a cosmopolitan centre for the arts than its ability to attract international celebrities?"

"There is that," he conceded.

"A great finale to a great day," I said. "I'd better get on with the posters. I'll bring them to you later on – how long will you be here?"

He turned away from me. "You'll find me at Chez Maman," he said in a low voice.

I wasn't surprised he was embarrassed. This really wasn't good from the point of view of reducing his alcohol consumption.

"Tell you what," I said. "Instead of me coming to you, you can come to me, chez Madeleine."

"Ah, Madeleine!"

I gave him a sharp look. He was attractive. And louche. "Is there anything going on between you and Madeleine?" I demanded.

He looked horrified. "Don't say that – Sylvain would kill me!" And then he let out a long sigh of relief. "But thank God, Sylvain's dead."

"So, there *is* something going on between you and Madeleine?"

"Not yet," he said. "But where there's life, there's hope."

I suddenly caught that faint radio play noise again, which I'd heard in this building on my arrival in Sans-Soleil.

The mayor grasped my arm and began leading me towards the door, saying, "I'd be very grateful if you could make the posters as soon as possible, so that I can put them up in good time."

"Wait, can you hear that?" I asked.

"No, I can't hear anything," he said, although he didn't stop to listen.

"That noise…" I said.

"Mice," he said. "We have a lot of trouble with mice."

It definitely wasn't mice, but I had more pressing things to worry about, namely the mayor's fingers pressing on my arm. From the moment he took hold of me, I had begun tingling again. Surely I had suppressed all romantic feeling for him?

We stepped out into the putative daylight, and I was relieved to find that the tingling stopped. It had been the same sort of low-level tingle I had felt from Madeleine. These weren't the people I was supposed to help, and yet there was some sort of signal coming from them. Perhaps they needed to be recharged in some way. Or I did. I really felt Miss Blaine should have ensured everything was working correctly.

There was a sudden sharp pain in my big toe, as though someone had trodden on it very heavily. I couldn't work out what might have caused it – I hadn't stubbed it on anything. I had been thinking about Miss Blaine, and now here I was, hopping about, squawking a bit.

"Gout?" said the mayor. "It's all that roast beef you English eat."

"I'm not English," I protested. "I eat porridge, haggis, short-bread, tablet, fish suppers. Haddock, not cod. With salt and sauce."

"Ah yes. Short bread. The small baguette you and the English milord both like."

I took a deep breath and changed the subject, returning to what I had been saying inside the town hall: "Did you hear the radio? The crystal set?"

He looked at me blankly, and I realised that broadcasting wasn't yet a thing.

"Back in there," I persisted. "Did you hear voices?"

He shook his head. "No, I told you, I didn't hear anything."

I was sure I had heard something, but on my previous mission I had suffered some visual disturbance. Perhaps this time it was my ears that were affected.

We headed back down into the village and into the main square, dominated by the statue of the monk with his hands upraised.

"Is that the village's patron?" I asked.

"We don't know who it is," said the mayor. "It's a memorial to the Unknown Abbot."

"Why are you commemorating him if he's unknown?" I asked.

"We don't know who he was, but we know what he did," said the mayor, sounding suddenly pious. I was surprised: I didn't have him down as a religious man. But I suppose there's no reason why someone can't be both louche and a person of faith.

"What did he do?" I asked. "Heal the sick, cleanse the lepers, raise the dead, cast out devils?"

"He discovered how to make cheese."

"Ah," I said, "blessed are the cheesemakers."

I expected the mayor to laugh, but he simply nodded. Of course, the first cinema in France opened in 1899, but it would be a while before it screened *The Life of Brian*.

The mayor gazed reverently at the statue. "The Unknown Abbot was in charge of the nearby Abbey of Sans-Foi. He capitalised on the unique characteristics of the area to create a local cheese, to tempt both the eye and the palate."

"Really? I didn't think abbots would approve of temptation. And do the monks still make the cheese?"

The mayor shook his head. "Shortly after taking up cheese-making, they also took up distilling eau de vie and died of alcohol poisoning. But according to legend, they went cheerfully."

"Alcohol can be more curse than blessing," I said, cringing at the memory of having missed That Book because of my hangover. "I suppose the recipes died with them."

"No," said the mayor, "thankfully – I mean, yes. Yes, gone. That is, the cheese-making survives because the monks taught the local farmers. But the brandy recipe, that's disappeared for ever."

"Probably for the best," I said. "It reminds me of a poem by Robert Louis Stevenson, called 'Heather Ale'. It's all about the Picts, who lived in Scotland before the Scots."

"When it was Pictland?" said the mayor.

"Let's not confuse things," I said. "Just focus on the fact that the Picts brewed ale from heather. Anyway, eventually there were just two Picts left."

"What happened to the rest of them?" asked the mayor.

According to the poem, the Scots had massacred them, but that's factually incorrect, so I wasn't going to mention it.

"They'd gone away," I said.

"Where to?" asked the mayor.

"Just – somewhere else. So, there were two Picts left–"

"What were their names?" asked the mayor.

I normally like people asking questions, but he was asking the wrong kind.

"We don't know," I said, a little sharply. "All we know is that they were a father and son, and they were very small. They were found under a stone."

"Like snails? They were as small as snails?"

"No, they weren't as small as snails. They were small, but they were still people. Just small people."

The mayor's brow creased. "Then it must have been a very big stone. Wouldn't it be better to call it a rock? So, they were found squashed under a rock–"

"Did you hear me say they were squashed?" I demanded. "They were hiding under the rock – the stone."

"Why were they hiding?"

I was going to tell him that he'd find out sooner if he didn't keep interrupting me, and then I thought this was probably useful preparation for teaching the pupils the next day.

"They were hiding from the new king. The king was upset, because he ruled over a land covered in heather, but he didn't know how to make ale out of it."

"This was the Scottish king?" asked the mayor.

It was just like the thing, that he'd finally cottoned on to national sensitivities at the time when it was least appropriate.

"The poem doesn't say," I hedged.

"But you said—"

"Never mind what I said, let's just stick to the poem. All we know is that the king was quite bad-tempered. His troops found the very small father and son under a stone."

"How?" asked the mayor.

"They just did," I said. "Look, do you know much about poetry?"

His Sans-Soleil pallor was darkened by a blush. "Oh no. We don't get involved with that sort of thing round here. We know that poetry is decadent."

"A lot of your nineteenth-century French stuff is, admittedly, but Robert Louis Stevenson wasn't French. Despite his middle name. People pronounce it in the French manner, but that's entirely incorrect," I said. "He was christened Lewis after his grandfather, but the spelling was subsequently changed. Returning to his poem, the point is, while it's perfectly proper to interrogate the text for meaning, you can't ask questions about things that aren't in it, like people's names, or how the king's troops happened to find two very small Picts under a stone."

"But I haven't got the text," he objected. "I don't know what's in it. That's why I'm asking."

"If there's anything you need to know, rest assured, I will tell you, so there's no need for you to ask any questions at all. In fact, I'm just reaching the relevant bit, which I thought you would appreciate, given the disappearance of the Unknown Abbot's brandy recipe."

The mayor looked down at the ground, and kicked a pebble with the toe of his shoe. I wondered if he was sulking.

"To recap," I said. "One bad-tempered king, two small Picts. The king says he'll spare their lives if they give him the secret recipe. The father asks for a private word, tells the king that he's happy to pass on the information, but that since he's promised never to tell anybody, he thinks his son will be cross with him."

I paused, but no questions were forthcoming. The mayor had now grasped how to approach the critical discussion of poetry.

"So, the father tells the king to tie the son up and throw him over a cliff into the sea. You may think these are extreme lengths to go to in order to avoid a family row, but in fact the father has an ulterior motive. Have you worked out what it is?"

The mayor shook his head.

"I'll keep going, then. Nearly finished. The son is duly thrown off the cliff to his doom. And then the father turns round and says he was actually worried about his son blabbing about the recipe, so that's why he had him done away with. The father knows that no matter what they do to him, he'll never tell, so the secret of heather ale is about to die with him. The end."

The mayor gave a kind of strangled cry and raced off down one of the narrow lanes between chalets. His reaction proved the power of poetry to move its hearers – and he had only heard my precis of it. He would probably have been in floods of tears if I had actually recited it.

With a final glance at the statue of the Unknown Abbot, I left the square and made my way to Madeleine's chalet.

She didn't seem overjoyed to see me. "I wasn't expecting you," she said. "You were jailed for a week."

"The mayor kindly got me out," I said.

"Ha!" she said. It wasn't a laugh. "Of course. How foolish of me not to think of that. And when did he get you out?"

"Some time this morning."

"This morning? Not yesterday?"

If she thought I had been released yesterday, where did she think I had spent the night? I was quite offended.

"This morning," I repeated.

"So, you have no idea what I got up to last night?" Madeleine asked.

"What you get up to at night is none of my concern," I said.

"Is it not?"

A conversation with Madeleine was rather like a strenuous game of ping-pong. It kept shooting off in unexpected directions and my opponent spent all her time lobbing and blocking.

"It most certainly is not," I said. "And while what I get up to at night is similarly none of your concern, I don't care for your insinuations about myself and the mayor. I admit, he's attractive. In a louche sort of way. But we continue to be nothing more than acquaintances, and I'm not here to help him."

"Of course not." There was a definite sneer in her voice. "You're here to help the poor widow."

I wasn't, but I couldn't exactly say that – it would sound both rude and hurtful. But I could retaliate with a ping-pong counter-hit stroke. "I thought you weren't a widow."

She didn't respond directly. "You were right, the vegetable tian was delicious the day after it was made," she said, and I realised I hadn't eaten anything substantial since my veggie burgers. Right on cue, my stomach rumbled.

"Anywhere in the village you recommend for a quick snack?" I asked. "Does Maman do food?"

"I thought it wouldn't be long before you called in at Chez Maman," said Madeleine, still in sneering mode. I didn't care for that. It suggested she thought I was a dipsomaniac.

"I believe I told you, I'm on a mission and therefore avoiding alcohol," I said. "Although right now, I wouldn't mind a glass of water if that's not too much trouble."

The next thing I knew, a glass of water thudded down on the table in front of me, closely followed by a plate of vegetable tian.

"I saved you some," she muttered. "It's probably gone off by now."

It was actually delicious, not that I was going to tell her that.

Once I'd finished, I asked if I could sit at the kitchen table to do some painting. I didn't mention the mayor in case that fuelled Madeleine's belief that there was something going on between us. I fetched the tin box of watercolours and opened it. It had its own brush in a groove inside, and the lid was sectioned into mixing palettes.

I flattened out the first sheet of paper and began. I couldn't have had a better subject than Mary Garden. The photographs I had seen of her highlighted her flair for the dramatic. She was elegantly sinuous, with elaborate headdresses, long flowing hair and exotic costumes. And in her cross-dressing role as Cherubino, she displayed a fine leg for stockings and satin breeches.

Taking my artistic inspiration from Toulouse-Lautrec's images of the bohemian stars of Montmartre, I was away. I based the first poster on his picture of Loïe Fuller at the Folies Bergère, prancing along with her head thrown back and her dress swirling round her. The second had Mary Garden as La Goulue at the Moulin Rouge, teetering on one leg, the other in the air. And in the third, I painted her as Jane Avril doing the can-can at the Jardin de Paris.

I suspected an undercurrent of xenophobia in Sans-Soleil, so I decided to stick with the name the mayor thought she had, to ensure that the punters actually attended. Using Toulouse-Lautrec's style of lettering, I added:

ALL THE WAY FROM PARIS
MARIE JARDIN
TOWN HALL OF SANS-SOLEIL
JULY 14 AT 19.30
(WITH PIANO ACCOMPANIMENT)

The mayor hadn't turned up, so I decided to take the posters to him, chez Maman. I didn't want them to get squashed en route, and once they were rolled up, Madeleine's wooden sewing box seemed the perfect container. She grumped a bit about having to take out all the needles, thread, buttons, scissors, ribbons, pins and thimbles, but then, she grumped about most things. I set off, the box under my arm.

As I approached the howff, I could hear a raised voice, the muscular, moustachioed schoolmaster. He shouldn't even be in the howff, since it wasn't yet the end of the school day.

"I tell you, she wants in on our action!"

"You mean she wants to buy in?" That was the chubby, florid young judge.

"No, she wants to take over our workforce."

"What? I hope you set her straight." Yet another voice, the tall, bewhiskered police officer.

"Not exactly."

"Why not, you fool?" The young judge again. "We've worked hard to set everything up. There's no place for a woman."

I bristled. I didn't know who this woman was, but I didn't see why she should be excluded on the grounds of gender.

"I'm scared of her," said the teacher, a slight shake in his voice. "She's dangerous. The police know all about her. You should have heard her when she told me – she was proud of it. It was a threat, pure and simple. We have to be careful."

Wanted by the police. I had a sudden terrible suspicion. They were talking about Madeleine. It wasn't clear what work the judge, teacher and policeman were involved in, but I imagined it was some charitable venture, perhaps a precursor of the Rotary Club, which would be established in Chicago in 1905.

Had Madeleine seen an opportunity to skim off the proceeds of their fundraising? By all accounts, Sylvain was a good, honest police officer. What if he had discovered that his wife was going around intimidating people? What if he had tried to remonstrate with her and she was having none of it? What if he had reluctantly concluded he would have to arrest her, and she had murdered him? And what better way for her to deflect suspicion away from herself than to keep insisting he wasn't dead? That way, she presented herself as a devoted wife, and the villagers would shy away from discussing the topic with her for fear of upsetting her. And if they thought she was deranged with grief, that would allow her the leeway to do pretty much what she wanted.

She had made some very odd remarks suggesting that she thought I was watching her. Perhaps she was beginning to crack up as a result of her evil deeds, like Lady Macbeth. Being locked up in the police station last night was probably a lot safer than being at Madeleine's. I would have to jam the chair under the door handle when I went to bed tonight.

It now seemed entirely possible that I was here to save the village from Madeleine. The slight tingling that I had felt with her and with the mayor – perhaps I was here to save the village from the pair of them. The mayor obviously had a *tendresse* for Madeleine and had been very relieved when he remembered that Sylvain was dead.

I was getting there, but I did feel it could have been a lot clearer. It had been simplicity itself to identify the subject of my first mission, but something seemed to be going wrong this time round. Perhaps the system had changed, and Miss Blaine had forgotten to tell me about it. She might easily be getting absent-minded – while she looked as though she was in her prime, she was in fact a very elderly lady.

There it was again, the sudden shooting pain in my big toe, bad enough to make me yelp.

"There's someone outside!" cried the teacher, and the next moment he was peering through the grimy window.

He was staring straight at me, his face chalk-white in comparison with the dark interior, so there was no opportunity to go into unobtrusive mode. I gave him a cheery wave, and walked into the howff.

It was important that they didn't think I had overheard them. Success on a mission depends on assimilating information without everyone knowing what you know.

"Hello," I said. "I'm just popping in to–"

I was about to say, "– hand these posters over to the mayor." But there was no sign of him. Only the teacher, the judge and the policeman were inside, clutching mugs of beer, with Maman muttering to herself in the background. It sounded impolite to imply I wasn't interested in talking to any of them.

I hastily amended my explanation to, "– agree the time when I come in to teach the children new skills." The word "skills" was deliberately chosen, given the teacher's obsession with vocational education.

He gave a gasp and looked round at the others. He had obviously forgotten all about it. This wasn't impressive. Most responsible teachers would be delighted to bring in an external educator so long as they knew the person had been properly vetted. But perhaps he had forgotten about that as well. I would have to explain again.

"There's a special scheme in my country, Protecting Vulnerable Groups," I said. "The police don't let you work with children if you're a convicted criminal. I don't mean minor stuff, obviously, but serious offences. I'm on their list. So, you can understand that I'm more than happy to work with the children here."

The teacher looked terribly uncomfortable at failing to remember all of this, as well he might. We needed to sort out a definite time here and now, or my mission would be over and I would be back in Edinburgh without having taught the pupils anything. It was important that they had a proper academic lesson for once. Given that it wasn't yet the end of the school day, and the teacher was drinking beer in the howff, the kids were obviously back out on work experience.

Using my prefect's voice that was friendly but firm, I said, "Let's make it tomorrow. Ten thirty."

"No, that's … no … that is to say, the pupils have a practical class tomorrow morning," he stuttered.

"My class will be practical too, in its own way," I said. "And the school day starts at eight thirty, does it not? Plenty of time for them to complete whatever task you've set them. So, we're agreed then, I'll come in at ten thirty."

"I don't … I don't know whether …"

"Whether that time's good for me? It's fine, or I wouldn't have suggested it. An hour's all I need, so I'm sure you can accommodate that within your plans for the day. Good, I'm glad we've got that sorted. I'll see you tomorrow morning."

While I was speaking, Maman had left her usual post at the back of the howff and sidled towards me, the manky dish cloth in her hand. She spoke now, in her ancient cracked voice. "You're supposed to be in jail."

She was apparently addressing me, but she was looking at the bushily side-whiskered police officer. He was an intimidating figure at the best of times, but right now he seemed to diminish before my eyes.

"No, I'm not," I said. "The mayor got me out."

She nodded thoughtfully. "Ah yes, the mayor. Our leading citizen. The learned judge may have sentenced you to imprisonment, but of course the mayor is in charge of the police."

"That's it," said the policeman eagerly. "The mayor insisted that I release her. I didn't have any choice in the matter."

He was making out that he had been under orders, concealing the fact that he was a bent copper. I was about to explain that money had changed hands when I realised that might get me put back in jail, especially as the chubby, florid young judge was paying keen attention to the conversation.

"Yes, the mayor, the main man," I said. "Whatever he says goes."

Maman's dish cloth must have been sodden, since she was tugging it tight and winding it round and round until it was practically a rope.

"How kind of the mayor to intervene," she said.

"It wasn't really kind, it was in his own interests," I joked. "After all, a hardened criminal like myself, I wouldn't have been too happy after a week in the clink, and who knows what I might have done?"

"What might you have done?" asked the judge in a perturbed sort of way. Judges aren't known for their sense of humour. Everyone has to laugh at their jokes, which aren't even funny, but they never understand anyone else's. It was safest to back off before he decided I could be rearrested for thought crimes.

"I wasn't being serious," I reassured him. "Honestly, I'm just glad I'm out of prison so that I can focus on the schoolchildren. By the way, do you know where I might find the mayor? I've got a spot of business to sort out with him." I flourished the wooden sewing box.

There was a sudden tearing noise, and Maman was left with the bulk of the twisted dish cloth in one hand, and a ripped-off dish cloth hem in the other. Muttering, she hobbled back to her customary place behind the bar where she produced a needle and thread and started repairing it.

"I'm not being rude, not offering you some of mine," I said, holding up the wooden container. "This might look like a sewing box, but it's not got any sewing stuff in it. It's to do with my business with the mayor. Speaking of whom, did you say where he was?"

"He's–" began the judge.

"He's not here," interposed the policeman.

"I gathered that," I said drily. "Which is why I asked where I might find him."

"You might find him in a field. You might find him in the river. You might find him down the mountainside. You might find him in the forest," said Maman.

"Thank you," I said, even more drily. "That's most helpful."

As I headed for the door, a thought crossed my mind. "Just one thing more, gentlemen – I don't like to ask Madeleine because she gets so disturbed at any mention of her husband being dead. But could you possibly tell me how he died?"

You could have cut the atmosphere with a sgian-dubh. The teacher, the judge and the policeman almost seemed to have stopped breathing. Perhaps it was just a preparation for sighing.

Maman piped up again. "He was torn to death by wild animals." A curious turn of phrase, but expressive. "In the forest," she added.

She had just said the mayor might be in the forest. The fool-hardy fool, I thought, succumbing to the tautology that was rife in the village. If anyone qualified as authorised personnel, that must be the mayor, but his civic title wouldn't save him if he came up against an angry wild boar.

Heedless of my own safety, I ran out of the howff and in the direction of the impenetrable forest. I didn't as yet have a plan, but I hoped the adrenaline rush would help me determine an appropriate strategy. At least I had a wooden sewing box, which I was sure would stand me in good stead.

As I sprinted round a corner, I cannoned straight into the mayor, the wooden box crashing into his chest and knocking him to the ground. It was a huge relief to see he hadn't been torn to death by wild animals.

"I'm so glad you're all right," I said.

"But I'm not," he groaned. "You've broken my ribs."

"Nonsense," I said. "I'm sure they're just bruised. And if they're broken, there's nothing you can do about it. You'll feel better in a month. Come on, up you get."

I put down the box and tried to pull him upright, but he just yelped. In the end, I let him stay where he was, and sat down beside him.

"It's a pity we missed each other," I said.

"The pity is that you didn't miss me," he said, massaging his chest and wincing.

"I mean on the road. I must have been going chez Maman to see you just as you were going chez Madeleine to see me."

"I wasn't anywhere near Madeleine's," he said, and I realised he must be in a bit of discomfort when he gritted his teeth rather than sighing. He looked so miserable that it was all I could do not to stroke his thick, lustrous hair. "I went to Maman's to ask about the cheese, but they couldn't – or wouldn't – help me, so I went to check things out for myself."

His obsession with cheese was a bit troubling. It was possible that he had some sort of hormonal imbalance or was suffering from a lack of nutrients. But there could be other reasons behind his food cravings. Excess cortisol can lead to increased appetite and a hankering for fat.

"Do you feel a bit stressed at the moment?" I asked.

He gave a hollow laugh. "More than a bit."

"Are you getting enough sleep?"

"No sleep at all. I can't sleep because of the stress."

Lady Macbeth had problems with sleeping as well. Perhaps both Madeleine and the mayor were cracking up. Madeleine was always so caustic about the mayor, and implying that there was something going on between him and me. Could that be to deflect suspicion away from him and her? Maman had said Sylvain had been torn to death by wild animals. But would the local CSI be able to tell the difference between someone who had been attacked by wild animals and someone who had been hacked to pieces by his wife and his wife's boyfriend? Only a few hours ago, I had thought the mayor was a cold-blooded killer and then I had decided he wasn't. Was I just vacillating because he had a pretty face? Framed by thick, lustrous hair. I sent a mental plea to Miss Blaine to stop me getting distracted.

The mayor prodded gingerly at his rib-cage and gave another groan. He was in pain, he was vulnerable, and I was going to take full advantage of it to get the truth out of him.

"Did you kill Sylvain?" I snapped in the voice that forced confessions out of even the most uncooperative third years.

"No," he quavered.

"Are you sure?"

"Yes, it's the sort of thing I would remember." His voice was still shaky, but emphatic.

"Did Madeleine kill Sylvain?"

"I don't know."

"Did wild animals kill Sylvain?"

"I don't know."

It struck me that I was rather good at conducting an interrogation. It's not the sort of thing I normally have the opportunity to do, since the questions I ask in the library are more along the lines of "Do you have photo ID or proof of address?" and "Do you know your PIN?"

"Why are you stressed?" I demanded.

There wasn't a second's hesitation. "Because of the cheese," he said. "I went to see the cheesemonger but the shutters were up and there was no answer when I knocked on the door."

That was odd. I had passed the cheese shop on my way to Maman's, and while the window still hadn't been cleaned, there had definitely been no shutters. Perhaps he was having hallucinations because of a lack of cheese. I wasn't dealing with a killer, I was sure of that, but I was dealing with someone who seemed to have a serious disorder; whether physical or emotional, I wasn't sure.

"You need to go to the pharmacy, and as quickly as possible," I said, letting him lean on me as I helped him to his feet. "First, get some arnica. It's a great anti-inflammatory and will sort out any bruising. But also get some nutritional yeast."

"Will that help my ribs as well?" he asked.

"It's very good for you," I said obliquely. He was so fixated on cheese that I couldn't risk telling him that it was an excellent cheese substitute and would reduce his cravings. They could also be reduced by adequate hydration. "And are you drinking enough water?"

He looked suddenly hangdog. "Lots and lots of water."

I couldn't understand why he thought this was something to

be ashamed of until I realised that he hadn't stopped speaking. We were talking in French, so I had heard him say "eau" when in fact he was saying "eau de vie."

"Brandy?" I said reproachfully. "You're drinking loads and loads of brandy? I said you had to cut down on your drinking for the sake of your liver, and that was when I thought you were just having the occasional half-bottle of wine."

"Don't worry," he said, a sad smile on his lips. "The supply of brandy is almost gone. Like the cheese."

I relented. He could do with something to cheer him up. "Here," I said, opening the wooden sewing box and taking out the posters. It was lucky they had been in a container – if I had bumped into the mayor when they were unprotected, they would have been crumpled beyond repair.

He unrolled them and looked at each one in wonderment.

"But these are – did you? – incredible!" he stuttered. "How very – yes, everyone will come to see her. The men, at any rate. Her legs – so very… And this is really what she looks like when she sings?"

I had been so busy trying to create a poster that was artistically striking that perhaps I had taken slight liberties with the actualité.

"Maybe not all the time," I said. Some of the punters might be a tad disappointed to find Mary Garden was primarily a singer, but I was sure I could persuade her to dance a wee jig in between numbers.

And before I knew what was happening, the mayor was bending towards me to give me a kiss. Perhaps it would have been a formal kiss on both cheeks, perhaps it would have been something more lingering, but I never found out, since I involuntarily cried, "Don't crumple the posters!" and he jumped back. The moment was lost for ever.

"I must put these up immediately," he said. He turned to go and spotted a brawny figure striding down the street towards us. It was Cart Woman.

"Look!" he called to her, flourishing the posters. "This is the young lady you have to collect for the celebrations."

She peered at my paintings and sniffed. "She looks a flighty piece. I'm not sure I want her in my cart."

The mayor shot me a pleading glance.

"These images are purely for publicity purposes," I said. "She's actually a very demure, polite young lady."

Cart Woman ignored me. "You said she would have a man with her," she said to the mayor. "A flighty piece with a man. I run a respectable cart. No, I'm sorry, you'll have to find somebody else."

"But there isn't anybody else," the mayor burst out. "You're the only one with a cart. And the only one who knows the route to the pick-up point."

I stealthily felt in my reticule for my purse. It opened.

"You can't get more respectable than the lady and gentleman the mayor has invited to perform for the celebrations," I said, balancing the open purse on my hand as though I was about to juggle with it. "The lady is modest and reserved, and the gentleman is of the utmost probity – he plays the piano."

Cart Woman's eyes were fixed on the purse.

"In fact," I said, "they each lead such a cloistered, contemplative life in Paris that I'm sure they've never been to the country before. They'll be quite overwhelmed when they find out how well we do things here. I imagine you're providing extra cushions? And a rug?"

"There was no mention of cushions and rugs when the mayor booked me," said Cart Woman.

I gave her a sympathetic smile. "Men, eh? No, he would never have thought of that. It's always up to us girls to sort things out properly."

There was nothing inappropriate or demeaning about my use of the word "girls": I was displaying sisterly solidarity. But Cart Woman stood stolid and unyielding.

"Oh," I said as a sudden thought struck me, "if the mayor didn't actually order the deluxe excursion, you're having to underwrite all the extras yourself. That's very kind, and I understand you want to show that Sans-Soleil has one of the finest carts in the land. But I'm a bit of a patron of the arts, and I wonder if I could make a small contribution to your expenses?"

I held out the open purse to her. At the sight of the contents, she gasped as Madeleine had done. "You must do a lot of patronising," she said.

After a moment's study, she extracted a couple of coins. "This should cover my costs."

"Then you'll meet Mademoiselle Jardin and the piano player at the pick-up point as planned?" I asked, briefly wondering whether I'd just invented a new tongue-twister.

She spat on her hand and held it out to me.

"No need for that," I said. "We have a gentlewoman's agreement."

The mayor spat on his hand and clasped Cart Woman's. "And we have a Sans-Soleil agreement. I must put these posters up immediately. Ladies, I'll see you later." He strode off, whistling a happy tune.

But Cart Woman didn't look happy. She surveyed me grimly.

"He may not always get it right, but he does his best. He doesn't deserve people attacking him in the street," she said.

"That was a misunderstanding," I said. "I was just being cautious, making sure that everything in the village was as it should be. You can't be too careful where vampires are concerned. They're very cunning."

She gave a snort. "That's as may be. But you wouldn't catch me attacking public servants in the street."

"Is that because you'd only do it when there were no witnesses?" I said to lighten the mood, but there was no repetition of the laugh, just a withering look.

"Anyway, he's forgotten all about it now," I said. "His mind's on more important matters, like where his next cheese is going to come from."

"I know how he feels," she said.

I was about to tell her to pop into the pharmacy and get some nutritional yeast when she snapped, "It's my livelihood. Week in, week out, I take the cheeses to the pick-up point, and get the other villages' produce in exchange. And now, no cheese, no produce."

"Barter schemes are very good," I said. "But in this case, it sounds as though in the short term at least, you'll have to buy what you need from the other villages."

"How can we?" she said. "Nobody here has any money."

That was why the mayor had said he couldn't raise taxes. But if nobody had any money... "Tell me," I said, "where did the mayor get the funds to build the town hall?"

A shrug. "I don't know, and I don't ask. None of my business. My business is taking cheese to the pick-up point. I've been promised coffins, but where are they?"

"Coffins?" I said. Call it Blainer's intuition, but I had a feeling this might be significant. "Tell me more about the coffins."

"I can't tell you anything about the coffins because I don't have any," she snapped. "It's a crying shame about the cheese shop. I always enjoyed walking past, seeing the cheesemonger hard at work making cheese. The kids loved it too. It was a village institution. And now it's all being done behind closed doors in the morgue. It's not hygienic, if you ask me."

"How do you make cheese in a morgue?" I asked, which sounded like the start of a rather unwholesome joke.

"How should I know? I tell you, this place is going to hell in a handcart."

I had heard that phrase before, the wee girl telling the policeman that her mum thought the place was going to hell in a handcart in the absence of Sylvain. It made sense: if anyone knew about handcarts, it was Cart Woman.

She strode off, leaving me to gather my thoughts. I could see that the undertaker and cheesemonger wouldn't want to be constantly running between two different sets of premises, but making cheese in the morgue did seem potentially unhygienic. On the other hand, would it be preferable to bring bodies into the cheese shop? Probably not.

What was the problem with the cheese? Cart Woman had had

a regular job transporting it to the pick-up point – why had that stopped? And what did coffins have to do with anything? A visit to the undertaker was in order.

I went into unobtrusive mode and set off for the rue Morgue. The wooden shed that I had seen the children approach had its windows shuttered. This must be where the mayor had gone to get some cheese. I sidled up to it. There was no sign of life, which seemed perfectly appropriate for a morgue.

And then I spotted three figures in the distance. If they got close, unobtrusive mode might not be enough to protect me. I crept round the side of the shed where I couldn't be seen.

I could hear their voices as they approached: the teacher, the judge and the policeman.

"How do you suppose he's doing?" said the judge.

"I don't suppose he's doing anything. He always says he can't do it without assistance," said the policeman.

"He can't do it even with assistance." The teacher this time. "Frankly, I don't know why the kids wasted their time."

"At least they weren't wasting your time," said the judge. "You're as good a teacher as he is a cheesemonger."

"And what about you two?" the teacher retorted. "Maman told me all about that so-called trial with the Englishwoman."

I bit my lip hard.

"It was a complete farce," the teacher went on.

"And I suppose you'd have been better," sneered the judge.

"No suppose about it. I bet I know more about the law than both of you put together."

I didn't find this remotely edifying, professional men bickering with another – in fact, in my view it was very unprofessional.

There was a thumping on the wooden door, and after a while it creaked open.

"Any luck?" asked the policeman.

"With the cheese or the coffins?" It was the undertaker and cheesemonger speaking.

"Both. Either."

"No. It's a disaster."

"We'd better come in and sort things out," said the teacher.

There was the sound of footsteps entering the shed, and the door closing.

I crept back round to the front of the shed and positioned myself beside a set of shutters.

"See what I mean?" asked the undertaker and cheesemonger.

I couldn't, since the shutters were close-fitting.

"You've got a model, can't you just copy it?" said the teacher.

"Of course, I would never have thought of that. Thank you so much." The sarcasm was palpable even through the shutters. "Perhaps you could show me how easy it is."

"Yes, why don't you do that?" said the judge. "You claim to be a teacher, so teach him. Your pupils have all gone home for the day, so you've nothing else to do. I'll get on my way."

"So will I," said the policeman.

"Hang on," said the teacher, "where are you off to?"

"I'm not like you, scarcely starting work before it's finishing time. I've got work to do," said the policeman.

"So do I," said the judge.

"What sort of work?" the teacher demanded.

"I've got to be on the lookout for that Englishwoman, in case she starts attacking anybody else," the policeman said.

For the second time, I managed to stop myself intervening.

"And I've got to be on standby in case there needs to be a court case," said the judge. "We'll see you later."

I could hear footsteps approach the door, and discretion won out over valour. There could well be a local by-law against loitering, not to mention eavesdropping, and I didn't want to spend a second night in jail. But as I sprinted down the nearest alleyway, I reflected that I probably didn't want to spend a second night chez Madeleine. There was every possibility that she was a cold-blooded killer, and she had definitely taken against me. If I took the next turning to the right, I would be going in the direction of the school, and that could be a good alternative. I could prepare the lesson for the next day and curl up in a corner somewhere. I can sleep pretty well anywhere after all those summer holidays in a tent. At least there were no midges in Sans-Soleil.

The playground and environs were deserted. The schoolhouse door was locked, but one window was slightly open, and I quickly scrambled through. The school room was dominated by the teacher's high desk on a raised platform. It was a model of practicality, with storage space under the lift-up writing slope, and a series of shelves down to floor level. I perched on the accompanying stool, and had a clear view over all of the pupils' double desks.

There was something odd about the room. The pupils' slates were all stacked on a shelf at the back of the room and were covered in dust, as though they hadn't been used for some time. But the desks and benches were clean enough. The inkwell on the teacher's desk was dry. Was any teaching going on in this place? I opened the writing slope and was shocked to find neither textbooks nor jotters but cigarettes, matches and a hip flask.

A bottle of ink was on the ledge by the blackboard, and I refilled the inkwell. The blackboard was covered in a detailed circular diagram of sines and cosines. The children were studying advanced trigonometry. I was back in an era when there was rigorous teaching of Euclid and Pythagoras. These children would know more about angles than the Venerable Bede.

But the diagram was smudged and smeared, as though a jacket had rubbed against it when someone had walked past. It was no longer a coherent lesson, so I had no qualms about taking the duster and rubbing it all out.

It took a while to find the chalk, which was stuck behind the hip flask. On the blackboard I wrote "Cardinal Numbers", listing one to twenty underneath, a similar list for "Ordinal Numbers", and then lists for "Months of the Year" and "Days of the Week".

That would be a start.

I took off my jacket, rolled it up to form a pillow, lay down and quickly fell asleep.

When the teacher unlocked the door the next morning, I was already at the high desk, having washed at the sinks in the cloak-room, and was making notes with a scratchy dip pen.

He did a double-take. "The door was locked. How did you get in?"

I waved my hand airily. "Didn't the police officer tell you? Locks are child's play to me. In fact, I might incorporate lock-picking into the children's playtime."

I had completely misjudged him when I first met him. I had him down as a macho type, and I thought he had been quite rude when I suggested taking an English lesson. But now I saw that he was actually quite a nervous, uncertain individual. He needed jollying along a bit.

I noticed he was holding a baguette stuffed with ham, lettuce and tomato.

"How kind, you've brought me breakfast," I joked.

"No, this is mine – I mean, yes, of course, it's for you – here, take it."

He scurried across the room and thrust the baguette into my hand. I was going to refuse, but he seemed very insistent, and I really was quite hungry.

He glanced at the blackboard.

"I hope you don't mind my rubbing off your maths lesson," I said.

"It wasn't my – that is, of course I don't mind. The classroom is yours."

"Ah, *mi escuela es su escuela*."

"Is that English?" he asked.

"No, Spanish – it's wordplay on the well-known phrase *mi casa es su casa*. I was imagining you saying that your school was my school. Just as you would say to me, 'my house is your house'." I realised I wasn't being terribly clear, especially as he didn't have the Spanish. I had been too optimistic in thinking that he would understand, given that French and Spanish were both Romance languages. He hadn't had the benefit of a Blaine education. "What I mean is, the school and your home are yours, but you tell me that they're mine."

"Why do I tell you that?"

His voice was positively shaking. What I had taken for hostility the previous day, when he had made an issue of English and Scottish, had stemmed from his embarrassment at not knowing any other languages. He was the teacher in a small village school – it was unreasonable of me to expect that he would reach the standards demanded by the General Teaching Council for Scotland. Especially as the GTC was only set up in 1965.

"It's a nice thing to say," I explained. "You're making me feel welcome by acknowledging that everything you have is mine."

He still seemed very ill at ease. I would move on to another topic.

"This is a lovely baguette," I said. "Fortunately, I'm not one of these people who's totally obsessed with cheese."

His face crumpled in dismay. Apparently, his lack of language skills extended to his own language and he had misunderstood me.

"It wasn't irony. I'm saying I like the baguette," I expanded. "I'm not complaining about the lack of cheese. Actually, right now, I'm more interested in drink."

"Drink?" he stammered.

He had good reason to be discomfited, an educator hiding a hip flask in his desk.

"Yes, I know all about your little secret," I said. "You're lucky it's me who found out – someone else might have gone to the authorities, but I'm not like that."

"What do you want?"

"Don't worry, I've no interest in drinking any of your precious stash. But I wouldn't mind a wee cup of tea."

His face recrumpled. He really needed to lighten up.

"It's all right," I reassured him. "I've had some water out of the tap. You can buy me a tea later. Right now, I've got a class to teach."

I waved him away as, on cue, the small pupils trooped in and stood behind their double desks. I recognised Cart Woman's daughter, and the wee scone who had been bullied by the policeman.

"Good morning, girls and boys," I said.

"Good morning, madame," they chorused.

"You may be seated."

They sat down quickly and quietly. These were well-behaved, attentive pupils, eager to learn. It would be a pleasure taking this class.

"Today we are going to have an English lesson," I said. "Who can tell me where people speak English?"

Every hand shot up.

I couldn't help it, I gasped in horror.

Every hand was covered in blood.

Six

"Your hands," I stuttered. "What on earth have you been doing?"

They sat silently, just watching me. Thankfully, they had lowered their hands so I no longer had to look on the ghastly sight. But there was something creepy about the unbroken silence. It took me a few moments to realise that these children were so well-behaved in class that they would only speak when addressed individually.

I nodded at Cart Woman's daughter. "You, girl. Why are your hands all … like that?"

She stood up. "We had our nature study lesson first thing, madame."

"Nature study? What on earth do you do in nature study to end up like that?"

"We crush the–" And there it was, that word again: "*sangliers*".

These well-behaved, innocent-looking children had just spent an hour or more vivisecting wild boar. The most we had done at Marcia Blaine was dissect an ox eye. And the rest of the ox had been nowhere around at the time.

I wasn't having the class sitting there like murderers in a Jacobean tragedy. It was distasteful.

"All of you, out into the cloakroom and wash your hands thoroughly," I said.

Obediently, they stood up and filed out. There was the sound of running water and splashing before they returned one by one.

When they were all in place, I singled out a small child in the front row. "You, boy. Where do you do this crushing of wild boar?"

He stood up. "In the forest, madame."

"I thought the forest was out of bounds except for authorised personnel?"

"We're authorised personnel, madame."

The children were being put in harm's way for the sake of a lesson. This wasn't education, this was appalling. It had also created a vicious circle: no wonder the wild boar were getting antsy if the schoolchildren were crushing them. I resolved to have a word with the teacher when next I saw him. And given his nervousness about the inspectorate, I could threaten to report him if he proved difficult. Yet another good reason to stick to classroom-based education.

"You may sit down again. Now, class, who can tell me where people speak English?"

The hands, reassuringly clean, went up again.

"England, madame," said the child I chose.

"That answer is correct, but only partially so," I said. "There are dozens of countries where English is the indigenous or official language. But there is one country in which that English is well-seasoned with French. And that country is where I come from, Scotland."

I took the long wooden pointer from beside the blackboard and went over to the map of the world hanging on the wall.

"There," I said, pointing. "Scotland."

I waited for the inevitable, which never came. These innocent, open-minded infants were simply sitting and listening to what I had to say without questioning it. Give me a child at an impressionable age and they are mine for life, I thought.

"We," I said, "the Scots and the French, you and I, are bound together through the Auld Alliance, which is why in my native city, Edinburgh, we have an area called Little France, and another called Burdiehouse, its name a corruption of Bordeaux House where some of Mary, Queen of Scots' retinue stayed."

The pupils, wide-eyed, hung on my every word. Sometimes when I'm explaining things to my colleagues in the library, I see their attention wander. I blame technology for ruining attention spans. But here I was addressing a pre-internet generation. I had never had such an interested audience, and I warmed to my theme.

"In Edinburgh, over a century ago, we built great stone tenements, up to fifteen storeys high."

They leaned forward on their desks.

"The plumbing was more basic in those days, in the sense that there wasn't any. So, the thousands of people who lived in the tenements relied on chamber pots. They obviously didn't want to trail up and down all those flights of stairs to empty them, so they just threw the contents out of the window."

They were scarcely breathing now.

"But in order to warn passers-by down below, they would shout, 'Gardyloo!'"

I smiled encouragingly, but there was no sign of any comprehension.

"They were speaking French," I said. "They were saying look out for the water, *garde à l'eau.*"

A small child raised his hand.

"Yes?" I said.

The child stood up. "But it wasn't just water, was it?"

Small children are greatly drawn to the scatological.

"No, it wasn't just water," I conceded. "But people in Edinburgh are very well-mannered, so they warned the passers-by in a polite way. You may sit down."

Cart Woman's daughter raised her hand.

"Yes?" I said.

She stood up. "It's not very well-mannered to throw …" She hesitated. "… *stuff* out of the window, is it?"

"Other times, other manners," I said firmly. "Sit down. And now, in honour of the Auld Alliance, we're going to learn some English."

Cart Woman's daughter raised her hand again.

"Yes?" I said wearily.

She stood up. "We already know a little," she said in passable English.

119

Why on earth hadn't the schoolteacher told me? I would have tailored the lesson accordingly.

"Including numbers, days and months?" I asked, and was relieved to see them look cagey. The lesson could go ahead as planned.

They were adept at rote learning and before long were reciting all of the words on the board in fine Edinburgh accents. I went round the class asking when their birthdays were in English, which met with reasonable success. I asked when Christmas Day was, New Year's Day and All Saints' Day, which went perfectly.

"And when is Bastille Day?" I continued.

They looked at me in incomprehension. Not a hand went up.

I indicated the wee scone. "You, boy. Bastille Day. When is it?"

He stood up. "I'm sorry, madame. I don't know."

I tapped the pointer at three words on the board. "What does that say?"

"Thursday, twelfth of July, madame."

"Very good. And now this?"

"Saturday, fourteenth of July," he said in a small voice.

There was furtive murmuring from his classmates, and I saw Cart Woman's daughter, who was sitting in the row behind, lean forward to rub his arm.

"Correct," I said. "Two days from now. And Saturday, fourteenth of July is?"

"The day of the celebrations," he said in an even smaller voice.

"And what do we call the day of the celebrations?"

His voice was now so small that I could barely make it out.

"No," I said, "you got it right first time. It's Saturday, not Tuesday. I want to know the special name of the day."

Cart Woman's daughter waved her hand in the air, clicking her fingers.

"Yes?" I said frostily. "You wish to speak?"

She got to her feet. "He didn't say Tuesday. He said Cheese Day. Which is the correct answer."

The others all nodded vigorously.

"I'm in the choir," she went on, going back to speaking French. "We all are. We're going to sing a special cheese song. May we sing it for you?"

I was flummoxed. Since when was Bastille Day Cheese Day? But the pupils were all watching me. From my experience as a Blainer, I knew that a teacher must never appear flummoxed. It's tantamount to displaying weakness, and when pupils sense weakness, they can be as vicious as wild boar. I quickly concealed my flummox.

"That's an interesting suggestion. Yes, I would like to hear your special cheese song."

They all rose to their feet and drew breath to begin. But the wee scone was waving his hand frantically.

"Yes?" I said.

"Please, madame, I don't know whether I'm allowed to sing or not."

He must have a dreadful voice, but it was unfair to be disbarred for that reason. I remembered our school singing classes, when we were divided into nightingales, thrushes and baby birds. Some pupils were permanently traumatised by their categorisation.

"Certainly, you may sing," I said.

"Thank you, madame."

There was the sound of clicking fingers again. Cart Woman's daughter.

"All you require to do to indicate that you wish to speak is to raise your hand," I said. "The clicking is superfluous. Do you wish to leave the room?"

"No, madame. Sorry, madame. I just wanted to ask, is he allowed to sing on Cheese Day as well?"

He must have a really dreadful voice. But even so. "I see no reason why not," I said.

Cart Woman's daughter patted him supportively on the back. "There!" she said.

Now the wee scone's hand was up in the air.

"Yes?" I said.

"But madame, the police officer said I wasn't allowed to join in the celebrations. How can I sing?"

That was why he had been so ill at ease when I asked him what was happening on the fourteenth. He was upset about missing the big day. There was concerned muttering from the rest of the class. They obviously thought as much of the police officer's diktat as I did.

"We'll worry about that later," I said, sitting down on the high stool behind my desk. "In the meantime, let me hear your song."

They all drew breath again, and I saw Cart Woman's daughter was counting them in. Their young piping voices filled the room with a remarkably familiar tune. Frère Jacques.

> *Cher fromage, cher fromage,*
> *Port Salut, Port Salut,*
> *Sainte-Maure de Touraine, Sainte-Maure de Touraine,*
> *Reblochon, Reblochon.*

"Well done," I said. "Is that a traditional song?"

Various hands shot into the air.

"We're going to have a new system," I said. "There's no need to keep raising your hands and standing up." I picked up the pointer again. "Here's what we're going to do. This is the Talking Stick. You can't talk unless you're holding the stick, but when you're holding the stick, nobody else can talk. Understood?"

They all nodded and I handed the pointer to the nearest pupil.

"It's not a traditional song, madame. Our teacher wrote it specially for us."

I was surprised. He hadn't struck me as a songwriter. "That was very good of him," I said.

Cart Woman's daughter grabbed the pointer. "You're not holding the Talking Stick," she objected.

My experience as a prefect enables me to pull rank when necessary, but in my current role, I found myself channelling Marcia Blaine's most formidable mistresses as I thundered, "I am your teacher, girl! The rules do not apply to me!"

She visibly quailed, as did the rest of the class, and the pointer clattered to the floor.

"Now," I said in a more measured tone, "would you like to learn the song in English?"

There were a few nervous nods, but nobody spoke.

"Have the wild boar got your tongues?" I snapped. "I'm waiting for an answer." For a moment, I wondered whether I had missed my vocation, and should have gone in for teaching rather than librarianship. But only for a moment. I'm where I should be.

A small boy scrabbled under the desk for the pointer and lifted it up. "Yes please, madame," he said. "We would like to learn the song in English."

"Very well," I said. "I'll write it for you. While I do that, class monitors, give out the slates and pencils, and everyone copy out what's already written on the blackboard."

I would have suggested an alternative occupation if I'd realised that slate pencils squeaked. Horribly. But I persevered despite the noise, and in a few minutes, I had the new version. I felt it had the additional advantage of actually rhyming.

"Everyone finished copying out? Good." I quickly cleaned the board and wrote up the new lyrics. We spoke them several times to get the pronunciation right, and then I led them in song:

> *Highland Caboc, Highland Caboc,*
> *Lanark Blue, Lanark Blue,*
> *Isle of Arran Cheddar, Isle of Arran Cheddar,*
> *Crowdie too, Crowdie too.*

"You can sing that at the celebrations after you've sung the original. Your parents will be very impressed," I said. "I see from the clock that it's nearly lunchtime. You've worked hard this morning – keep it up. Class dismissed."

A small child grasped the pointer. "Please, madame, can we have some more lessons?"

The pointer was seized by the child next to her. "Yes please, madame. We haven't had any lessons for such a long time."

I looked at the blackboard, which now had nothing but the English verse of the cheese song on it.

"You've just had a maths lesson," I said.

The pointer was passed to the row behind. "That was ages ago, madame. It was the last lesson we had. It wasn't with this schoolmaster, but with the one before."

Cart Woman's daughter appropriated it. "The one who taught us English."

Another hand gripped the pointer. "The one who was torn to death by wild animals."

"In the forest?" I asked.

"Yes, madame."

"The forest that's out of bounds?"

"It wasn't out of bounds then, madame. It only became out of bounds afterwards."

"After your teacher and Officer Sylvain were torn to death by wild animals?"

Nods all round. But silent nods, since nobody had the Talking Stick.

Cart Woman's daughter leaned across and took charge of the pointer. "Not just our teacher and Officer Sylvain. My dad as well." There was a touch of pride in her voice.

"That's dreadful," I said. "I'm most terribly sorry."

"It's all right," she said. "My mum says Madame Madeleine has gone quite mad with grief because she's not from here, and that here we just have to get on with it when someone's torn to death by wild animals."

This was philosophical but worrying. "Torn to death by wild animals in the forest. Where you still go?"

More nods.

The pointer changed hands again. "We go in, do our lessons, and come out again."

I'm always impressed by the pragmatism of country folk, and their lack of sentimentality about animals. These children were off massacring wild boar in the name of nature study, and thought nothing of it.

The pointer had reached the back row. "But we like this sort of lesson better. We like history and geography and Euclidian geometry."

They could almost be Blainers.

"Do you go home for lunch?" I asked.

Universal shaking of the heads and patting of knapsacks.

"Let's go and sit outside while you have something to eat, and then we'll have a lesson," I suggested.

It would have been nice to sit under a tree, but the only trees were in the forest, which was out of bounds.

"Before we go out," I said, "we'll finish the morning with an art lesson. I'd like you all to draw a tree."

The boys spat on their sleeves and the girls spat on their pinafores in order to clean their slates. Saliva seemed to play a key part in Sans-Soleil life. The ghastly screech of slate pencils started up again.

I walked between the desks with my own pencil, squeakily adding a leaf here, straightening a branch there, always with a word of encouragement so that nobody would feel inhibited from pursuing an artistic career in later life.

And I harboured great hopes for them. It was a pleasure to see that they were already *au fait* with contemporary trends, and felt no need to create Realist images. There were Expressionist trees, their shapes distorted and exaggerated. There were Pointillist trees made up of a series of dots. There were Symbolist images with the merest suggestion of a tree. There was even a proto-Surrealist tree that looked like a fish.

We went outside, and sat down on the rough gravel of the playground. It was a dreary setting, without a blade of grass or a single flower, so I got them to hold their slates with their tree drawings above their heads.

"There," I said. "It's as though we're sitting in beautiful woodland, shading us from the…" The Sans-Soleil dusk enveloped us. "Sitting in beautiful woodland," I repeated.

After a while they were getting tired of holding their slates over their heads, so I let them put them down, and they started on their sandwiches.

A small girl was studying me curiously. She got up, ran back into the schoolhouse and returned with the Talking Stick.

"Are you a soldier, madame?" she asked.

"Only for truth and literacy," I said. "Why do you ask?"

"You're wearing soldiers' boots."

I was so impressed by this generation. Not only studying complex mathematics but also free from preconceptions about geography and gender-specific footwear.

"I wear them for comfort and practicality. Now, over the lunchbreak, would you like me to tell you a story?"

Multiple hands seized the pointer. "Yes please, madame."

"Very well. Let me tell you a strange and disturbing story that has its roots in my country, Scotland. You know the gentleman who lives in the castle?"

"The English milord," they chorused.

I unconsciously rechannelled the Blaine schoolmistresses. "Never let me hear you say that again! Do you remember the map you looked at earlier? What country was it?"

The hands were still on the pointer. "Scotland," they chorused.

"Correct. Which means Lord Erroll is not English. He holds the title conferred by James II, King of Scots, in 1453. He is a Scot from the bottom of his kilt to the top of the eagle feathers in his crest badge."

They let go of the pointer and sat attentively.

"A few years ago, Lord Erroll was visited by a writer called Bram Stoker, who came from London for his holidays because holidays in Scotland are the best holidays. Mr Stoker found Lord Erroll's clifftop castle so inspiring that he wrote a whole novel as a result. It's about a very wicked nobleman–"

A tiny hand clutched the pointer. "Lord Erroll? The milord is very wicked?"

The unsophisticated reader so often conflates fiction and real life. It was a salutary reminder that Mrs Spark's egregious fantasy of precocious schoolgirls and their criminally negligent teacher must not reach the general public.

"This is nothing to do with Lord Erroll. The earl is a perfectly pleasant gentleman. The wicked nobleman Mr Stoker wrote about is called Count Dracula, and he is a vampire. Does anyone know what a vampire is?"

They shook their heads. Euclid and Pythagoras, but no *Buffy* or *Twilight*.

"Vampires live for ever," I said. "They are called the undead. They have eyes that glow red, and very long sharp teeth. And when they feel a bit tired or elderly, they sink their long sharp teeth into the neck of the nearest human and suck out all of their blood."

The children hugged themselves in delighted terror. If there's one thing children like more than the scatological, it's the hideously gruesome.

"Then the people they've bitten become undead as well and go around biting people," I went on.

The pointer was appropriated. "And then do the new human people the new undead people have bitten go undead as well and start biting more people?"

"Yes," I said, "of course."

"So, at the end is everyone undead?"

"The story stops before that happens," I said. "It ends with Count Dracula getting killed properly. The popular belief is that vampires can be killed only by driving a stake through their heart…"

I was going on to explain that this never happened in the novel, and that Dracula had actually been despatched with a Bowie knife, when the child grasping the pointer said, "How long do you think it would take for everyone to be undead?"

"It would depend," I said.

"Depend on what?"

"The size of the total population, and the frequency with which vampires bite people," I said. "It's easier if we pose the question slightly differently. Let's ask how many people a vampire bites per month. Then we can work out how many vampires there are in however many months have passed after our starting point."

There was a mass seizing of the pointer.

"Please may we have a sum?" asked Cart Woman's daughter.

"Yes, please, madame!" said her neighbour.

"A sum?" I said. "This isn't a maths lesson. This is your lunch hour. I'm telling you a story."

"We like sums." It was the wee scone this time. "We haven't been able to do any sums for ages."

Who was I to say that stories were superior to sums? The children looked at me expectantly, their half-eaten baguettes discarded beside them. I appropriated a spare slate and wiped it clean with my lace-trimmed cotton handkerchief.

"Very well. Let v represent the number of vampires and B represent the number of people who are bitten. Let's suppose that Dracula, and all other vampires, bite B new people every month, and these people all turn into new vampires by the next month. If at the start of the month you have v vampires, then at the end you have the original v, plus v times B. So, altogether you have … " I wrote carefully on the slate, trying not to let the pencil squeak too horribly. "… $v \times (B+1)$. And a month later, you have?"

There was an outbreak of spitting as they cleaned the tree drawings off their slates, followed by a screeching of pencils. The wee scone and Cart Woman's daughter scribbled like the clappers. And in a photo finish, they both held up their slates, with identical formulae: $v \times (B+1) \times (B+1)$.

"Exactly," I said. "Everyone clear how we got that?"

A few of the other children looked baffled, and the next thing, the wee scone and Cart Woman's daughter were talking them through it until their brows cleared.

"Let's start with Dracula on his own," I said, writing $v=1$ on my slate. "After n months, we have…" I wrote $(B+1) \times (B+1) \times … \times (B+1)$ n times vampires.

The wee scone's eyes were shining. "Madame," he whispered, "what is the population of the world?"

Cart Woman's daughter grinned at him. "Oh yes," she said.

They were both way ahead of the others.

I made a quick estimate of the world population in 1900. "About two billion," I said, and they nodded. I wondered whether the Founder had a scheme through which one could become an honorary Blainer.

"Let's say the vampires are very restrained and only bite one new person every month," I said. "Then it's not just $v=1$, but $B=1$ as well. In that case—"

Suddenly all the children dropped their slates and scrambled to their feet. The schoolmaster was approaching.

"What is the meaning of this?" he shouted. "You're all late for your practical biology lesson!"

I got up as well, standing head and shoulders taller than the tallest pupil. I had the satisfaction of seeing the schoolmaster's eye twitch when he caught sight of me.

"Madame," he stammered, "I thought you said you would only be an hour or so."

I had, and I had gone well over, but I wasn't going to apologise.

"Time is irrelevant when one is imparting knowledge," I said, even though the Marcia Blaine school day was divided into precise fifty-minute periods. "But, in fact, I've finished teaching and we are merely amusing ourselves with a little light algebra over the lunch break."

"So I may take charge of the pupils again?"

"For the moment. They're bright little things, quick learners. There's a lot more I can do with them."

The children were still standing to attention, apparently deaf to the exchange, but the wee scone and Cart Woman's daughter gazed wistfully at their slates.

"Get the slates back in the classroom and go and find your buckets," the schoolmaster snapped. "These cows won't milk themselves."

I wondered if I should tell him about robot milking parlours, but I knew he wouldn't believe me.

He set off like a non-musical Pied Piper, the children trailing after him. I was left alone in the playground, surrounded by bits of filled baguette. I was still quite hungry. It was too late to invoke the five-second rule, but it's also important to eat a peck of dirt over one's lifetime, so I ate my way through them.

It was beginning to prey on my mind that I still didn't know what my mission was. There was so much talk about the forest that it must surely be a place worth investigating. The children showed no fear of it, and while perhaps I wasn't as fleet-footed as they were when it came to evading wild animals, I could think more strategically and I packed a punch.

Not that I could investigate yet. It was crucial to avoid getting into any more trouble with the law in case I was jailed again. I would wait until it was dark, and then sneak in unobserved. But first I would have to go back to Madeleine's to retrieve my head torch. It would be dangerous, given the likelihood of her being a cold-blooded killer, but that meant I was already on my guard and in the right frame of mind to go into the forest.

I set off in the direction of Madeleine's, in unobtrusive mode, and was thrilled to see a group of elderly men congregating around my Jane Avril poster and chattering excitedly. I strolled by them to hear what they were saying.

"They're right racy, these can-can dancers."

"You're telling me. You get to see their drawers."

"I wasn't planning on going, but if there's going to be drawers on show–"

I stopped being unobtrusive. "How dare you talk like this about a distinguished performer? In fact, how dare you talk like this about any woman? This casual sexism is outrageous, and I want you all to apologise right now."

"She's the one showing her drawers," said one of the elderly men, pointing at the poster.

"No, she's not," I said. "That's her petticoat."

"It looks like her drawers."

"I'm the one who painted it, and I can assure you, it's not

her drawers, it's her petticoat. Really, I despair – seeing drawers where there aren't any."

"Where there aren't any?" repeated another elderly man in a hopeful sort of way.

I didn't even speak. I just turned my prefect's gaze on them.

"Sorry, madame," he gabbled. "I spoke out of turn."

"Sorry, madame," they all mumbled. "Very sorry."

"All right," I said. "Now stop leering at a work of art that you've completely misinterpreted and move along."

They backed away, but one whispered to another, "I'm still going, just in case."

"Oi!" I shouted. "I heard that! I'll be checking people at the door."

I waited to be sure they weren't returning to do more leering, and spotted the mayor trudging up a lane, looking thoroughly entangled with the cares of this world.

"Hello," I called, making my way towards him. "I've had a great morning in the classroom with the schoolchildren."

He looked aghast. "In the classroom? What about the milking?"

This anti-intellectualism was disturbing.

"They're away to do that now," I said, hoping that he would pick up on my disapproval. "We achieved a great deal in the classroom through cross-curricular studies designed to create successful learners, confident individuals, responsible citizens and effective contributors. We also sang. Yes, I meant to ask you about that. They sang me their cheese song for your Cheese Day."

The mayor let out a terrible groan.

"Gout?" I said facetiously. "It's all that cheese you French eat." I sacrificed accuracy for the sake of humour. It has long been thought that gout sufferers should avoid dairy products, but the latest studies suggest that these can actually reduce the levels of uric acid and hence the risk of an attack.

"The cheese," he moaned. "What if ..." His words tailed off.

"What if what?" I asked curiously.

"No – nothing – it would be too dreadful. There's still another full day. It will be fine. The celebrations will go perfectly." It was as though he was talking to himself.

"It's the celebrations I wanted to talk to you about," I said. "I wondered if you could clarify them for me a wee bit."

"Of course. They will be great celebrations. The best celebrations ever."

A real politician's answer.

"I have to say, I'm confused," I said, which was something I rarely had to say. "The fourteenth of July is Bastille Day. France's national day. Celebrated across the country. But apparently not here."

"Bastille Day!" The mayor looked as though he was about to spit, but fortunately didn't. "Madame, we in Sans-Soleil have had a cheese festival on the fourteenth of July since the Middle Ages, when the monks of Sans-Foi took up cheese-making at the behest of the Unknown Abbot."

He genuflected in the direction of the main square with its sacerdotal statue. "And then, as always, Paris dictated to the provinces and told us that from now on, the fourteenth of July would be called Bastille Day. The villagers tried it for a year – they made a model of the Bastille and threw cheese at it, except nobody was quite sure what the Bastille looked like. It got squashed by the cheese anyway, so the next year things just went back to normal, and so they've continued."

"And what exactly is normal?" I asked. "What happens?"

The mayor looked nonplussed. "We celebrate cheese."

"What kind of cheese?"

"Every kind. But in pride of place is our own unique local cheese."

"And how do you celebrate?"

"The usual way. We look at it, we examine it, we discuss it, we throw it, we eat it. Not the bits we've thrown, obviously."

"For a whole day? There must be a lot of cheese."

The mayor ran his fingers distractedly through his thick, lustrous hair leaving it attractively tousled. "Yes," he muttered, "there must be. There must be!"

"And it's not just cheese. You've got the international singing star," I reminded him in the hope of cheering him up.

It worked. "Yes, that's right," he said. "That was my idea, to expand the events in order to draw a bigger audience."

"A bit like the Edinburgh Festival and the Fringe," I said.

He looked blank.

"I mean it's a really good strategy, and I'm sure it will keep getting bigger and better," I said.

"Yes," he agreed, "that's exactly what's happened. When the teacher found out I'd hired the singer, he said he would write the song for the children."

"I was quite surprised by that," I said. "The teacher is so obsessed with manual work that I didn't have him down as a lyricist."

The mayor grimaced. "Not the current teacher. The previous teacher."

That made more sense. The teacher who had taught them English, history, geography and Euclidian geometry. "The one who was torn to death by wild animals."

"Perhaps," muttered the mayor, staring at the ground.

Perhaps?

"You mean he wasn't torn to death by wild animals?"

"I don't know. I don't know how he died. I just know he's dead. I wonder how I'll die." He gave a bitter laugh.

"I've already told you, if you want to minimise your chances of heart attack and stroke, cut back on the booze and the cheese," I said.

"Ah yes," he said, laughing again. "Such good advice. Advice I fear I shall have to follow."

He glanced down the road and gave a despairing exhalation. "I must go. I have no work to give her. How can I give her work when…" He disappeared back down the side lane without saying goodbye.

It was Cart Woman who had caught his attention. Now I caught hers. She indicated that she wanted to talk to me, so I stayed where I was.

"I'm looking for my daughter," she called as she got within earshot. "She's got work to do."

More anti-intellectualism.

"She's off milking cows," I said.

Cart Woman rolled her eyes. "She should have finished doing that ages ago."

"Sorry, I think that might be my fault," I said in a tone that contained not a trace of apology. "I was teaching them. She's smart, your wee girl. Particularly in maths."

Cart Woman put her hands on her hips. I thought she was about to object to my suggestion that there should be education in a school: but it was quite the opposite. "Teaching them? Thank goodness someone is. The teaching has gone to hell in a handcart with this new schoolmaster. Our mayor's a good man, but he's done some crazy things recently."

"What's it got to do with the mayor?" I asked. "Education is the responsibility of national government."

"This is Sans-Soleil, madame. We don't hold with national government. The mayor appoints the schoolmaster. And the judge. And the police officer. And a pretty mess he's made of it." She paused. "Did he appoint you?"

I didn't like the implication. "The mayor had nothing to do with my teaching. It was a private arrangement between myself and the schoolmaster."

Her eyes narrowed. "What exactly were you teaching them?"

I thought back. "Literacy, numeracy, history, geography, communication skills, urban design, fine art."

Her expression changed to somewhere between disbelief and awe. "You know about all these things?"

"I do," I said. "I have had the finest education in the world."

"Ah, education!" She clasped her hands to her chest as she sighed; then, spreading her hands wide, she said, "Look at me, madame, I'm not an educated woman, although I do like my books. That's why all I can do is pull a cart. Education, that's the way forward for my girl."

This was casting a different light on things. "You said you were looking for your daughter because she had work to do. What sort of work?"

"Homework, of course."

"Housework?"

"Studying! It's hopeless now because all she's doing are these stupid practical lessons. But I make her go over the lessons she did with the previous teacher so that she doesn't forget."

I mused on the advice not to judge a book by its cover, axiomatic in librarianship, but which I felt I had been guilty of in relation to Cart Woman.

"You said you liked your books? What sort of books?"

Shrug. "Just the usual. Balzac. Dumas. Zola. Stendhal."

"That sounds like an expensive hobby."

"I haven't got money to waste buying books. No, I get them out of the library."

For a moment, I couldn't respond. I had seen no sign of a library as I'd walked round Sans-Soleil, and that in itself worried me – I can usually sense libraries before I see them. But this was the solution to all of my problems. Where there is a library, there is a librarian. And if ever you want to know something, a librarian is the person to ask.

I swallowed hard. "Where's the library?"

She pointed over my left shoulder. "Miles away. Not the next village but the one after that. Well beyond the pick-up point. I don't think anybody else in Sans-Soleil has ever been that far."

Cart Woman could take me in her cart. "What's the librarian like?" I asked, trying to control the excitement in my voice.

"There's a library with books, and that's not enough for you? You want a librarian as well?"

A library without a librarian – it was inconceivable.

"How do you take books out?" I demanded. True, the City of Edinburgh libraries now had self-service machines, but they definitely hadn't had them in 1900.

"There's a woman with a mop," she said. "I tell her what I'm borrowing. She can't read, but she's quite good at remembering. I go with the cart once a week. I don't take out so many books now, of course. I used to get them for my husband as well. He was a great reader. An educated man."

I had forgotten that she too was a widow. "I was very sorry to hear about your loss," I said.

Another shrug. "Oh well, I just have to get on with things."

She seemed remarkably phlegmatic.

"You do believe he's dead?" I said. "I know Madeleine doesn't believe her husband's dead."

A third shrug. "Madeleine's not from here. She's full of silly notions about love and romance. If that's how people think in Sans-Saucisse, I'm glad I live in Sans-Soleil where we just get on with things. But who knows what to believe any more?"

This was interesting. "You mean you don't believe your husband was torn to death by wild animals?"

She folded her brawny arms. "All I'm saying is that I've never known anyone to be torn to death by wild animals, apart from those four ages ago, and they were years apart. Now suddenly everyone's being torn to death by wild animals, and the forest is out of bounds. Unless you're 'authorised personnel'." She put the phrase in derisive quotation marks. "Though how a wild animal would know the difference between an authorised personnel and an ordinary villager is beyond me. Hell in a handcart, that's where this place is going to. Meanwhile, I just get on with things."

I was impressed by her stoicism. "It can't be easy when you're not getting as much work as before. I suppose you still have to keep feeding your horse, or pony."

Her brow creased in a frown.

"Or donkey."

"A horse or pony or donkey?" she repeated incredulously.

"Or … cow?" I ventured.

"You don't come from here either," she declared. "The people in your village must have more money than sense."

I was going to explain that the Scots were noted for their thriftiness, but she was still speaking.

"Why would I waste money feeding an animal to pull the cart when I've got two strong arms and two strong legs?"

"You pull the cart yourself? Like a rickshaw?" No wonder she had brawny arms. And her glutes must put mine to shame.

"Of course. I just have to get on with things."

She made it sound as if she had no choice, but there was one question I had to ask.

"Why do you take the cart to the library? Wouldn't it be easier to walk?"

She gave me a scornful look. "But then I'd have to carry the books back. This way, I can just throw them in the back of the cart."

"Of course," I said. "And any luck with the coffins?"

"None. It's always just getting sorted out and then nothing happens. Hell in a handcart, I'm telling you."

She strode off, leaving me with nothing to do but go back to Madeleine's. I entered the house cautiously, as appropriate when encountering a suspected cold-blooded killer. I felt quite full after eating all of the baguette remnants, allowing me to refuse any food and drink she offered, just in case she decided to poison me. I would also be sure never to turn my back on her.

She was sitting in the kitchen with her head in her hands and she looked as though she was crying. I would normally treat an individual in that situation with sensitivity and sympathy. But it could just be a ploy to get me to go closer to her, and then she would shove a hunting knife between my ribs or toxic mushrooms in my mouth.

"Hello," I said, staying in the doorway.

She gasped and turned away, rubbing her face with her apron. Clever. She was pretending she didn't hear me come in.

"I didn't hear you come in," she snapped. "I've got no food prepared. I had no idea whether you were coming back or not."

"It's OK, I ate earlier," I said.

She faced me, her eyes red and puffy, her cleavage as defined as ever. "And I told you before, you don't get a rebate for not staying the night."

I was incensed to read the subtext: "dirty stop-out". Even more clever. She was trying to needle me, so that I would lose focus and concentration. I did a bit of abdominal breathing before saying calmly, "I believe we agreed that what each of us got up to at night was none of the other's business. I didn't expect a rebate when you kindly facilitated my imprisonment and I don't expect a rebate for last night either. I'm going to my room now, and I'll see you in the morning."

I sat on the bed, gazing out at the dark, dense forest, trying to marshal my thoughts. But it was impossible. Madeleine had decamped to the parlour and was playing the first of Satie's three *Gnossiennes* in the most poignant, heartbreaking way. All I could do was listen. She really was gifted. I would have paid good money to go and hear her in the Usher Hall. Then she moved on to the second one. And after that, the third.

By the time she stopped, night had fallen. I was about to go downstairs to offer my sincere congratulations when I remembered she was more than likely a cold-blooded killer. I had almost fallen into her trap. She was trying to hypnotise me with music, just as Kaa hypnotised Mowgli in *The Jungle Book* cartoon.

I stayed in my room, avoiding lighting the candle in case the light seeped under the door: she had to think I was already asleep. I stood behind the door with the chair in my hand, ready to hit her over the head with it if she burst in to kill me. But when she came upstairs, she went straight into her own room, and after a while, all that could be heard was gentle snoring.

I couldn't risk her suddenly waking up and bumping into me on the stairs, especially when she might try to push me down them. I took the top and bottom sheet off the bed and knotted them together before tying them to the chair, which I wedged under the windowsill. The window was quite small, and it was tricky getting through. Had there been any butter, I would have considered greasing myself, but there wasn't, so I just struggled and eventually managed to shin down the sheets to the ground and slip over the wall without being detected.

I made my way through the village with the help of glints of candlelight through the chalets' wooden shutters, and once I was safely out of the villagers' sight and near the forest, I switched on my head torch. It was all a bit eerie, the soughing of the wind through the branches, the branches themselves casting weird dancing shadows, the crack of twigs. But the thing that was bothering me was the wild boar.

In principle, I'm very pro wild boar. They live in a matriarchal society. What they lack in looks, they make up for in personality. But those tusks are pretty dangerous. And if a boar decides to gore you, it just keeps goring until it's quite sure you're not going to give it any more trouble. I didn't know how easy it would be to convince a boar that I too was a good feminist, so as I went into the forest, I made sure I kept very close to trees that I could shin up at a moment's notice.

The torch lit my path, illuminating not only the trees but also mosses, ferns and shrubs, picturesquely dotted with small red flowers. Pretty though they were, I follow the countryside code – respect, protect, enjoy – so I certainly wasn't going to pick a plant that might be endangered. In any case, I wasn't here to admire vegetation, so I continued my journey to the interior.

I could hear something creeping through the forest in my direction, so I switched off the head torch. Whatever it was didn't sound like a wild boar – they have hooves, and this thing sounded as though it had paws. And as it got closer, I could see two red, gleaming eyes in the darkness. For safety, I tried to clamber up the nearest pine tree, but since I didn't have climbing spurs or a winch pulley, and the pine trunk didn't have branches, I quickly found myself slithering back down again.

The red eyes had a satanic glow. I put the head torch back on in the hope of scaring away whatever the creature was. And I found myself confronted by a massive shaggy-haired wolf, chief predator of the wild boar. If it could make quick work of an animal that was thirteen stone and had tusks, I didn't give much for my chances if I had only a head torch.

The great grey wolf blinked when the light came on and stood there, panting slightly, its jaws stained with blood, its scarlet-spotted tongue lolling out of its mouth. It almost seemed to be smiling, and I couldn't help thinking what big bloody teeth it had.

And then I mused, what is a wolf but a big dog? I'm very good at training dogs. I once trained a ghastly little lapdog in less than a minute. It's all about dominance and showing you're the alpha animal.

Training Dogs the Woodhouse Way was one of my favourite television programmes in the 1980s. Putting out my hand, palm aloft, I brought it sharply up to my shoulder while saying "Sit!"

The wolf sat. It was obviously nothing to do with the language, since this was a French wolf and I was speaking English: it was everything to do with the right signal and the right tone. Channelling my inner Barbara Woodhouse, I held out my arm and lowered it quickly as I said, "Down!"

The wolf lay down. It gave itself a quick lick round the jaws, removing all of the blood, and I could see now that it didn't look remotely ferocious. It was watching me with an alert but compliant expression, which proved the efficacy of the Woodhouse Way.

"Good wolf!" I said, and its tail thumped on the ground, displacing moss and lichen. If I went further into the forest, I might meet the rest of the pack. That could mean more than twenty wolves, and I wasn't sure how many I could train simultaneously. There was also the risk of meeting the wild boar. I had found nothing significant in the forest, no clues to anything, let alone anything untoward, so the wisest thing was to go back to the village. But I wasn't entirely sure which way I had come.

The wolf was watching me. It really looked remarkably intelligent and I found myself saying, "I don't suppose you know how to get back to Sans-Soleil?"

I knew how absurd it was even as I said it. I almost laughed when the wolf scrambled to its feet and set off, for all the life as though it had understood me. But this was far from a humorous situation. Miss Blaine had failed to provide me with a compass, so all I could do was wait for what passed as dawn to work out where east was, and orienteer accordingly.

There was a tug on my skirt. The wolf had returned and had sunk its teeth into my clothing. I knew it wasn't being aggressive, it was simply trying to initiate play, but this was still totally unacceptable. I used the training method of turning away to show the wolf that it had to modify its behaviour if it wanted to get my attention.

The tug on my skirt intensified. This wasn't supposed to happen. I maintained my aloofness and then, success. The wolf let go. I turned to see it bound away. And stop. It looked at me expectantly before returning and sinking its teeth into my sleeve.

"Naughty wolf!" I said severely, and it loosened its grip, looking abashed. It ran forward, ran back to me, ran forward, ran back to me until I finally understood what it wanted. To be taken for a walk.

"Walkies!" I said, stepping forward. The wolf came to heel and must have had a favourite route since it periodically nudged me in a particular direction.

Serendipitously, the trees began to thin. We were reaching the edge of the forest.

"Clever wolf!" I said, even though it had no idea it had inadvertently led me exactly where I wanted to go. But tone being everything, it wagged its long tail. I bent down to scratch it behind the ears, but it shied away, looking apprehensive.

I obviously appeared too dominant. "It's all right," I said. "I wasn't going to hurt you. Go back home now. That's what I'm doing."

I had expected to have to use the head torch to get back to Madeleine's, given the lack of electricity. But as I emerged from the forest, I was puzzled to see a glow of light where the village began. I switched off the head torch and made for it. As I got closer, I saw a large group of villagers holding flaming torches. And pitchforks.

"It's her!" shouted one. "And look, it's true, she's got a wolf with her!"

I hadn't realised the wolf was still with me. It bared its sharp teeth and gave a long, low growl.

The crowd began moving towards us, still wielding their torches and pitchforks.

"Everything's fine," I shouted back. "I've trained the wolf so it does what I tell it."

I was just wondering what else I could do to reassure them, perhaps get the wolf to balance a pine cone on its nose, when it gave a final growl and bounded away back into the forest.

"There, you've frightened the poor thing away," I said accusingly.

But still they came on, and before I realised what was happening, I was seized and pinned to the ground by half a dozen pitchforks, which fortunately went over my limbs rather than through them.

I tried to struggle free, but another pitchfork slammed down across my neck. Thankfully, the pitchforks were only two-pronged, and while I was pretty well immobilised, I wasn't skewered. But no wonder they never got visitors if this was how they treated them.

"What do you think you're playing at?" I croaked. "Let me go."

"Never," said the nearest villager. "We must destroy you. You are evil."

"You're confusing me with perfidious Albion," I said. "I keep telling you, I'm not English, I'm Scottish. You and me, we're the Auld Alliance. Just let me up, and we'll say no more about it."

"Vampire!" he snarled at me.

"Oh, is this because of the misunderstanding with the mayor?" I asked. "I've already apologised, but I'm very happy to apologise again, in writing if necessary."

It all seemed quite anarchic, and I thought it would be wise to invoke some sort of officialdom.

"I wonder, could someone call the police?" I asked. "Or the judge? Or perhaps the mayor?"

The response wasn't the one I'd hoped for. "Burn the witch!" someone shouted and flaming torches were waved in my direction. I tried to struggle free, but it was no good.

"Fools! She's not a witch! You mustn't do that!" shouted another villager.

"Exactly," I agreed. "I'm not a witch. You mustn't do that." It was good that someone was talking sense.

"That won't kill her," the villager went on. "She's a vampire."

"Now just hang on a minute," I said. "I'm not a vampire."

"Then why do you look like one?" said the villager next to me, and everybody nodded.

"Why do I…? I look nothing like a vampire. Do you know the first thing about vampires?"

"I do!" I recognised the voice. It was Cart Woman. "I know all about them," she said. "When my girl came home from school, she was full of it, said you'd been telling her about a book on vampires, so I went straight to the library and got it out."

"It's good, isn't it?" I said, glad of the chance to compare literary notes with another aficionado. "What did you think of the narrative structure? I really like the way it incorporates diary entries and letters, and newspaper articles and ship's logs."

"It's a clever technique for getting the information over," she agreed. "And it's a gripping story. I liked it. Yes, it's very good. Even though it's by an Englishman."

There was an outbreak of spitting among the villagers.

"Bram Stoker is not an Englishman!" I said. "He's Irish. Irish!"

I wondered whether the confusion was arising from the Summer Olympics in Paris, in which the United Kingdom of Great Britain and Ireland were competing as Great Britain. But in that case, it would be more appropriate for us all to be lumped together as British, not English. I was about to help them sort out the various nationalities when someone shouted, "Why are we wasting time? Kill the vampire! There was never any talk about vampires until she came here and started talking about them. That proves she is one."

I gave a weary sigh. "Where's the logic in that? Why on earth would I have been talking about vampires if I was one? I'd just be drawing attention to myself."

"Vampires are cunning," said Cart Woman. "That's exactly what you told me. And what's more cunning if you're a vampire than talking about vampires so that people think you can't possibly be one?"

The other villagers took a while to process this, and then one shouted, "You may be cunning, but we're more cunning than you!"

There was loud agreement from the rest of them.

"I'm quite sure you're more cunning than me," I said in a placatory way. "But I'm really not a vampire." Since I couldn't swivel my head, I swivelled my eyes to look at Cart Woman. "You've read the book. You know all about vampires."

"I certainly do," she said. "I know vampires can turn themselves into wolves, and we just saw you with one. I know vampires are rich, and you've got a purse with lots of money in it. I also know that vampires sleep in coffins, and you keep asking me about coffins."

The villagers muttered darkly.

"I don't keep asking you," I remonstrated. "I just mentioned them in passing. You were the one who talked about them to begin with. And since you know so much about vampires, you'll know I wouldn't be able to eat anything with garlic in it. I can prove I'm not a vampire. Ask Madeleine. I made fabulous sweetcorn and chickpea burgers the other night – well, not real ones because I didn't have any sweetcorn or chickpeas. But they were very good. And I used a clove of garlic."

Somebody spat on the ground right next to me. "A clove! That proves nothing – that's scarcely any garlic at all."

"Then bring me lots of garlic, as much as you've got, and I'll eat it all." Though the thought didn't give me much pleasure.

Fortunately, I then had another thought. "If I was a vampire, I wouldn't be reflected in a mirror," I said. "Get a mirror, and you'll find I reflect perfectly well."

"All right, I'll go and get one," said Cart Woman, but she was stopped by the people round her.

"It's a trick. Don't listen. She was out at night and she had a wolf with her. What more proof do we need?"

"Destroy the vampire!" shouted someone.

The villager next to me raised his pitchfork and prepared to strike.

"Stop!" yelled Cart Woman. "Don't do that!"

I breathed a sigh of relief, even though my breathing was somewhat compromised by the pitchfork across my neck. Cart Woman had finally recognised that I wasn't a vampire and was going to save me.

"A pitchfork's no good," she said. "It has to be a stake."

Just when I thought things couldn't get any worse. I locked eyes with her. "You haven't finished the book, have you?"

She looked a bit uncomfortable. "Not quite. I only got it this afternoon, and I've had other things to do. I've read the beginning."

"If you had read it all, you would know that Dracula didn't get killed by driving a stake through his heart."

Cart Woman folded her brawny arms. "You told my girl that the only way to kill a vampire was by driving a stake through its heart."

"I said no such thing. I said that was the popular belief." I was stalling for time. The popular belief was also held by vampire hunter Van Helsing in the book; it's just not what finally did for Dracula.

"Don't listen to her," shouted a villager. "She's being cunning again. She's telling us driving a stake through her heart isn't the way to kill her because that's the way to kill her."

I had to concede the point. Driving a stake through my heart would definitely kill me.

And then unfortunately somebody found a stake.

There was only one thing that could save me now. A miracle.

Seven

"A miracle!"

The cry came from my landlady, who was pushing her way through the crowd.

A collective male sigh: "Ah, Madeleine!"

She threw herself on top of me, and I felt something other than the pitchfork scratching my neck.

"Look!" She scrambled to her feet. "I only just saw it in the torchlight. We nearly committed a terrible sin, murdering this saintly woman."

She had certainly changed her tune.

The villagers peered down at me, muttering.

"What?" asked one.

"She's wearing a crucifix," said another.

Cart Woman gasped. "She can't be a vampire, then. They can't abide crucifixes. She'd be hissing and all sorts."

I tried to look like someone who never hissed, let alone all sorts.

"We weren't to know. She had a wolf with her," said one sullenly.

"Of course, she did!" said Madeleine. "That proves how holy she is. Don't you remember the story of Saint François and the wolf of Goubillot?"

She was telling it all wrong. She had misappropriated the story of Saint Francis and the wolf of Gubbio.

"That's not–" I began.

She surreptitiously kicked me in the ribs, which was pretty sore as she was wearing her wooden sabots. Perhaps I should have been more sympathetic when the mayor claimed his ribs were broken.

Madeleine was now in full flight. "The wolf terrorised our neighbouring village of Goubillot, devouring the villagers if they strayed outside, and people faced starvation in their homes. It was then that the good Saint François..."

I really had to bite my tongue at that point.

"...Saint François went out to the wolf and commanded it to stop attacking people."

"Wolves are just big dogs," I said. "You have to let them know who's boss."

She gave me another surreptitious kick with her sabot and went on, "It placed its forepaw in his hand in agreement and followed him into Goubillot where the villagers agreed to feed it in return for its promise of peace. This saintly woman–"

"That's me," I said.

Madeleine smiled, but it looked a little sickly. "This saintly woman had made such a pact with the wolf–"

"Brother Wolf," I said. "That's what I call him."

"–with the wolf and was bringing him here to accept our forgiveness and goodwill."

"Is this the wolf that's been tearing people to death?" demanded a villager.

"Forgiveness and goodwill," I said. "Whatever it's done in the past should be forgotten. I've had a word, and you're all safe now."

Madeleine lifted the pitchfork off my neck, and nobody stopped her. Then other villagers lifted the pitchforks off my arms and legs. I sat up, rubbing the sore bit on my neck, and my fingers touched the chain with the crucifix. Glancing at Madeleine, I saw that she was no longer wearing hers.

People were helping me to my feet, with words of apology. I tried to look saintly.

"Bless you," I murmured. "Bless you."

"She's very religious," whispered an elderly man. "She doesn't approve of can-can dancers. Tore strips off us when she heard us talking about them."

147

"Did she indeed?" snorted his equally elderly wife. "Good for her. I'm not having a husband of mine talking about can-can dancers." She gave him a clip on the ear.

"Bless you both," I said, smiling benignly. "Marriage is an honourable estate."

I clutched hold of Madeleine's arm – there was tingling, yes, but very, very slight – and leaned heavily on her, limping, as we made our way back to the chalet while the crowd dispersed.

"Are you badly hurt?" she asked once we were safely inside.

I straightened up and did some back stretches and hip rotations. "I'm fine. I'm a bit bruised from your sabots, but otherwise OK. Thanks to you." I went to unfasten the crucifix.

"No," she said harshly. "You keep it. They'll be watching for it."

"Not as closely as they watch you – the blokes at any rate." I indicated her bosom.

"I'll wear beads instead. It's not the crucifix they're looking at. Sit down, I'll get you something to drink. Some tea."

"Tea? You have tea? Where did you get it?"

She looked away. "I've always had it. Sylvain loves tea."

Still talking about her late husband in the present tense. Worrying.

"That's very nice of you," I said as she began to make the tea. "Although in case you think hot sweet tea is good for shock, that's an urban myth, and I'm not actually in shock, I'm just a bit startled. But tea is proven to have a calming effect, so I'm very grateful."

She didn't reply. She didn't say anything until she'd brought two bowls of tea to the table. She didn't bring any milk or sugar and I didn't like to ask.

"That story," I said. "The one you told about Saint François and the wolf of Goubillot. That was quite similar to, one might almost say identical to, the story of Saint Francis and the wolf of Gubbio."

"I know."

"But you said Goubillot was the neighbouring village. So has the story taken root there as well because of the similarity of the names?"

Shrug. "I don't know if there's any neighbouring village called Goubillot."

"But they all accepted what you said."

"They don't know if there's any neighbouring village called Goubillot either. Nobody ever goes out of Sans-Soleil. Apart from my Sylvain."

"And the woman with the cart," I said. "Although only as far as the pick-up point and the library."

There was another silence while we drank our tea and then Madeleine suddenly burst out, "I'm sorry."

"It's OK," I said. "I'm sure tea is expensive and you didn't want to use it up."

"I mean about what happened to you."

"You've got nothing to apologise for. It wasn't your fault."

"It was," she bit out. "I knew you had gone out."

Now I did feel shocked. I had been so careful to be quiet.

"I thought you were asleep," I said accusingly. "I heard you snoring."

"I was snoring, but I wasn't asleep," she said, and, as we sat there at the table, she began snoring gently while remaining wide awake.

"Very clever. So, you knew I had gone out."

"You made quite a lot of noise when you were going through the window. You were swearing."

"I wasn't swearing exactly," I said. "Just using robust language."

"And if those sheets have been damaged, you'll have to pay for them." She looked down at the table. "I followed you until I realised you were going into the forest. I went to alert my husband's temporary replacement that you were breaking the law, but he wasn't at home. Neither was the judge. So, when I couldn't find either of them, I roused the other villagers." Her fingers tightened round the bowl. "You had been going on about vampires, so I told them you were a vampire. It was even better when you turned up with that wolf. I thought they would just frighten you and you'd go away. I didn't think they'd try to kill you. I couldn't let them do that."

149

I laid down my bowl. "I wonder, could I have a wee bit of sugar to put in my tea? And maybe a wee dash of milk?" I asked. Urban myths sometimes have a basis in truth.

"No milk," she said dully, but she fetched some sugar.

I stirred the sugar until it dissolved.

"You could just have asked me to leave," I said.

She gave a short laugh. "And what good would that have done? I'm tired of pretending, madame, that you are a passing stranger who needs board and lodging. I know you're a spy."

I closed my eyes. Why do people misunderstand the simplest thing? "No," I said. "No, no, no, no, no. You've got it all wrong. I'm on a mission, but that doesn't make me a spy."

"You tell yourself that, do you? Well, do your worst. Creep into the forest trying to find where I've been. Or just come with me, I don't care. But you will never be able to stop me. If you try…" She left the words hanging. "I swear to you, I will find my Sylvain and when I do, it will be the end for you and your paymasters."

It really sounded quite threatening, and I had to remind myself that she was grieving and her emotions would be unpredictable.

"Listen," I said, "what I do is entirely altruistic. I'm here to help. I'm not yet entirely clear about whom I'm here to help, but that's by the way. I'm certainly not here to hinder, and if you want to look for your Sylvain, you go right ahead."

I took a sip of tea, which was really quite good now there was some sugar in it. "Also," I said, "I don't have paymasters, unless you count the City of Edinburgh Council. I'm carrying out this mission pro bono, although I'm allowed reasonable expenses."

She stared at me and then her expression hardened. "You lie so convincingly. Just like the men. But you, you betray your sex by such behaviour."

"Excuse me one moment," I said. "If men can lie convincingly, there's no reason why women can't. But I'm a little offended that you think I'm lying when I'm not."

"It was pure coincidence, then, that you came to our little village and the mayor had the happy idea that you could stay with me?"

"It was," I agreed.

She slapped her hand down on the wooden table, making me jump. "Stop lying to me, madame! I know you're the mayor's creature."

Now she had gone too far. In the voice that had quelled the outburst when Bruntsfield House beat Marchmont House at netball, I said, "I am not the mayor's creature. I am my own creature."

She proved tougher than the Marchmont mob. "I found you with all five of them, plotting. And then the mayor suddenly had the brainwave that this mysterious visitor should lodge with me. Do you think I'm stupid, madame? Do you think I didn't realise you were there to spy on me as I searched for my Sylvain? I can tell you now, you haven't stopped me, nor will you. I shall not rest until I find my beloved."

Angrily, she dashed tears from her eyes. "I can't bear to think what has happened to him. He's lying injured somewhere, wondering why his Madeleine doesn't come for him. All because of your friend the mayor, the murderer."

I pushed aside my tea bowl. "It's funny you say that. For a while, I thought he was a murderer as well. I was quite wary of him, and then we had a good chat, and I realised I was entirely mistaken. He's a decent public servant, trying to do his best for the community."

"Then why," demanded Madeleine, "was my Sylvain investigating him?"

"I don't know," I said. "Why was your Sylvain investigating him?"

"I don't know! He just said he was convinced there were ongoings."

Ongoings were rarely good. But she had said something that didn't make sense. I put on my gentlest voice. "You said the mayor was a murderer. So, you really do accept that Sylvain is dead?"

She jumped to her feet. "Do I have to tell you again and again? My Sylvain is not dead! When my Sylvain had a cold, I felt as though I was encased in a block of ice. When my Sylvain was stung by a hornet, I felt as though I had been pierced by a thousand arrows. The instant my Sylvain dies, my own heart will burst with grief and we will be united in the afterlife."

She seemed to have a remarkably sensitive nervous system.

"That's good to hear," I said. "But if he's not dead, it's a bit unfair of you to call the mayor a murderer."

"I'm not talking about my Sylvain," she snapped. "I'm talking about the deaths of the others."

"What others?" I asked in bemusement.

She threw up her hands. "The others! The judge! The teacher! The undertaker and cheesemonger!"

Grief had made her lose the plot entirely. "They're all fine," I said. Until I remembered it was a full day since I had seen or heard them. "Did something bad happen today?"

"Not today! I thought we had decided to be frank with one another at last, but it seems you are determined to keep up this pretence of ignorance. Very well, I shall spell it out for you. The men I found you with chez Maman have replaced the men who are dead. The forest has been safe for years, apart from the four separate incidents years ago. And then suddenly, one after the other, the judge, the teacher, the undertaker and cheesemonger are torn to death by wild animals. Does that sound plausible to you?"

"Well," I said, "it could be a mutation in the forest fauna. Or the wild animals might have been eating ergot or magic mushrooms and gone mad. You say the judge, the teacher, and the undertaker and cheesemonger were torn to death by wild animals. That's what I heard happened to Sylvain as well."

She sank back in her chair. "That's what they told me. That was why they said I couldn't see his body, because it would be too distressing for me." Her voice got quieter. "I couldn't under-stand why I hadn't died of grief when I first heard the news of his death, and then at the funeral I realised it was because he was still alive. Had he been dead, I could not have stopped myself jumping into his grave onto his coffin, and letting them throw the earth over us both.

She stood up. "It's been a long day. I'm going to bed."

I sat at the kitchen table a while longer, watching the candle burn down. She seemed genuinely convinced that Sylvain was still alive. But there had been a funeral. With a coffin. And if Sylvain wasn't in it, who or what was?

Eight

It was midnight the following night. I flitted unseen along the dark streets of Sans-Soleil. My unlit head torch was pressing into my forehead, and I carried another couple of pieces of equipment I had found in my suitcase. In some ways, Miss Blaine was remarkably thorough; in others, notably telling me what I was supposed to be doing, not so much.

Everyone was tucked up in bed, in readiness for the cheese celebrations the next day. All of the chalets were shuttered and silent, so I was navigating by memory and night vision.

But as I rounded a corner, I saw a tiny chink of light. I calculated that I must now be in the rue Morgue. The light came from the wooden shack: one of the shutters wasn't quite closed. I could hear voices. Voices I had heard in there before. The judge, the teacher, the policeman, and the undertaker and cheesemonger. As I got closer, I could pick up what they were saying.

"It can't be done," said the undertaker and cheesemonger.

"You don't say," said the judge. "It certainly hasn't been done. And unless you work it out in the next seven hours, it won't be done."

"Why don't we go and dig out the proper stuff? At least that would be something," said the teacher.

"Don't even suggest that," snapped the policeman. "That would just make the genius's failure all the more obvious."

"Why am I getting the blame?" said the undertaker and cheesemonger querulously. "Fat lot of use you lot have been."

"How could I help?" asked the judge. "I'm a judge."

"I'm a teacher," said the teacher.

"And I'm a policeman," said the policeman.

"Yes, very funny," said the undertaker and cheesemonger. "So, what are we going to do?"

"What are we going to do?" said the judge. "We're going to do exactly what we've been doing. We lie low."

"Why should we listen to you, you young whippersnapper?" demanded the policeman.

"Because I'm the only one talking sense. You think wisdom comes with age? Can I point out that the eldest of us is the one who-"

At this point, I decided I had heard enough. The bickering was as unedifying as it had been last time, and I had things to do.

I had slept late that morning, as had Madeleine, after the little *contretemps* with the villagers. Breakfast was awkward, with both of us being civil but wary. I tried to give her back the crucifix again, but she insisted on me wearing it when I was going out. The emphasis was very much on my going out: she obviously didn't want to spend more time in my company than was absolutely necessary.

So I went out. The villagers were bustling about at their various tasks and I beamed at them, but they were too shamefaced to meet my gaze.

"Love your enemies and pray for those who persecute you," I murmured, just loud enough to be heard. I was anxious for them to know I didn't bear a grudge, and it was also helpful to remind them of my saintly, non-vampiric status.

Cart Woman was oiling the wheels of the cart and she at least was prepared to talk to me. "I've made cushions, so it's all ready for the floozie and her fancy man," she said.

"I've told you," I said, "Mademoiselle Jardin is propriety itself, and the relationship between herself and the musician is above reproach."

"Rubbish. They're from Paris, aren't they?" said Cart Woman, as if that settled the matter.

Aberdonians don't put up with any nonsense: I could imagine Cart Woman saying something inappropriate, and Mary Garden heading straight back to Paris, accompanied by her accompanist.

"You're right," I said. "I've been to Paris, and you wouldn't believe how rude everyone is."

"I would," she said.

"And what's really ironic," I went on, "is that they say the most awful things about people in the provinces. Especially villagers. They say villagers have got no idea how to behave, that they're so ignorant they don't even know how to say 'please' and 'thank you'."

"Do they indeed?" said Cart Woman. "Well, these two will get a surprise when they meet me. They'll never have met anyone so genteel and refined in their lives. I'll treat them like royalty."

The French guillotined royalty. "Treating them as honoured guests is perfectly adequate. Oh, and could you point me in the direction of the cemetery?"

"What?" said Cart Woman.

"The cemetery," I repeated. "You know, where people are buried. I just fancied seeing it."

"Odd place to fancy seeing," she said. "Is it because you're religious?"

I latched on to this. "Exactly. A cemetery's a great place to ponder one's mortality. A real memento mori."

She looked blank.

"That's a Latin phrase meaning 'remember you must die'," I explained.

Cart Woman shrank away from me.

"It's not morbid," I said, "it's realistic. It encourages you to make the most of the time you have left."

But she wasn't listening. She fished something out of her apron and held it out to me at arm's length. "Has this anything to do with you?" she said through dry lips.

It was a piece of paper. On it was written "*Souviens-toi, tu dois mourir.*" Remember you must die.

"No," I said. "No, nothing to do with me."

"Or someone else in your religious order?"

"No, I'm more of an anchoress, a solitary practitioner. Where did you get this?" I asked.

"I didn't get it. My husband did."

"He didn't know who sent it?"

"I don't know. He never mentioned it to me. I found it on his desk after he was supposedly torn to death by wild animals."

"You really don't think he was torn to death by wild animals, do you?" I said.

"I can't understand why he would have been anywhere near the forest. He always kept to the village streets. He was hylophobic."

I had encountered people with all sorts of odd phobias over the years, but this was the first time I had heard of someone with an irrational fear of forests.

"Was this the result of early trauma?" I asked.

Cart Woman nodded.

"Fairy tales can be very frightening for children," I said. "I can understand that he would be scared of woods after hearing about Hansel and Gretel, and Little Red Riding Hood."

"It wasn't fairy tales," she said. "A tree fell on his house when he was a child and missed him by centimetres."

That did make a forest walk sound implausible.

"It was lucky that he survived," I said. "But you are sure he's dead now?"

"You asked me about this before," she said testily. "Don't confuse me with Madeleine. I told you, she's not from round here, and she has some crazy notions. Of course I'm sure my husband's dead. There was a funeral."

"And how was the wake? I'm sure everyone came round to say their goodbyes."

She shook her head. "No. I was told there couldn't be an open coffin. It would be too distressing, since he had been torn to death by wild animals."

"That's … that's so sad," I said. I had been about to say "interesting", but I thought she might take it amiss. Cart Woman hadn't seen her husband's body because he was said to have been torn to death by wild animals. Madeleine hadn't seen Sylvain's body because he was said to have been torn to death by wild animals. Cart Woman's husband had received a memento mori note. Sylvain had received a note as well. The mayor had also had a note, although he hadn't been torn to death by wild animals. Gradually, I was building up a picture – so gradually that I couldn't actually see anything yet. This was day five of my mission. I definitely needed to make the most of the time I had left.

"So, if you could give me an idea of where the cemetery is?" I prompted. "I'll say a wee prayer for your husband while I'm there."

"Don't bother," she said. "He was a militant atheist."

I followed her excellent directions to the kirkyard and rather wished I hadn't. The smell of decay I detected on my arrival in Sans-Soleil intensified the closer I got. There were a number of new graves, but as yet they didn't have memorial stones or any other identification. All but one had candles on them. I deduced that the candle-less one was Sylvain's: Madeleine would see no reason to tend it. I carefully noted where it was, and returned to Madeleine's to wait for nightfall.

Night refused to be rushed, but fell eventually: and here I was, having left behind the unedifying bickering of the teacher, the judge, the policeman, and the undertaker and cheesemonger, heading back to the kirkyard with my head torch. The smell of decay was worse than ever. I ignored the graves with feebly flickering candles, and made for Sylvain's.

"Thank you, Miss Blaine," I murmured as I extended the spade's retractable handle and locked it in position.

I started digging, pushing the blade into the ground with my foot and levering it. It was a lot easier than I had expected – whoever had filled the grave had failed to pack the soil tight. Far in the distance, I heard the howl of a wolf. I kept digging, piling the earth neatly beside me. Suddenly, the spade hit something solid. Not a stone. I peered downwards, directing the head torch, and saw it was a wooden lid. This definitely wasn't six feet under:

it was relatively close to the surface.

I started digging with renewed vigour and then whirled round as I heard heavy breathing behind me. A massive shaggy-haired wolf stood there, its tongue lolling and its tail wagging.

"Hello," I said, "is that you?" and it lowered its head in the lupine equivalent of a nod. Before I could even say "good wolf" it started scrabbling at the hole I had been digging, sending the earth flying. It was an impressive worker and before long, we succeeded in uncovering the coffin. The stench was horrific. It smelled exactly as I imagined a decomposing body would smell.

The wolf sat on its haunches, panting, its eyes shining red in the light of the head torch. I hesitated, afraid of what I was going to find. The wolf padded up to me and nudged me with its head in the direction of the coffin. I picked up the claw hammer that Miss Blaine had sent along with the spade, and began easing out the nails securing the lid to the coffin base. Only half were out when the wolf began whining and pawing at the lid. Trying not to breathe, I pulled out the rest of the nails.

Leaning over the hole I had dug, I grabbed hold of the top edge of the lid and lifted it. The wolf gave a howl of triumph. It bounded past me straight into the coffin, salivating. It opened its jaws, revealing its long sharp teeth.

The coffin was full of cheese. Wheels of pungent, red-veined cheese. The wolf fell upon it, gulping down huge mouthfuls as though it hadn't eaten for years. It was a first-hand example of the expression "to wolf it down".

There was a sudden tinkling noise and the wolf leaped backwards with a startled yelp. In the middle of one of the cheeses was a bottle. I carefully eased it out, brushing off bits of cheese, which the wolf gobbled up.

The contents looked a bit like red wine, but not exactly. I was studying the bottle, turning it round, when I heard the wolf give a growl and saw it bare its teeth.

There, at the edge of the kirkyard, was a petrifying sight. Four mutant scarecrows. They were coming towards me with their strange blank faces and my mind raced – how to tackle them? My martial arts skills are second to none, but I'd never had to deal with mutants before. And then I realised that they were simply four ordinary people with hessian sacks over their heads, who had cut little eyeholes so that they could see out.

"What are you doing here?" I said sharply, conscious that they could ask me the same question.

They didn't speak, but kept advancing on me. Each of them was carrying a spade, a spade that looked more weighty and deadly than my retractable one. I thought back to my kendo training, wishing I was wearing the helmet with its metal grille, and the padded gloves and breastplate.

The silent foursome were circling me now, raising their spades and preparing to strike. With an inferior weapon, and hampered by my long heavy skirt, I had little chance.

"Wolf," I called in my best Woodhouse way, "you get the one at the back, and I'll tackle the rest of them."

There was no answering howl or bark or even snuffle. I glanced round and saw to my horror that the wolf had disappeared. And then the assailants were on me.

"Kiai!" I shouted, stepping forward and striking. The first assailant crumpled as I parried blows from the other three. I felled another one. But the odds were against me. As I parried again, my spade's retractable handle shattered. I sent a thought wave to Miss Blaine suggesting that she provide better-quality equipment next time when a spade caught the back of my knees and I fell forward.

And then there was a hessian sack over my head as well, with no eyeholes or mouth-hole, and the ghastly stench of decay was so overpowering that I had no strength to retaliate. Some sort of binding went round the sack, fastening it tight round my neck and over my mouth so that I couldn't call for help.

As though from a great distance, I could hear a conversation. It was difficult to make it out. The scarecrows' hessian sacks meant they were even more muffled than Lord Erroll with his scarf, and my hessian sack was an additional level of deafening, quite apart from my head swimming from the awful smell.

This is how the conversation went:

"[inaudible] so dark [inaudible] sure it's her?"

"Of course it is. [inaudible] husband's boots."

"[inaudible] big feet."

"I don't like this. Men [inaudible] but this is a woman."

"Not a pretty one. Not like Madeleine."

[Long pause, possibly for a sigh.]

"[inaudible] got our orders. [inaudible] buried and dead."

"Well, get on with it."

"I can't do it."

"Neither can I."

"Stop arguing and just [inaudible] get on with it."

"Oh, give it here. I'll do it."

There was a searing pain at the back of my skull, and I lost consciousness.

When I came to, I had so many questions. Who were my assailants? Why did they persist in thinking that men and women should be treated differently? Why on earth did they say "buried and dead" instead of "dead and buried"? And where was I?

I tried to wiggle around, and found that I couldn't. I was in some sort of receptacle, my hands folded across my chest. It was so snug that I was stuck fast. I unfolded my hands and tentatively began a fingertip investigation of my surroundings. I was encased in wood. Completely encased. There was wood beneath me, at my sides, and just over my head.

I was in a coffin.

I had been buried alive.

Nine

Exactly how buried was I? If I was six feet under, that was roughly six tonnes of soil. My breathing was already impeded by the hessian sack. How much longer would I able to breathe?

I tried to do a calculation. The internal volume of the coffin minus my own volume would give me the amount of air available, which I could then divide by the amount of oxygen I would require each minute. A simple sum, which would normally take me no time at all, but for some reason, I couldn't concentrate.

I remembered my instructions to the mayor to be more zen. That was exactly what I needed, to slow everything down, so that I was using up the minimum amount of oxygen. But despite that, I was breathing quite fast.

I had never imagined I would be a victim of vivisepulture. If it was going to happen, the nineteenth century was the best time – following the cholera epidemic, there was a lot of nervousness about being buried alive. It even had its own word, "taphophobia", and was much more common than hylophobia, with people devising some very ingenious safety coffins. The simplest and most effective was a bell that the interree could ring, alerting the cemetery night watchman. The only problem was that my coffin was lacking a bell, and I was pretty sure the Sans-Soleil cemetery was lacking a night watchman.

I felt around with my fingertips, and again came across traces of earth and grit in the coffin joints. Was this the very coffin I had found myself in on arrival? On that occasion, it was a vivid enough reminder of my mortality when I hadn't even been enclosed; but now, to be buried alive in it – that was the ultimate memento mori.

I reached up to touch the lid above me, and met two metal handles that I could grip. Oh, the irony. Of course, they had been installed because of the rampant taphophobia, but six feet under, much good would it do you.

I had no hope of Madeleine coming looking for me. She would just be delighted that I wasn't there, while my rent money was. Cart Woman knew of my interest in the kirkyard, but would she know I was missing?

Brother Wolf. If only he could sense where I was. The earth would still be workable. If he could scrabble down to me and howl a bit, he would alert the villagers to come and rescue me. I focused. Brother Wolf ... Brother Wolf ... Brother Wolf ...

Even as I thought it, there was a scraping sound, not of earth, but of wood against wood. The coffin lid was lifted off, and through the hessian sack I could faintly discern a light.

"Good evening, madam. If you would allow me?"

It was Lord Erroll's voice. Gentle fingers felt around my head and neck, and within moments, he had removed the hessian sack. I blinked in the light of the lantern.

He extended his hand to me and helped me out of the coffin.

"Thank you so much," I gasped. My reaction was part relief, part embarrassment. I wasn't in a grave. I wasn't in the kirkyard. I was in a room. The coffin lid hadn't even been nailed down: I could have kicked it away.

I investigated my surroundings. We were in some sort of workshop. Jagged pieces of timber were stacked against the wall, a saw and a container of nails on a stool beside them. The lantern stood on a workbench alongside all sorts of strange paraphernalia, including metal-bound wooden hoops and a contraption with cross-bars, moveable arms, levers and handles. A cheese press.

The stench from the hessian sack was slowly leaving my nostrils, and instead I could smell sour milk. I spotted a row of large metal buckets, some full of milk, some empty. And with a horrified shudder, I saw still more were filled with blood.

I turned to share my horror with Lord Erroll. He was smiling. Perhaps he hadn't yet spotted the gory sight. Or perhaps he had. He wasn't wearing his muffler, and in the lamplight, I could see his long, sharpened fangs.

I thought I had been rescued, but now I wasn't so much out of the frying pan into the fire as out of the coffin into the realm of the undead.

"You're not the Earl of Erroll," I said bitterly. "You're a vampire."

He gave a slight bow. "Indeed so, madam. My name is Dracula."

Every one of my muscles weakened in shock. "Count Dracula," I whispered.

He waved a self-deprecating hand. "Oh, please don't call me that. I don't think it's right to use a title that's been conferred through an accident of birth. Just Dracula will do."

I was scarcely listening to what he was saying. I couldn't take my eyes off those canines, glistening in the lamplight. He was about to turn me into a vampire. What sort of missions could I carry out for Miss Blaine if I had an uncontrollable urge to go around biting men, or, if I could persuade the authorities not to be so gender-specific, anybody? And the council would undoubtedly fire me as a librarian for reasons of health and safety.

There was only one solution. I had to prevent Dracula from biting me. He would find that a Blainer wasn't one of these droopy, swooning women he was used to. When I was a schoolgirl, I was well able to deal with unwanted attention from the boys of the Royal High School and Heriot's – a vampire surely couldn't be much more difficult. My teenage status of Ballbreaker McMonagle could be upgraded to Toothcracker McMonagle.

If Dracula could be killed with a Bowie knife, a saw should work equally well. I grabbed the saw off the stool, scattering the nails on the floor, and dropped into a martial arts stance, the saw in one hand, and the stool in front of me like a shield.

"What are you doing?" he asked.

"Protecting myself," I said.

"From what?"

"Don't play the innocent with me. Are you saying you didn't order your henchmen to kidnap me and put me in there?" I nodded towards the coffin.

He gasped. "In there? In my bed? Good gracious, my mama would never condone such a thing!"

"Yeah, well, we don't always do what our mothers would like." I held the stool more tightly. "Just so as you understand, I'm not going to let you bite me."

"I beg your pardon?"

"Sorry, I'll try to be a bit clearer. You make a move on me, and I'll shove your teeth so far down your throat that you'll have to brush them in a very unusual way. Comprenez?"

"Madam!" There was no doubting his shock. "I am not in the habit of biting people. My mama would not tolerate such behaviour."

I doubted his shock. He was play-acting, trying to lull me into carelessness.

"Nice old lady, is she, your mama?" I asked. "Don't suppose she's bitten anyone in her life – or her afterlife, or whatever it is you lot are in. I know all about you. I've read my Bram Stoker."

His mouth dropped open, displaying his fangs to best advantage. "That…" he whispered. "That … that…"

His legs seemed to give way and he collapsed on the ground. He looked quite dreadful, his face at least two shades paler than it had been. Had he been anyone else, I would have rushed over with the stool, and helped him to sit. But I could see his plan. He was trying to lure me closer so that he could sink his fangs into me.

He was curling up into a foetal position. "That…" he repeated, "that…"

He was barely audible now, but I have remarkably acute hearing. "That … that book…"

I shuddered. I had frequently used those very words myself.

Now I knew he wasn't faking – we librarians can always tell.

Nobody better understands the power of books. It was my duty to promote good reading experiences. I hadn't time to speculate what had upset him so much: if someone was traumatised by a book, it was up to me to put things right as quickly as possible.

With no further concern for my own safety, I went and knelt beside him, putting a comforting hand on his shoulder. "There, there," I said. "Did a nasty book upset you? Nasty book! Don't give it another thought. There are lots of lovely books around. Lots and lots. We'll get you a lovely book that you'll like, and you won't have to think of the nasty book ever again."

He looked up at me pitifully, showing absolutely no sign of wanting to bite me. "Really?" he asked.

"Really," I confirmed. I wondered what book to get him. He seemed to be a bit of a mummy's boy, so something with a strong mother figure. Medea. No, she killed her children in revenge for Jason cheating on her. Mrs Bennet in *Pride and Prejudice*. No, she was a total pain. I was looking for a nice mum. Mrs Weasley would have been ideal, but she wouldn't appear until 1997. *The Railway Children*, featuring Mrs Waterbury. Sadly, we were just too early for that – it wouldn't be published until 1905.

And then I had it. *Little Women*, with the saintly Marmee, had already been in print for several decades. "There's a lovely book with a lovely mum, set in America. Have you heard of America?"

He nodded.

"Good. You'll enjoy it. Well, Beth dies, but she's quite boring, so it doesn't really matter." I realised too late that I should have said "spoiler alert" but he was still recovering from his agitation, so I hoped he wouldn't remember.

He hauled himself up to a sitting position against the wall. "Thank you," he said. "You're very kind."

"Just doing my job," I said.

Now that the immediate literary crisis was over, it struck me that another crisis was still pending.

"You're sure that you had nothing to do with my incarceration?" I asked, and he shook his head.

"In that case," I said, "the thugs who smacked me over the head and dumped me in there are liable to come back. They're planning to bury me. I think we should leave. Quickly."

I got up and went to the door. It was locked.

"How did you get in?" I asked Dracula in puzzlement. "Have you been here the whole time?"

"I'd only just arrived when I found you," he said. "I came in through the window."

The window was shuttered. He must have closed the wooden panels after he came in. I wrenched the shutters open. Only the lower sash windows opened, and it was too small for either of us to get through.

"How did you get the upper sash to move?" I asked.

"I didn't," he said. "I got in there, and then climbed over the top of the shutters." He pointed to a tiny area of broken glass in the top pane.

"There's no need for sarcasm," I said. "How did you really get in?"

He stood up, and then before my very eyes, he disappeared. In his place was a brown bat, which flapped around the room a few times, then hovered on the opposite side of the room to the broken window. Suddenly, it shot past me so quickly that I couldn't register where it had gone. Except it was no longer there.

I peered at the fractured pane and saw two tiny brown ears wiggling in from the outside, followed by a cute wee brown furry face. The bat seemed to breathe in, and then it was through, its wings outstretched, making great whirling circles round the room.

And just as suddenly as the count had disappeared, the bat disappeared, and there was Dracula, descending lithely to the floor like Nureyev performing a jeté.

"That, madam," he said, panting slightly, "is how I really got in."

I had to applaud. "That's very good," I said. "Although it doesn't help me much." I examined the window. If the entire thing was removed, we would be able to get out, but the wood round the two sashes was solid. If I battered it with the stool, I was sure it would be the stool that splintered. A thought struck me. "Are you able to give me just a wee bite, enough to turn me into a bat, but not enough to turn me into the undead?"

He started to curl up again, moaning, "That book … that book…"

"OK, OK," I said. "Plan B. You fly off whenever you like, I'll hide behind the door, and when the goons come back, I'll nip past them and run away. I always won the four hundred yard race on sports day."

He had uncurled and was looking at me in bemusement. "But I need to take this – that's why I'm here."

He indicated the coffin I had so recently vacated.

"Take it where?"

"I'm taking it home," he said. "Back to the castle."

I looked at him, a slight, delicate figure, quite unlike the brawny Cart Woman, who had the additional advantage of a cart.

"That's impossible," I said. "You can't carry that."

"Allow me to contradict you," he said. He put the lid back on top of the coffin and I saw there were grooves enabling it to lie flush. If the body inside was alive or undead, the lid could be closed neatly and effectively from within. With a deft movement, he picked up the top end of the coffin and pulled the whole thing upright, then whisked it across the floor in an elegant figure of eight.

"My own design," he said.

I now saw that there were wheels attached to the base of the coffin, allowing it to move effortlessly.

"That's very clever," I said. "Have you patented it? You really should, or someone else could steal your idea."

"The way they stole my coffin?"

"Exactly," I said. "And if I could make a suggestion – there's been another invention recently called the suitcase. If you could modify your wheels to fit that, you would make your fortune."

He looked a little uncomfortable. "I already have a fortune. It's thoughtful of you to suggest that I involve myself with patents and modifications, but I dislike bureaucracy almost as much as I dislike confrontation."

I understood his reluctance, especially as bureaucracy and confrontation can go hand in hand.

He sent the coffin spinning round, demonstrating its impressive turning circle. "I really should go."

"But it will take you hours to get back to the castle, and you'll have to wait until dawn to see where you're going," I said.

He gave a small, self-effacing laugh. "The distance and the dark are no problem – I've taken it on much more complicated journeys. But I would be very grateful for your help to begin with. Then perhaps you would like to come back with me and have a cup of tea?"

This was an offer not to be refused. "Of course," I said. "What do you need me to do?"

He blushed a fetching shade of pink. "Are you – are you wearing undergarments?"

This male preoccupation with women's underwear was pathetic. We Morningsiders have never been amused by the Weegie jibe, "all fur coat and nae knickers". I gave Dracula the sort of look that could incinerate a Royal High boy at ten paces.

"I believe that's a private matter," I snapped.

"Forgive me for asking such an intimate question," he stammered. "I merely thought you might have been able to tear off a strip of your petticoat."

We had been talking at cross-purposes.

"Not a problem," I said. I went to lift the hem of my skirt and Dracula swiftly turned away, shielding his eyes. I was coming round to the view that he was quite shy, really not the type to bite bosoms. There were rows of tucks at both petticoats' hems, so it was easy to rip away the bottom edges.

Once my skirt was decently covering my ankles again, I waved the lengths of cotton at Dracula. "Will these do?"

"Perfectly," he said. He rapidly tied each length to the top handles of the coffin while he outlined what he wanted me to do once we were outside. It didn't make any sense – in fact, it sounded total nonsense – but his tone was exactly that of a form teacher. When you hear that voice, you know that however daft the instructions, your job is just to obey.

"Won't it hurt?" I asked.

"I can tolerate a degree of discomfort if it is necessary for the task in hand," he said.

Or task in teeth, I thought. I admired his attitude. It was the sort of thing I would expect a Blainer to say.

"So now we smash our way through the window with the coffin?" I asked.

Dracula winced. "We do not. I don't wish my bed to suffer any more damage."

"Then how do we break the window? The stool isn't going to be strong enough, and there's nothing else around that looks suitable."

"There's me," he said, "I'll jump through it."

I looked at him. He was so slight, he would make even less impact than the stool.

He noticed my scepticism and gave a small smile. "There's a technique to it," he said, wheeling the coffin to lean against the wall near the window. "Ready? We'll need to move fast since the breaking glass will probably alert your kidnappers."

"Ready," I said.

And for the second time that night, Count Dracula disappeared and was replaced by a massive shaggy-haired wolf. It backed up slightly, tensing its hind paws, then suddenly gave a mighty leap, crashing through the window, sending splinters of glass and wood everywhere.

I whacked at the debris round the window frame with the legs of the stool, pulled over the coffin by its new cotton petticoat cords, and quickly manoeuvred it onto and over the windowsill. Then I clambered out myself, pulling my thick skirt tightly round me to avoid getting cut by the remaining shards of glass.

Lights were being lit in distant chalets. We had to get away. I balanced the top end of the coffin on the wolf's hindquarters. I took the cotton cords, crossed them over in the wolf's jaws to form a bridle, and fastened the ends to the coffin's carrying handles. I clambered into the coffin, grabbing the handles in the lid to pull it closed over me, and shouted, "Go! Go! Go!"

The wolf went. It wasn't the best journey I've ever experienced. Given the lurching from side to side over uneven terrain and the sounds of disturbed undergrowth and branches, I guessed we were going the direct way through the forest. I was feeling quite groggy by the time we slewed to a halt outside what I must now call Castle Dracula. I pushed the handles to open the coffin lid, my knuckles white with tension.

The phrase "a braw bricht moonlicht nicht" could have been coined for the occasion. The castle was a black Gothic silhouette, however recent its construction. Dracula stood there panting, no longer a wolf, but still fastened to the coffin by the cotton cords in his mouth. Perhaps it was a trick of the moonlight, but his face was paler than I had ever seen it.

"You were a little heavier than I expected," he gasped.

"Muscle weighs more than fat," I snapped. Not true, of course – a pound of muscle weighs the same as a pound of fat – but it's amazing what you can get away with if you say it confidently enough.

"I think you are the most muscular lady I have ever met," he said.

I accepted the compliment with a gracious bow once I had scrambled out of the coffin. "I work out a lot," I said, untying the cords from the handles and freeing him. He spat out a few loose threads.

"Thank you," he said. "Welcome to my house. Enter freely and of your own free will."

I wondered if I should tell him about the tautology, and also remind him that he'd said this all before. But I worked out it must be his traditional greeting to guests, the vampire equivalent of "You'll have had your tea."

He lifted up a terracotta flowerpot from beside the entrance and produced a massive iron key with which he unlocked the great wooden door. He returned to pick up the top end of the coffin, preparing to lug it into the castle. He was obviously exhausted and, conscious of all the steps we would have to go up, I grabbed the other end. He demurred a little, but not too much. We got the coffin upstairs and into a large room that looked like a bedroom, except that it had no bed. There was a large ornately carved wardrobe against one wall, and a chest of drawers with a jug of water and a glass on it. There was a stepped plinth in the centre of the room, covered in a purple velvet cloth. Between us, we hoisted the coffin on top of it.

With a deft move, Dracula unclipped the lid, lifted it off and leaned it against the wall. For the first time, I noticed a brass plaque on it. There were no dates on it, merely the name Draculek.

Dracula saw me looking at it. "It's what my mama calls me," he said with his small self-deprecating laugh. "I know it's a bit babyish and I should change it, but I've got used to it over the centuries." He adjusted a fold of purple velvet and looked on the scene with a critical eye.

"Well, well," he said in an undertone. "It can't be helped."

He sounded exhausted and despondent.

"Is something wrong?" I asked.

"I shouldn't complain. I have my bed back. It won't be as comfortable as it was before, but I'm sure I shall get used to it in time."

"What you need is a wee cup of tea," I said. "Point me in the direction of the kitchen, and I'll make it."

After a token protest, he let me go off. It was a proper Victorian kitchen with whitewashed plaster walls, a stone floor and a solid-fuel range, where a tea kettle was already bubbling away. But in the middle of the room was something I hadn't expected.

"Dracula, there's a cow in your kitchen," I called.

"Yes, that's Ermintrude," he called back. "Don't worry, she's not dangerous."

"I'm more worried about the hygiene element."

"It's fine, she's house-trained. Actually, if you wouldn't mind, could you let her out? She's been cooped up for quite a long time."

I had heard that cows couldn't walk downstairs, but nobody had told Ermintrude. Her descent wasn't elegant, but it was efficient. I unlocked and unbolted the castle's massive doors, and, with a moo of relief, Ermintrude lolloped away into the darkness.

I couldn't see where she had gone. I was going to feel totally daft stumbling around yelling, "Ermintrude!" and heaven knows what I might stumble into.

But just as I was about to go looking for her, she reappeared and licked my face. I felt I was being lightly sandpapered. It struck me that if more cows were house-trained, they could be useful exfoliants in beauty salons – but since I don't hold with beauty salons, which encourage women to be dissatisfied with their looks and pursue unrealistic images of beauty, I decided to keep this insight to myself.

Ermintrude waited patiently while I locked up again, then led the way upstairs, galumphing through the main hall and into the windowless octagonal room where Dracula was slumped in one of the high-backed leather armchairs. She set about licking his face.

"Good girl," he said. "Lie down."

She bent her forelegs until she was in a downward dog pose, then folded her hind legs under her, and laid her head on Dracula's knee.

"I'll get the tea," I said. "And anything for Ermintrude?"

The cow looked at me hopefully, but Dracula said she'd had quite enough grass already. I returned to the kitchen, whose shelves made Mother Hubbard's look well-stocked. I wondered if he ate out a lot. Sans-Soleil seemed short of eateries, but perhaps as a bat he flew further afield – Michelin guidebooks first came out in 1900, which could have given him an idea of where to go.

There was tea, oatmeal, flour, sugar, a few rounds of shortbread and a tiny lump of pink-veined cheese with some teeth marks in it, but that was it. A colander lined with a loosely woven cloth sat over a pan, exuding a stench of rancid milk. On a shelf nearby stood several jugs of fresh milk, the first I had seen in Sans-Soleil, and very much more than a thimbleful.

I brewed the *Camellia sinensis* tea and brought it through with the shortbread and a large jug of milk, large enough to make a point. I was miffed that he had been so stingy when he obviously had enough. He should have heard enough digs about mean Aberdonians to encourage him to defy the stereotype.

"You've not got much food in," I said.

"I manage," he said. "I haven't been getting as much protein as usual. I normally eat the local cheese, which is excellent, but – well, I'm sure you understand the situation. I was terribly pleased to be able to have a soupçon this evening."

His idea of a soupçon and mine were very different, given that he had demolished virtually an entire wheel of cheese.

"It's been very awkward no longer being able to access it," he said. "I have very few alternatives, since I'm a vegetarian."

"A vegetarian?" I echoed in disbelief. That didn't sit well with the blood-sucking. And I remembered when I had met him as a wolf, his jaws dripping blood.

"Yes, for centuries now. It creates difficulties, but it's a matter of principle. I've been having to get my protein from the–"

For a moment, I didn't understand him, and then realised he had spoken in French. *Sangliers.* So that was how he defined being a vegetarian. He might not eat meat while he was in human form, but he devoured whatever was around when he was a wolf.

He needn't think it was acceptable just because he said it in a foreign language. I was conscious of a tinge of sarcasm in my voice as I translated, "You mean wild boar?"

"Like hellebore?" he asked.

"Up to a point," I said, reluctant to spell out the dissimilarity between wild animals and flowers. It confirmed me in my view that home education is no substitute for proper schooling.

"I've been trying to make my own cheese," he added. "But it's not very good. My mama never taught me how to make cheese. I suspect she doesn't know how to make it herself – she's never taken an interest in culinary matters."

"I suppose you can't teach an old dog new tricks," I said, and then realised how rude that sounded. "Sorry, I didn't mean to suggest your mama was a dog. I should have said you can't teach an old bat new tricks."

That sounded even worse. I cast around for a change of subject.

"I was worried I'd lost Ermintrude when I took her out," I said. At the sound of her name, the cow looked up at me. "Shouldn't she be wearing a cowbell?"

"Oh no," he said. "I don't want anyone to know she's here. That's why I keep her indoors."

Now everything was clear.

"Oh my God," I gasped. "You're going to eat Ermintrude!"

Dracula sprang to his feet, his hands over the cow's ears. "How dare you suggest such a terrible thing! I would never dream of eating Ermintrude."

His eyes glowed red and I found myself edging back in my seat.

Just as suddenly, he subsided. "Forgive me, madam. I had no right to speak to you like that. If my mama knew I had been so discourteous to a lady, particularly one who is my guest, she would thrash me to within an inch of my life."

That would be a pretty bad thrashing for someone who was undead.

"Please accept my apologies – I was distressed in case Ermintrude picked up what you were saying."

"No apology necessary," I said. "But you needn't worry. Ermintrude can't understand what I'm saying. She's a cow."

"Animals understand," Dracula said. "Are you suggesting that a cow is a lesser creature than a wolf?"

I had never thought of it quite like that. In my mind, I have a hierarchy of animals, with guinea pigs fairly near the bottom, but I found it difficult to make a comparison between cows and wolves.

"When we first met in the forest," he said, "had I not understood English, how would I have known what to do when you said 'sit'?"

"It's all to do with the tone of voice," I said. "And hand gestures. It's nothing to do with the words."

"Really?" he said, with slightly more than a tinge of sarcasm. "I heard you make a noise and wave your hand, and somehow I intuited that you meant for me to sit? And to show you the way out of the forest? I assure you, madam, I know from direct experience as a wolf that human speech is perfectly comprehensible."

I was going to argue that he wasn't a real wolf, he was a man masquerading as a wolf. That led me to question whether, being one of the undead, he could be classified as a man. I was no longer at all sure of my ground, so I kept quiet. I still thought he was being completely disingenuous about the vegetarianism.

But there was one point that was worth clarifying. "When you're a wolf, you can still understand everything I say in English?"

"Of course. I was trying to explain precisely that – forgive me for being unclear."

"You were perfectly clear," I said. "I was just puzzled. Because when I was attacked by those thugs, I definitely remember saying, 'Wolf, you get the one at the back, and I'll tackle the rest of them.' Perhaps you have selective deafness?"

Dracula flushed. "I heard you," he said in a low voice. "As I told you before, I have a great dislike of confrontation, particularly when there may be a threat of violence."

He had his good qualities, but he would never match a Blainer unless he became a lot more proactive. I remembered that he had also run away when the villagers set upon me.

"So, what happened to you?" I asked.

"I'm afraid I hid behind a tombstone. Since you were insensible, they were obliged to pick you up and carry you. They had a little difficulty because of the weight, and in the end it took all four of them. I followed at a safe distance and saw them take you into the morgue. They left shortly afterwards, which was when I was able to make my ingress through the broken window. I was astonished and, I may say, delighted, to find my bed. I had missed it dreadfully."

He saw the expression on my face, and added hurriedly, "Of course, my key purpose was to ensure that you were safe and well."

It wasn't fair of me to make an issue of it; he had, after all, got me out.

"What I don't understand," I said, "is why your coffin – your bed – was there in the first place?"

"I don't understand either," he said. "It was stolen recently. It was a particularly pleasant day, completely overcast, and I had decided to have a little siesta in the garden. My bed is of my own design, as you have seen, the wheels enabling it to be transported easily. The handles inside the lid let me keep myself protected during a journey, and also to lift it back on if there's a sudden ray of sunshine."

Ermintrude nuzzled up against him.

"Yes, girl, you tried to warn me, didn't you?" he said, bending down to scratch her head. "She was very good, you know. I had come upstairs to make myself a cup of tea when I heard her mooing. I ran back down to find her snorting and pawing the ground, and my lovely bed gone."

Ermintrude licked his hand in sympathy.

"I went to the village to report the theft to the police," he said. "But the officer couldn't have been more unhelpful."

"What did the officer look like?" I asked. "Was he young and very handsome?"

"Oh, no, by no means. A tall, severe-looking man with bushy side whiskers."

Sylvain's replacement. "And what did he say?"

"He said it was my own fault for leaving it unattended, and there was nothing he could do. So, then I went to see the judge–"

"A chubby, florid young man?" I asked.

"That's the fellow. He threatened to put me in jail. He cared even less about my stolen bed than the police officer did, but he said it had come to his attention that I had a cow, and that all milk was now being requisitioned."

"That's very interesting," I said thoughtfully. "You're very isolated here. How would he know you had a cow unless someone had told him? Perhaps someone who had seen Ermintrude when they stole your bed. Or perhaps the judge himself was involved in the theft."

"Good heavens, madam, you can't be suggesting that a jurist would be involved in something clandestine?"

"I'm beginning to think there's something odd going on with these men," I said. "You know the judge actually jailed me for what was an extremely minor incident? The mayor got me out."

Dracula's face brightened. "Ah, the mayor! What a sympathetic gentleman. I went next to seek his help. He asked me such detailed questions about my bed, what it looked like, what its dimensions were, whether I had left a note in it saying, 'Remember you must die'. He was so moved by my predicament that he became quite tearful."

"When was this?" I asked.

Dracula thought. "My bed was stolen last Sunday. I didn't think there was any point in going to the village then. They're not religious, but they do believe in their day of rest. So I went on Monday. Around lunchtime, I think."

Monday. I had arrived in Sans-Soleil on Monday morning. I had found myself in a coffin in the town hall, a coffin containing a note saying, "Remember you must die". A coffin whose confines had felt remarkably similar to the one now in Dracula's bedroom.

"So, you went from the police station to the court to the town hall?"

"No, that wasn't necessary. I sought advice from a lady who had a cart, and she explained that the people I needed to talk to were all in a local establishment called Chez Maman. I spoke to them there."

"And did the mayor say anything about getting your bed back?" I asked.

"I'm not sure. It was difficult to make out what he was saying because he was crying so much. I thought he said he would do what he could as long as he was still alive, but that didn't make a great deal of sense."

"He does get a bit gloomy," I said, but my brain was working overtime. The coffin in the town hall hadn't been the mayor's; it had been Dracula's. And the note in it – the same note that had gone to Sylvain and Cart Woman's husband. There was something linking it all. I was sure of it.

Dracula interrupted my thoughts. "I must apologise for being so brusque the day you called on me. Please excuse my stupidity, but I became suspicious of you."

He bent down to scratch Ermintrude's head again, which I realised was just to avoid looking at me. "I'm afraid to say I told the judge an untruth. I couldn't risk losing my supply of milk. I take it in tea, I need butter to make shortbread, and I've been trying to make my own cheese."

Of course. It was cheesecloth lining the colander in the kitchen. But the repulsive smell suggested that he wasn't being at all successful in his enterprise.

Dracula gave a small embarrassed cough. "I told the judge that Ermintrude wasn't mine, that she was just a stray who was passing through."

The cow gave a reproachful moo and shifted away from him.

"I wasn't being disloyal, girl – I was trying to protect you," said Dracula. He glanced at me contritely. "When you turned up, asking if I had any milk, I thought you might have come to requisition my supplies. Or even…" He dropped his voice and put his hands over the cow's ears again. "…requisition Ermintrude."

"Why on earth would you think that?" I asked.

"Nobody comes to visit me here. You turned up out of the blue, and while I was initially very pleased to have a guest, I thought you might be an inspector enforcing the new laws."

Everybody seemed to mistake me for an inspector. I supposed it was something I would just have to live with, the consequence of my natural air of authority.

Suddenly, I had one of the flashes of insight for which we Blainers are famous. "That must be what's happening in the village – all of the milk is being requisitioned. And I know why. It's needed to make cheese. Tomorrow is their cheese festival."

"Cheese festival?" said Dracula, suddenly animated. "What happens at the cheese festival?"

I would have thought that with his love of cheese he would have been a regular at the festivities. He really didn't get out much.

"I understand they look at cheese, they examine it, they discuss it, they throw it and they eat it. Apparently, they don't eat the bits they've thrown."

"Can anyone attend?" he asked, his voice shaking slightly.

"It's not for me to say, but I'm sure you could sneak in."

"I'd had no cheese for so long," he murmured. "And then, last night, when you kindly opened the coffin and I was able to eat some at last – it revived me. I've really not been feeling at all well, without the cheese, and not getting a good night's sleep."

"It's good that you've got your bed back, then," I said. "You'll get a proper sleep now."

He shook his head. "Not without my mattress."

"What's happened to your mattress?" I asked.

"Who knows? Scattered to the four winds, I dare say. My lovely Aberdeenshire soil, brought over specially."

"Of course!" I breathed. "You're a vampire. You can rest only in your native earth. But shouldn't it be Transylvanian?"

"No!" he shouted, alarming the cow. "Madam, I will thank you not to perpetuate the fallacies and calumnies of that ... that book."

"Are we talking about Bram Stoker's *Dracula*?" I asked, just to make sure.

He collapsed back into the wing armchair, wringing his hands. "I liked Mr Stoker very much when he came to Port Erroll. I enjoyed chatting with him, particularly as he had such a very keen interest in vampires. I found he had some quite extraordinary ideas about us, and I explained to him that they were entirely misconceived. Naturally, I thought he would listen to me and then that ... that book appeared and I found he had deliberately contradicted everything I had told him."

His eyes glowed red. "I wish I could have introduced him to my mama. He wouldn't have dared to ignore her. But, of course, he was a writer, and my mama would never converse with a tradesman. I have been let down, deceived, betrayed."

"I understand exactly how you feel," I said gently. "If it helps to talk, I'm here for you."

"Mr Stoker and I would walk along Cruden Bay beach for hours," he burst out. "I'm a vampire. What better source could he have? And yet he preferred to take unverified, unsubstantiated and positively unbelievable material from some lady."

"Yes," I said, "Emily Gerard. She wrote *The Land Beyond the Forest*, subtitled *Facts, Figures and Fancies from Transylvania.*"

Dracula was struggling to keep his temper. "So I understand. When Mr Stoker told me how helpful and instructive this lady's book had been on the subject of vampires, I asked what qualified her to write it. He informed me that she had spent some years in Romania. Romania, forsooth!"

A word forever associated in my mind with Miss Blaine. Not "Romania", "forsooth". I immediately felt an indissoluble camaraderie with Dracula, undead though he might be. But I still wasn't quite following.

"Forsooth indeed," I said, before adding, "and that was a problem because–?"

"Yes!" he cried. "Exactly! What did she know about Aberdeenshire? Mr Stoker could give me no reassurance that she had ever been to the north-east, or indeed the east."

"Why?" I asked uneasily. "Where was this lady from?"

Dracula was a gentleman. But had he been a villager, I had no doubt that, at this point, he would have spat on the ground.

"Airdrie," he said.

I felt dreadful, burning shame. I'm a librarian; I'm supposed to know all about books. I knew, of course, that this particular volume had been published in 1888 by William Blackwood and Sons. And I had taken it for a serious, scholarly work. I should have been more vigilant, knowing that, in 1901, Ms Gerard would write a work entitled *The Extermination of Love, A Fragmentary Study in Erotics*. Airdrie is a mere fifteen miles from Glasgow. The woman couldn't be relied on to tell you accurately whether the cat was sitting on the mat.

"The things Mr Stoker wrote in that book," said Dracula, shuddering. "I admit, there are certain members of the family who don't behave well, but my mama certainly does not approve and we have very little to do with them."

"Do they bite people?" I asked.

"I'd really rather not discuss it," he said. "Suffice it to say there are lurid and scandalous descriptions in that … that book with which no self-respecting vampire would ever wish to be associated."

This exactly mirrored the Blainers' chagrin as a result of Mrs Spark's pernicious work.

"Tell me about it," I said.

He looked at me in incredulity. "Certainly not! Why would I repeat slanderous claims about my family?"

"Sorry, I didn't mean you to actually tell me about it. It's just an expression," I explained. "I was indicating that I understood what you were saying. Some authors have absolutely no scruples, and I'm afraid sex sells."

He winced. "The language he uses."

Certainly the bit about Jonathan Harker waiting in languorous ecstasy, and the soft, shivering touch of the female vampire's lips on the super-sensitive skin of his throat was very explicit. And as a feminist, I believe in equality of the sexes. This was no less exploitative because it was a male victim. I had previously judged the book to be a harmless Gothic horror, but I was radically revising my view of it.

"Please don't be offended, but could I ask you a few things?" I said. "I've read Mr Stoker's book and I think I've been guilty of making assumptions." I hoped Miss Blaine wouldn't find out. Her instructions to me before my first mission reverberated in my skull: "Never assume. When you assume, you make an ass of you and me."

Dracula gave a weary smile. "I ascribe no blame to you, madam. Readers are credulous beings."

I was going to protest that I was no mere reader, but a librarian.

However, my professional certainties had been shaken by the discovery that I had been giving authority to a book written by a woman from Airdrie.

"I understand now that you left Aberdeenshire because it's too sunny," I said. "Is that because your powers dwindle in daylight?"

His lips tightened. "Madam, I can assure you that there is no diminution of my powers at any time of the night or day."

I would have to remember that although he was the undead, he was the male undead. I've found that even the most right-on man gets a bit fretful when he thinks his powers are being impugned.

"So, what's the problem?" I asked.

"I get a dreadful rash," he said. "If I go out in the sun, within a few days I get blisters that just get worse and worse."

"You poor thing," I said. "You suffer from photoallergic eruption. Tell me, are you going to live for ever?"

"I don't like to tempt fate but yes, probably," he said.

"In that case, it's a while to wait, but in the great scheme of things not that long – in about fifty years, you'll be able to get corticosteroid cream that should help to sort things out."

"How do you know?"

"It's just informed speculation. I keep an eye on medical developments and you get a feel for these things. You'll probably find the cream nips a bit when you first put it on, but persevere and it will almost certainly get better."

He gave a shy smile. "Thank you. That's very encouraging. Please, do have some more shortbread."

I was happy to have as much as was on offer. He might not have mastered cheese-making, but he was an excellent baker. Once I had demolished another piece, I asked, "Can you turn into mist?"

"Can you?" he retorted.

I took that as a no.

But there was one question likely to get a yes. I remembered how he had gurgled when I mentioned how useful garlic was in treating toothache.

"Do you have problems with garlic?" I asked.

He shrank back, his eyes gleaming red. "Yes! I abhor garlic. I've never understood why people pollute their food with it. I believe in plain eating, madam."

Including entire wild boar. I supposed if you were tearing apart animals in a forest, there wasn't much opportunity to whip up a Cumberland sauce to go with it.

According to the book, there was something that was worse than garlic. I had put Madeleine's crucifix inside my high-necked blouse when I went off to exhume Sylvain's grave. Hesitantly, I pulled it out and held it for Dracula to see. "Does this bother you?"

He glanced at it in a long-suffering sort of way. "Really, madam. I admit that I do place more emphasis on individual spirituality than organised religion but I find the supposition that I would be repulsed by Christian iconography somewhat offensive."

I began to wonder whether there was anything at all in the book that was accurate.

"About the earth in the coffin," I said. "Not Transylvanian, then?"

"I confess I cannot understand why people have such an obsession with Transylvania, a faraway country of which I know little. No, madam, the earth was local to Port Erroll, it was familiar, it was comfortable, and the louts who stole my bed simply tipped it out somewhere. There is no respect nowadays for other people's property. I'm glad to have my bed back, of course, but without the mattress, I shall continue to sleep badly."

It was still a bit of a struggle coming to terms with this revisionist history.

"You actually lived in Slains Castle?"

"I was born there. My mama had always wanted to live by the seaside, and of course my papa agrees with whatever she wants."

"Of course," I said. I felt Dracula's mama and Miss Blaine would get on well together.

"My parents had been looking for a suitable home for some time when they found the earl embarking on a building project; they paid him a considerable sum to include accommodation for themselves."

"Ah yes," I said. "The eighteenth earl remodelled the castle in 1836."

Dracula gave me a startled look. "Madam, that was less than seventy years ago. I'm not a child. I'm referring to the ninth earl building New Slains Castle in the sixteenth century."

I tried to recover from my blunder. "And do your mama and papa get on with the current earl?"

"It's quite a big castle," said Dracula. "The families don't get in one another's way. Of course, Mama and Papa spend a lot of their time in the octagonal room, hanging upside down from the ceiling."

This conjured up quite a startling image until I realised what he meant.

He gave a sigh. "Actually, it's a little bit awkward these days. Part of the reason I moved here was, as you know, because of the dreadful Aberdeenshire sunshine. And partly it was because I felt that at my age I should have a place of my own, rather than living with my parents. But over the years, the earls seem to have forgotten our arrangement. Now they seem to think the castle is…" he dropped his voice, "…haunted."

"They think you're ghosts?" I asked.

He gave a despondent nod. "Whenever any of us tries to engage them in conversation, they scream and run away. That's why I enjoyed chatting to Mr Stoker so much."

"He knew you were a vampire?" I asked.

"Of course. I told him my family had lived in the castle since the sixteenth century."

I could see that Bram Stoker might not necessarily equate "family" with "mum and dad".

"How exactly did you introduce yourself?"

Dracula thought for a moment. "We met in a corridor. I remember him bowing and saying, 'Good day, my lord,' and I said, as I always do, 'Oh, please don't call me that. I don't think it's right to use a title that's been conferred through an accident of birth,' and he said he would be very uncomfortable calling me anything else. He told me he was manager of the Lyceum Theatre in London, but he was writing a novel about vampires while he was on holiday, and I said if there was any help I could give him, he only had to ask."

"Did he ask?"

"No, but I told him anyway."

Bram Stoker had mistaken Dracula for a member of Lord Erroll's household. And when Dracula started bending his ear about vampires as they walked along Cruden Bay beach, Bram just thought it was the usual meaningless waffle of the upper classes rather than pure gold, first-hand information. And he had preferred the balderdash of a woman from Airdrie.

"Dracula," I said, "I don't think Mr Stoker knew you were a vampire."

He was yawning, so loudly that he didn't hear me. He settled himself in the armchair and closed his eyes. This was awkward. I had been hoping for a lift back – I would never find my own way through the forest, and I would have to wait until dawn before I could navigate Madeleine's route.

"Would it be all right if I stayed?" I asked diffidently. "I'll leave as soon as it starts getting light, and I don't need any breakfast or anything. I'll get some cheese at the festival. Do you have a spare room by any chance?"

It was quite a sizeable castle: he must have several. But he didn't respond. He was snuggled up in the vast leather armchair, fast asleep. Ermintrude, lying at his feet, was asleep as well.

I found a footstool under one of the occasional tables, which let me stretch out, and nodded off.

***

I was wakened the next morning by Ermintrude indicating that she wanted to go out. I took her downstairs to the garden, after which she bounded back up to rouse Dracula.

He blinked when he saw me. "Have you been here all night?" he asked.

I had a suspicion his mama would definitely not approve.

"It's all right, I sorted myself out," I said. "And now I'm off to the cheese festival. Thanks for your hospitality and for rescuing me."

"I'm planning to go to the cheese festival as well. Perhaps you'll allow me to escort you."

I hoped he didn't think we were now an item. But going with him would be quicker than going on my own.

"I'll get back in the coffin," I said.

He tried and failed to hide his expression of alarm. "I'm afraid that won't be possible. I'd prefer to keep it safe here. Losing my bed once was a misfortune: to lose it twice would look like carelessness."

The Importance of Being Earnest had premiered in London in 1895; I wondered if Dracula had been in the audience.

But he was giving one of his small coughs. "I shall be delighted to have you sit on me."

Toothcracker McMonagle very nearly went into action. Fortunately, I saw from his expression that the remark had been made in all innocence. And before my eyes, he transformed himself into a massive wolf. Minutes later, we were hurtling through the forest, me clinging desperately to his shaggy grey coat. He careered to a halt just before the trees began thinning out, and I toppled into the undergrowth as he became himself once more.

"I'm so sorry," he said, helping me to my feet. "I'm unaccustomed to passengers."

He was wearing a double-breasted black frock coat and a black silk top hat. He looked very dashing, but nobody else in the village dressed like that.

"Do you have anything more ordinary?" I asked.

"What do you mean?" he asked, taking the black muffler out of his pocket and winding it round his face so that only his eyes were visible.

"You just look a bit unusual."

"You think they might not admit me to the festival?" he asked anxiously, and the next moment he had disappeared completely. I looked around for mist, even though he had claimed that wasn't in his repertoire. Something brushed past my hair. Something with a cute wee brown furry face. I hadn't realised that bats flew in daylight, but Sans-Soleil's daylight was as close to night as you could get.

I made my way to the main square, my airborne companion alongside me. Trestle tables had been set out all round the village square, covered in white linen cloths. But nothing else was on them. The villagers were standing around in disconsolate little groups. Their gloom was evident from the fact that they weren't even looking at Madeleine, who was standing observing the scene with grim satisfaction.

I went to join her. She looked me up and down. "Another night out?" she said. "There still isn't a rebate."

"I wasn't expecting one," I said. "I've come back for the cheese festival. It is today, isn't it? July the fourteenth."

"The cheese festival is on July the fourteenth," she confirmed.

I looked again at the trestle tables, covered in white linen cloths and nothing else.

"There is no cheese," I said cautiously.

Ten

Madeleine nodded. "There is no cheese."

"Where is the cheese?" I asked.

She gazed round her, giving her Gallic shrug. "Where is the cheese?"

I could feel my patience wearing thin. "Do you know where the cheese is?"

She gave me a hard Paddington Bear stare. "Do *you* know where the cheese is?"

The parrot thing really was very irritating. I wasn't surprised that Miss Blaine got tetchy with me. Something brushed past my hair with a peevish squeak and disappeared into the distance. Dracula was tetchy too.

There was a small platform between two of the tables for the MC. The mayor, visibly trembling, sidled into the square and stepped onto the platform, to be greeted by loud booing.

"We've been waiting for ages! What's the hold-up?" shouted a villager.

"I ... that is ... I... " the mayor stuttered, his louchely attractive face paler than I had ever seen it. "The ... I... "

"We'd pelt you with cheese if we had any," shouted another villager.

"Let's pelt him with something else," a third suggested.

The boos resumed. The mayor held up his hands in a plea for silence, and the booing diminished slightly.

"Yes, the cheese... " he said. "I ... that is ... yes, the cheese..."

Someone took off a sabot. It seemed more than likely that the pelting-with-something-else was about to begin. I leaped onto the stage and addressed the crowd in the prefect's voice that could carry to the back of the bike sheds.

"Citizens! The mayor has had the brilliant idea of doing things slightly differently this year in honour of Sans-Soleil becoming an international tourist destination. I myself have come all the way from…" I didn't want my message to be diluted by a debate over what did or didn't constitute a nation state. "…from across the Channel."

Muttering, tinged with curiosity.

"Some of you may have noticed that Paris is currently hosting the summer Olympics."

The muttering was now matched by spitting.

"And anything Paris can do, Sans-Soleil can do better, am I right?"

The response this time was a roar of approval.

"So, citizens, the mayor welcomes you all to the inaugural Sans-Soleil Sans-Fromage Olympic Games!"

The crowd burst into loud applause. I did a quick mental run-through of how I could organise things.

"The Paris Olympics," I said, and waited until the spitting stopped, "have only sporting events. But the Sans-Soleil Sans-Fromage Olympics are superior in every way since they encompass sport, cuisine, agriculture, the fine arts, maths and music."

The great thing about isolated Alpine villages in 1900 is that the inhabitants have excellent practical skills. We had the village square and nearby pastures set up for track and field events in next to no time. They were raring to go, and despite their pallor, they had the physique of people well-used to manual work. I would have expected them all to have rickets because of the lack of sun, and I could now understand their obsession with cheese. They would have to eat industrial quantities of it to get the requisite amount of vitamin D.

I was anxious to have gender-neutral races, but the villagers were having none of it. The crêpe-tossing race was strictly women and the sack race was all men. The latter was simple enough, although I started hyperventilating at the sight of the hessian sacks, and the mayor had to take over.

But the crêpe tossing was satisfyingly multidisciplinary. I ascertained that as the villagers had all been waiting since the early hours for the cheese festival, the cows had not yet been milked. Making crêpes required milk, and there was universal excitement when I pointed out that the villagers could now keep their milk since requisitioning was no longer necessary. It crossed my mind that the undertaker and cheesemonger was nowhere to be seen, but I had better things to do than to worry about that.

"So, we've to get back home, milk the cow, make a crêpe, and come back here for the race?" a villager asked.

"Exactly," I said.

"But that's not fair! Some of us have further to go than others."

"And that's why," I said, "we will have a handicap system to ensure a level playing field."

Another villager squinted at the pastures. "But they're not level," she said.

"It's just an expression," I explained. "I mean there will be equal opportunities."

I signalled for the schoolchildren. "Run and get your slates. I have a sum for you." It was only as they scampered off that I realised they were one child short. The wee scone. Something caught my eye. There he was, in a chalet overlooking the main square, his face pressed against the window, and a tear trickling down his cheek. I signalled for him to come down and join us. He pointed at himself in a questioning way and I nodded. A few moments later, he was standing at the top of the steps of his chalet but showing no sign of coming down. I crossed over to him.

"I'm setting a maths question. Don't you want to join in?"

"Yes," he said in a small voice, "but I can't. The policeman said I wasn't allowed to come to Cheese Day."

"This," I said firmly, "is not Cheese Day, but the Sans-Soleil Sans-Fromage Olympic Games, and I am personally inviting you to take part. Now go and get your slate."

"Thank you, madame!" he breathed, and ran off.

It crossed my mind that the policeman was nowhere to be seen, but I had better things to do than to worry about that.

When the children had gathered, I checked that they knew all of the competitors and where they lived.

"I need you to calculate distance along with average speed. The ladies all look pretty fit, so we'll say eight miles an hour. So if Madame A has half a mile to go to her cow, Madame B has one mile, and Madame C has two miles, then Madame A should be given three minutes forty-five seconds to reach her cow, and the same to come back with her crêpe, Madame B needs seven and a half minutes, and the same back, and Madame C needs fifteen minutes, twice."

The pupils looked at me in some confusion.

"What's wrong with you?" I demanded. "You've done much more complicated things than this in the past."

The wee scone put up his hand. "Please, madame, what's a mile?"

"I don't know what they teach you children these days," I said. It crossed my mind that the teacher was nowhere to be seen, but I had better things to do than to worry about that. "A mile is 1.6 kilometres. You can do the conversion easily enough, can't you?"

Their faces cleared, and their slate pencils squeaked. They soon devised a handicap system and the first competitors sped off to milk their cows, the mayor and his pocket watch checking the times. The men meantime were sprint-hurdling, using barrels as hurdles. The children, having sorted out the maths, had three-legged races and wheelbarrow races. Cart Woman wanted to join in until I explained that you upended your teammate in order to make a wheelbarrow, and no carts were involved.

The men decided they wanted a wheelbarrow race as well, and I tried to instigate an egg-and-spoon race for the children. But the mothers wouldn't allow them to have the eggs because they would break them, and insisted that in any case, they needed them for the next cooking challenge. So the children had a *pommes-de-terre-en-cuillère* race instead.

In one pasture, men were using boules for the shot put, while in another, two teams were battling in a tug of war.

The mayor went from one competition to another as judge. It crossed my mind that the actual judge was nowhere to be seen, but I had better things to do than to worry about that. When it came to the crêpe-tossing competition, he wisely decided it was a dead heat.

The women, fresh from this triumph, decided they were going to make as many things as possible with their unexpected supply of milk. My organisational skills were not required: they organised themselves. They got the children shaking milk to make butter. They produced chicken in mustard sauce with potatoes au gratin, they produced spinach and bacon quiches, omelettes aux fines herbes, onion tarts, tarte tatin, blancmanges, crème brûlée. I was disappointed that there wasn't a competition for sauce Béarnaise, but, realistically, my organisational role gave me no time to be a competitor as well.

The hitherto empty tables were now laden with food, and wine and beer appeared from the back doors of chalets, although I stuck to water. We all had a long, leisurely meal, during which the wee scone and Cart Woman's daughter came up to me holding their slates.

"We've been calculating," Cart Woman's daughter said, and the wee scone displayed his slate to show the working-out.

"You said if the vampires only bit one new person every month, then we had $v=1$, and $B=1$," said Cart Woman's daughter. "And you said the population of the world is about two billion. When $n = 31$, 2 to the power of n is just over two billion."

The wee scone could no longer contain his excitement. "That means that if vampires all bite just one new person each every month, then in thirty-one months, which is two years and seven months, we'll all be vampires!"

He seemed quite enthusiastic about the prospect. I wondered whether I should tell him that well-behaved vampires didn't bite people (I couldn't speak for Dracula's rogue relatives), and that the undead had been defamed because of a woman from Airdrie.

Instead, I praised their keenness, and told them that maths helped develop skills in thinking logically, solving problems and making decisions, which would greatly enhance their employment opportunities.

After we had eaten, we had the prize-giving. Armed with my watercolours, the children had expanded on their tree-drawing skills to create the awards, and the prize winners duly won Expressionist gold medals, Pointillist silver medals and Symbolist bronze medals. There was even a proto-Surrealist runner-up medal that looked like a fish.

"And now," I said, "the children are going to pay tribute to the olden days, when this was simply a cheese festival, by singing a specially written song about cheese."

Their little voices rang out, clear and true.

The parents applauded enthusiastically.

"As a special surprise for you, the children are going to sing a second verse," I said.

"My lad's been practising his song for weeks, and there isn't a second verse," said the nearest parent.

"There is now," I said, and I began to conduct. Their accents were perfect: they could have performed in any Morningside venue and been taken for locals.

When the children finished singing my verse, there was silence.

Then a parent said, "What was that?"

"A verse in English," I said. "I've been teaching them English."

"Why?"

"It's good to learn other languages."

"Why?"

"Because then you can communicate with different nationalities."

"I already can. I speak French. If other people can't, that's their problem, not mine."

There was vigorous agreement with this. I was about to outline some of the other benefits of language-learning, such as boosting the cerebral cortex, promoting multi-tasking, enhancing your CV and boosting creativity, but the parents were already shoving past me to praise their little darlings for their singing, if not for their linguistic skills.

People started drifting away from the village square to have some downtime before the evening concert. The mayor looked anxiously at his pocket watch.

"I don't understand it," he said. "I expected them to be here by now."

He glanced round the square as though looking for something. Suddenly, he gave a strangled cry and ran off. I followed.

He ran after Cart Woman, who was walking away with her daughter.

"Where are they?" he panted. "What have you done with them?"

"What have I done with what?" asked Cart Woman.

"Not what, *who*," said the mayor. "The singer from Paris. The man who plays the piano."

"Oh, them," said Cart Woman. "Don't worry, I haven't done anything with them. I got your message."

"My message?" queried the mayor

"The message not to pick them up."

"Not to pick them up?"

I was going to suggest that he stop just repeating things, because of the irritation factor, but I could see he wouldn't be receptive.

"Yes, the policeman explained that you had made other arrangements," said Cart Woman. "Frankly, I'm getting a bit sick of people making other arrangements. That cart is my livelihood, especially now that I'm a widow."

The mayor didn't reply. I turned to see why not, and realised he was in the process of fainting. Fortunately, I have excellent reflexes, and was able to grab him before he hit the ground.

"Quick," I said to Cart Woman, "take his other arm, and we'll get him to Madeleine's."

Between us, we half-dragged, half-carried him to the chalet, Cart Woman's daughter following in fascination. We needed her help to manoeuvre him up the steps and over the threshold, where we were confronted by Madeleine.

"How dare you bring that man here?" she snarled. "I will not have him in my house."

"You will," I said, "and you will also make him a cup of tea with sugar and milk."

I used my prefect's voice, not the loud one, but the quiet one, and she knew better than to argue.

Cart Woman and her daughter helped me prop him up on a chair in the kitchen and then took their leave. The mayor was beginning to revive, although since he came from Sans-Soleil, I couldn't say the colour was coming back into his cheeks.

"Take it easy," I soothed. "You'll feel better once you've had a nice cup of tea."

Madeleine shoved the tea towards him.

"Murderer," she declared.

"What?" he quavered. "I'm not ... I never ... why would you say that?"

"She's talking about the former teacher, judge, schoolmaster and cheesemonger and undertaker," I explained.

"I am." Still standing, she put her hands on the table and leaned forward. She wasn't talking to me. "You know what I think? I don't think they were torn to death by wild animals at all. I think they were murdered."

The mayor put down his bowl and shrank back in his seat. "Now, Madeleine. You mustn't say things like that."

"Or what? You'll murder me too?"

"I haven't murdered anyone!" he protested, sounding quite upset.

"I'm sure you haven't," Madeleine sneered. "You get your creatures to do it."

"My creatures?"

"She's got a thing about creatures," I explained. "She thought I was your creature, but I put her right."

Madeleine was still in sneer mode. "You deny that they're your creatures? That pathetic replacement for my Sylvain, and the so-called judge, teacher, schoolmaster, undertaker and cheesemonger?"

The mayor stared into the bowl of tea as though he was planning to dive into it. Eventually, he said, "You've got it all wrong, Madeleine. I'm not running them. They're running me."

"Those idiots, running you? You've been dealing with them for so long that you must think I'm as stupid as they are."

Slowly, I was gaining an insight into what was going on. Since I had only one more day to complete my mission, it was about time I was given all the information I needed. I really must suggest a new system to Miss Blaine.

"He's telling you the truth, Madeleine," I said. "When I first arrived here, and called in at Chez Maman, they looked really threatening. I thought they were about to beat him up. And before you start, I say that as a disinterested spectator, not as a creature."

"You're the mayor," said Madeleine stubbornly. "You're in charge of this village. How can they tell you what to do?"

"They discovered something that gives them a hold over me," said the mayor in a low voice. "They stole my business."

"What did they discover?"

"I can't tell you."

Madeleine started pacing round the room. "I knew it. I knew you were up to something. My beloved Sylvain was too professional to discuss his work with me, but I knew he was putting the town hall under surveillance. And one night he went out and I never saw him again."

She approached the table, and for a second time I thought the mayor was about to get beaten up. But instead she sank onto a chair and put her hands over her face.

"Madeleine, I swear to you, I had nothing to do with Sylvain's dea – disappearance," said the mayor. "By that time, they had forced me to hand everything over at the town hall. They took my keys. I couldn't get in."

"Couldn't get in where?" I asked. "There's only one door, and I thought you told me it was always unlocked because it was the people's hall."

"There's only one front door," he said with a bitter smile. "And it's unlocked because the front-door key was attached to the others, and they took the lot."

Madeleine's hands were now gripping the edge of the table. "This is all linked to my Sylvain's disappearance, isn't it?" she hissed. "Tell me about this business of yours."

The mayor cowered. "Everything I have done is for the benefit of this village," he whispered. "Everything."

Madeleine smacked her hand down on the table in front of him, making us both jump.

"What business? Keys to what?" she demanded, just like a television Bad Cop. I wondered if she'd considered teaming up with Sylvain.

The mayor's voice could barely be heard. "I have the recipe."

"Recipe for what?" snapped Madeleine.

It was all falling into place. "Heather ale," I said. "Or rather, the Unknown Abbot's brandy. Your mayor has been distilling hooch. And he's been smuggling it out in wheels of cheese."

"How could you possibly know that?" he said through dry lips.

"An educated guess," I said.

He bowed his head. "I found the recipe in an ancient record book. Nobody here has any money, and I thought this would be the best way to get some."

"How many people were in on this?" I asked. "The woman with the cart, obviously, and–"

"No, no," he interrupted. "Nobody in Sans-Soleil knows anything about it, apart from…" He stopped, a haunted look on his face.

"Apart from the judge, the teacher, the police officer, and the undertaker and cheesemonger," I said. "And now Madeleine and myself."

Madeleine was staring at him. "Who else knows?" she said sharply. She really would make a very good Bad Cop.

"I have contacts in other villages," he gabbled. "They take delivery of the cheese, which is sold on the open market, and the eau de vie is sold under the cheese counter."

"I'm not interested in your contacts in other villages," said Madeleine. "I want to know who else knows in Sans-Soleil." I could see her as a Detective Chief Inspector.

The mayor started tousling his thick, lustrous hair. I managed to stop myself saying, "Here, let me do that for you."

Suddenly he stopped, with a laugh verging on the hysterical. "It's all over for me," he said. "My dream was to build a town hall worthy of Sans-Soleil. When I found the recipe, it was as though the Unknown Abbot had blessed my plan. I began distilling small amounts of eau de vie in my little chalet, setting up my distribution network, and saving every centime towards construction. I needed bigger premises, and it struck me that I could combine the two projects."

He indicated a rectangle with his hands. "The town hall. The front door leads into the auditorium. But the auditorium is surrounded on three sides by a secret corridor, whose only access is a back door concealed by the forest."

That explained the lack of windows, and why the town hall seemed smaller on the inside.

"So that's why you built it so close to the forest?" asked Madeleine. "Everyone in the village just thought you were stupid."

"Perhaps I was, to think I would ever get away with it," he muttered. "It went so well, so smoothly. I set up all the latest equipment in the corridor, and I had an excellent workforce. They could slip out into the forest after dark for supplies, and then return to their distilling duties, with the door not only concealed but locked for safety."

Madeleine was eyeing him the way a Weegie eyes an unopened bottle of Buckfast. She would be an ideal Detective Chief Superintendent.

"This workforce of yours – who are they?"

He opened his mouth to speak, then closed it. "No – I can't – that's what they found out, the four of them: Jean-Voix, Jean-Tant, Jean-Chante and Jean-Jambe."

"Who?" I asked.

Madeleine flapped an impatient hand at me. "The Jeans. The so-called judge, teacher, undertaker and cheesemonger, and the useless replacement for my beloved Sylvain. But never mind that. I want to know about this mysterious workforce."

"Please, Madeleine. Don't ask me that," pleaded the mayor. "I can't tell you." He gave a long exhalation. "Then again, why not? I have nothing left to lose. The Jeans have already stolen my business. And now they're threatening to slit my throat and feed me to the pigs."

"We don't have any pigs in Sans-Soleil," said Madeleine.

"You've got wild boar," I said.

"What?" said Madeleine.

"What?" said the mayor.

It wasn't the most tactful thing I could have said. "Sorry, carry on."

"This workforce," Madeleine reminded him.

The mayor took a deep breath. "Jean-Jambe was out having a late-night cigarette when he spotted one of them heading into the forest. The next thing I knew, the Jeans had discovered what I was up to and demanded that I hand over the business to them, so that they could feather their own nest."

"Surely you could have exposed them?" I said. "Admittedly, you were doing something a bit illegal – something totally illegal – but you were doing it for the best of motives, trying to help Sans-Soleil. If the Jeans are just out for themselves, wouldn't the villagers support you?"

"It's more complicated than that," said the mayor. "Because of what the Jeans discovered."

"They discovered your workforce," said Madeleine.

The mayor nodded. "It's the fathers. I've been giving them refuge."

Madeleine's eyes widened. "What, all of them?"

The mayor nodded again.

Her gaze was a mixture of shock and pity. "You're a dead man," she said.

"I know," he said with a bleak smile. "One way or another, this is the end."

"Sorry, who are the fathers?" I asked.

"My beloved Sylvain told me about them," she said. "They just disappeared, ages ago, one by one, and everyone presumed they had been torn to death by wild animals. So how–?"

"I found them in a *grotte*," said the mayor. "They were happy enough, as you can imagine, but not terribly comfortable. It's basically just a cave. They had got used to living on wild berries, which meant they were very low-maintenance. They were delighted to move somewhere wind- and water-tight, and of course they enjoyed the distilling because they got paid in kind."

"And now the Jeans are doing the distilling?" asked Madeleine.

The mayor raised his head, looking suddenly noble instead of louche. "They're trying. But they will not succeed. I refused to give them the recipe."

"Quite right too," I said.

"They tried to pressurise me by sabotaging the cheese festival."

"I don't think they did," said Madeleine.

"Of course they did," said the mayor. "Why else would they have hidden all the cheese? If it hadn't been for Madame Maque, there would have been no celebrations, and the villagers would have risen up against me."

"Yes, your jacket would definitely have been on a shoogly peg," I said.

"What?" said Madeleine.

"What?" said the mayor.

"It's just an expression," I said, "indicating that your job is insecure."

"I think that was merely a side effect, rather than the purpose," said Madeleine. "You said they don't know how to make the brandy. They're such fools, I don't think they know how to make the cheese either. With the amount of milk the children have been taking to the morgue, there should have been enough cheese to feed the whole of France." She snapped her fingers. "And of course! That explains why the forest is out of bounds. They don't want anyone else crushing the *sangliers*."

I froze at her words. Even though I had heard it from the children, I had tried to tell myself that somehow I had misunderstood.

"Crushing the wild boar?" I asked, hoping she would contradict me.

"Exactly. It's a delicate manoeuvre, getting the liquid out. All those little hands are just perfect."

"But why do they need the bl – the liquid?" I persisted, repeating the euphemism.

"That's what gives the cheese its beautiful red veins and its unique flavour," said the mayor. "And without it, the brandy would just be boring and clear – but the liquid from the *sangliers* gives it a beautiful pink colour."

I felt quite nauseous at the thought of cheese and brandy laced with blood.

"I'm sure I'm right," said Madeleine. "The Jeans haven't hidden the cheese; they've gone into hiding themselves because they haven't managed to make any. If they wanted the crowd to turn on you and depose you, wouldn't they have come to watch?"

The mayor rubbed his eyes. "You may be right about the cheese. But as for the brandy, they gave me a final ultimatum of this evening." He turned to me. "And thanks to you, Madame Maque, my mind is made up."

"Thanks to me?"

"Yes, the poem, about your Scottish king murdering the snail people."

"That's not quite–" I began.

"The Jeans have said they will kill me tonight unless I give them the recipe. But if I give them the recipe, there's nothing to stop them killing me anyway. My decision is made. When I die, the recipe dies with me."

Eleven

"Never say die," I said. "Go home and get ready for the concert this evening."

"But–"

"The concert this evening," I repeated firmly. "It will take place as billed. We'll meet you at seven thirty outside the front door of the town hall. Everything's going to be all right."

The mayor, looking both attractively louche and nobly optimistic, took his leave.

"What are you going to do?" asked Madeleine.

"Not me, us," I said.

She snorted. "Not me. I'm not getting involved."

"What would your beloved Sylvain think of that attitude? Does he go out in the morning telling himself he's not going to get involved?"

"He's a police officer," she snapped. "I'm not."

"You're a police officer's wife," I retorted. That newspaper headline appeared again before my eyes: "Schoolteacher's Wife Wins *Mastermind*." I hoped Miss Blaine wouldn't find out.

But the politically incorrect marital link worked. "What are *we* going to do?" she asked.

I was already formulating a plan. "Do you know who Mary Garden is?"

"Of course," said Madeleine. "She's Debussy's muse."

"Do you know anything about her?"

"She's young and she's English."

I glared at her. "Scottish."

She didn't speak but that shrug was a definite "whatever".

"Do you know what she looks like?" I asked.

"No."

"Does anyone else here know anything about her?"

"Of course not. Sans-Soleil is not cultured like Sans-Saucisse."

"In that case, I'm going to be Mary Garden, and you're going to be my accompanist."

"You?" The incredulity in her voice was really quite insulting.

"Yes, me. I sing a bit."

She gave a sarcastic laugh. "How fortunate that nobody here knows anything about Mademoiselle Garden. Imagine if they had been attracted by the chance of hearing a celebrated diva and found instead a woman who could sing a bit."

It would be immodest to tell her I was being modest. She didn't know about the standing ovation for my solo performance of "Ca' the Yowes" at the school concert.

"Also," she said, "they all know you, so how can you pretend to be someone else?"

"I not only sing a bit, I also act a bit. And I'm going to be in costume. Do you have a spare bed sheet and some thread?"

Presently, I was installed in front of the treadle sewing machine. I had learned to sew on a very similar one in primary school, and it struck me that they should be reintroduced since not only are they eco-friendly, requiring no electricity, but they also give the feet and calves a good workout. I began creating a dramatic robe.

Meanwhile, Madeleine was leafing through her stack of music to find suitable songs. She started to play and I started to sing along.

She stopped abruptly. "You know it?"

"Of course," I said. "Verlaine's 'Clair de Lune', set by Debussy."

She harrumphed. Then she said, "You might as well come and see which ones you want to sing."

I compiled an excellent programme of Debussy songs, entirely appropriate for a Mary Garden performance, and Madeleine practised them while I put the finishing touches to my costume.

"I'll just try it on," I said, slipping out of my suit and underskirts.

Madeleine gave a shriek. "Mother of God! Are you a demi-mondaine?"

"I most certainly am not," I said. "I'm from Morningside, which is the acme of respectability."

"Respectability? When you're not wearing drawers?"

I was wearing extremely respectable M&S high-waisted full briefs. But to Madeleine, they must look like a dental-floss thong.

"It's fine," I said. "The sheet isn't see-through."

"You're not going out dressed like that," she declared, sounding exactly like my mother in the 1970s. She went out of the room and returned with a spare pair of bloomers, but it became apparent that they were slightly too snug for me.

"You can't even get your leg in them," she said accusingly.

"Don't worry about it," I said "I'll stick with my own under-wear. No one will know."

"I'll know," she said grimly.

I had some offcuts from the bed sheet, and before I knew it, I was being obliged to make myself some knee-length lingerie with a drawstring and lace trimmings. It was beyond me that such a baggy and shapeless garment could cause such excitement among the elderly gents of Sans-Soleil.

She looked at me critically once I had added my new flowing robe. "You still look like you."

"I'm going to use my watercolours as make-up," I said. "But what I really need is something on my head. Mary Garden wears all sorts of exotic headdresses."

Madeleine grabbed one of the sheets of music. "Here, this lyric of Leconte de Lisle – 'Crowned with thyme and marjoram' – we'll crown *you* with thyme and marjoram."

"Do we have any?" I asked cautiously. "I thought this area wasn't great for herbs."

"Of course we don't have any. But that means nobody here has ever seen them – they don't know what thyme and marjoram look like."

She picked up some discarded music and started ripping it up.

"Stop!" I yelled. "What do you think you're doing?" Admittedly, it wasn't a book, but I still can't bear to see misuse of printed paper.

"I'm making thyme and marjoram," she snapped. "Stop complaining. You need to be disguised, don't you?"

She was trying to sound brisk and businesslike but I'm very sensitive to nuance, and I realised she was as distressed as I get when I find a borrower's been folding over the edge of a page rather than using a bookmark.

I put my hand on hers. "Thank you," I said. And I meant it.

That faint tingle again, but still not enough to be the subject of my mission. Miss Blaine was getting on a bit. She must have forgotten to give me the key information about my mission. She had better hurry up and remember, given that I would have to leave the next day.

I gave a howl of pain and took off my DMs so that I could nurse my big toe.

"Gout?" said Madeleine. "You English eat too much roast beef."

I didn't even bother to correct her. She was sacrificing her beloved music for me. She was transforming the pages into flowers and leaves, and once she had a pile of them, she got two darning needles and more thread.

"Sew," she said.

We created a monochrome frondescence of blossom and leaves to drape round my head and frame my face.

"It's great," I said, "but I'm not sure that it's going to stay on."

"Your fascinator," she said. She put my head torch on top of our handiwork, then skilfully arranged swathes of music over it.

"OK, that works," I said. "Now take it off."

She stared at me.

"I can't walk through the village like this, can I?" I said. "And people will see me coming out of your house and work out that it's me. I'm going to go behind the town hall, change there, and then meet you and the mayor at the front door at seven thirty."

"How will you walk through the village without being seen in the first place?" she demanded.

"I have a technique. I become unobtrusive. All I need is a basket to carry my costume in."

"I'll come with you," she said. "You need me to paint your face."

She was right. I was adept at putting on stage make-up, but using watercolours was a different proposition, especially when Miss Blaine hadn't equipped me with a pocket mirror. I needed Madeleine, but there was no way I could have her with me. Her undulations affected the menfolk of Sans-Soleil so considerably that I suspected they might still be felt through wood, bricks and wood. As we headed for the back of the town hall, I didn't want dozens of doors opening to sighs of "Ah, Madeleine!"

"I'll manage on my own," I said, trying to sound convincing. "That's the best way. When *you* walk around you're a bit ... obvious."

She looked at me with a degree of her previous loathing. Then she picked up a shawl and tied it on as a headscarf. Her shoulders slumped and her bosom became concave rather than convex. She walked across the room without a hint of an undulation.

"Oh, you're good," I said.

"I know." It was said without the slightest conceit. She was simply stating a fact. "I had to teach myself to be unnoticeable when I started looking for my Sylvain. Before that, it was 'Oh, Madeleine, let me carry your basket', 'What luck, Madeleine, just the direction I'm going', 'You can't remain a widow for ever, Madeleine.' Fools!"

I was reminded of Glenda Jackson on *The Morecambe & Wise Show*: "All men are fools, and what makes them so is having beauty like what I have got." Madeleine, whom I had dismissed as someone interested only in making an impression, was capable of giving the impression that she had no beauty at all.

"I've looked for him everywhere," she muttered. "I've covered every centimetre of that forest, I've been along every road, path and track. And he's nowhere to be found."

The tremor in her voice suggested that she was close to tears.

"Don't worry," I said. "At least you know he's not in the grave-yard."

She gaped at me, and I suddenly realised that with all the excitement of the Olympics, I had completely forgotten to tell her.

"When I went out last night, I exhumed his grave," I explained. "The coffin was there all right, but it was full of cheese. Cheese with bottles of hooch in it, which is how I worked out what the mayor was up to."

She flung her arms round my neck. "Thank you! Oh, thank you! He's alive! My Sylvain's alive!"

"Of course he is," I said, managing to free myself from the unexpected embrace. "You've always said so."

"I wasn't sure," she faltered. "Sometimes, in the bleakness of the night, I fear my love for him may not have been strong enough, that he might have left me, and I wouldn't know."

"Of course he wouldn't leave you," I said heartily. "You're good-looking, you play the piano well, your vegetable tian is really tasty."

"I didn't mean leave me for someone else," she snapped. "I meant die."

That was embarrassing. "I'm sure he's fine," I said. "He's probably in a *grotte* somewhere."

"But why hasn't he come home?" she burst out.

"I'm sure there's a good reason," I soothed. "Especially since we're both certain he wouldn't leave you for someone else. Tell you what, let's get this concert out of the way, then we can go and look for him together. I've got my fascinator to help light the way. OK? Now, we need some water to energise the pigment in the watercolours. Do you have something we could carry it in?"

She went and fetched a battered leather-covered water bottle with a strap. "My Sylvain's," she said brokenly. "He brought it with him when he came to my village, and refilled it at our village well. His beloved lips have touched it, as have mine."

"Lovely," I said, hoping she had rinsed it thoroughly.

We put my costume, the watercolours, the water bottle and the sheet music in Madeleine's wicker basket and, unobtrusive and unobserved, reached the back of the town hall, bypassing the hordes of villagers going in the front door. With difficulty, we eased ourselves past the screen of conifers, and by luck rather than judgment found a tiny path leading to a solid wooden door secured with half a dozen locks and padlocks.

Madeleine gave a sudden shiver and looked all around her.

"Oh!" she said. "I thought … no, it's nothing … it doesn't matter."

I quickly changed into my flowing robe and got out the water-colours.

"I want something dramatic," I said. "Black eye liner, blue eyeshadow, carmine lips, bit of rouge on the cheekbones. If it looks too red, dab a bit of green on top to tone it down."

Madeleine set to work with the brushes and eventually decided I looked sufficiently dramatic. She sorted out my paper coronet, securing it with the head torch. I prepared to go, but Madeleine pointed down at my feet.

"They'll recognise your boots."

I took them off and gingerly followed her to the front door. There was no sign of the mayor.

"He knew we were meeting outside, didn't he?" I asked. "You heard me say that?"

Shrug.

"Maybe he's waiting for us inside," I said, pushing the door open.

The town hall was packed, and everyone turned to look at us. There was still no sign of the mayor, but I couldn't delay. I raised my arms high.

"Good evening, Sans-Soleil!" I called.

There was utter silence as the villagers continued to stare at me.

"I said," I said, raising my voice still further, "'Good evening, Sans-Soleil!'"

I made encouraging circles with my hands until there were some scattered mutters of "Good evening".

Nodding from left to right, I processed up the centre aisle and onto the stage, followed by Madeleine, who took her place at the piano, putting the first song on the music stand.

"It's a genuine pleasure to be with you all tonight," I said. "For those of you who haven't seen me in Paris, I am Mary Garden…" I paused for an ovation which never came. "And let us have a generous round of applause for the lovely Madeleine…" I was forced to pause not only for the clapping but also the sigh. "… who has agreed to be my accompanist. I shall perform a series of songs written by the eminent composer Claude Debussy. The first features lyrics by the Parnassian poet Charles Marie René Leconte de Lisle, beginning with the beautiful words 'crowned with thyme and marjoram.'" I indicated my headdress and nodded to Madeleine to begin playing.

There was a puzzled muttering from the audience as I sang. When I finished and bowed, one or two people clapped, but that was it.

"You're supposed to be a dancer," called an elderly man. "Let's see a bit of leg."

There was excited muttering from the men and rustling disapproval from the women. They had completely misinterpreted the posters. For a moment, I forgot I was Mary Garden and turned into my default prefect persona. "I am not a dancer, I am a singer," I said, fixing him with a gimlet eye. "Sit quietly and listen."

He subsided, and they all sat quietly and listened while I sang songs about the snow-coloured butterflies, the twilight falling on the sea, and the woodland covered in frost.

"Thank you, thank you, you're too kind," I said, even though only about half of the audience were applauding. "And now a charming song that Debussy has based on the Spanish dance, the seguidilla, entitled 'A Tight Petticoat on the Hips'."

"That's more like it!" shouted the elderly man. I was about to do the gimlet eye thing again, but Madeleine was already playing the opening chords and I had to start singing. It was quite a catchy number, and the audience were soon clapping along.

When I finished, another elderly man bellowed, "Dance! Dance!" The men all took up the cry, with an obbligato of tutting and the occasional "Disgraceful!" from the women.

I looked down at Madeleine for support, but she just shrugged and started playing. To my horror, I realised it was Offenbach's *Galop Infernal* – otherwise known as the can-can. The lecherous elderly men were already straining forward, anxious for a glimpse of my drawers.

I was still swithering about what to do when the front door burst open, and the judge, the teacher, the policeman, and the undertaker and cheesemonger rushed in.

"Terrible news!" shouted the teacher.

"Terrible, terrible news," intoned the policeman.

"The mayor is dead," proclaimed the judge.

Twelve

The hall erupted in consternation.

"What?"

"The mayor?"

"Dead?"

"The mayor's dead?"

"What happened to him?"

The undertaker and cheesemonger shook his head. "You don't want to know. His injuries are so terrible that I've put him in a closed coffin."

"Of course we want to know! Tell us!"

The policeman stepped forward. "I'm afraid he was innocently going about his business in this very village when he was torn to death by a wild animal. A wolf, to be precise."

The earlier consternation was as nothing compared to this one.

"In the village?"

"Not in the forest?"

"A wolf?"

"It's that Englishwoman's fault – she brought the wolf here!"

"Let's get her!"

I hastily draped more of the musical flowers over my face, but my disguise had worked – they were heading towards the door rather than the stage.

"To arms, citizens!"

"Where are the pitchforks?"

The mob rushed outside, carrying the Jeans with them.

I looked at Madeleine. "I don't believe the mayor was torn to death by a wolf," I said.

"Nor do I," she said. "They've killed him, just as they killed all of the others."

"Apart from Sylvain," I said. She had been absolutely certain that he was still alive, and if she was now wavering a bit, it was up to me to be absolutely certain for her. "I'm going to change back into my proper clothes and then we're going to find him, even if we have to search every *grotte* in the province."

She shot me a small grateful smile.

The village was in uproar, the mob prowling the streets and lanes, wielding their flaming torches. Madeleine and I escaped unnoticed down the side of the town hall and into the conifers. I quickly put on my blouse, jacket and tulip-bell skirt with its petticoats, and sat down to put on my DMs. That was my mistake.

There was a sudden rustling in the conifers behind us.

"Get them!" said a voice. It was the teacher.

Clutching my DMs, I leaped to my feet. My bare feet. Pine needles pierced my soles and I found myself tumbling to the ground. Beside me, Madeleine was grappling with the judge and the policeman. And before I could get back up, a rope was looped over my shoulders and pulled tight, pinioning my arms, while my hands, still clutching the DMs, were tied behind me. After that, everything went black – for the second time, a hessian sack had been thrown over my head.

"Monsters! Murderers!" I heard Madeleine scream, followed by a choking sound suggesting that she too was stifling in a hessian sack.

I was manhandled to my injured feet.

"Be careful of her!" I heard the policeman say. "She can walk through locked doors."

The teacher laughed. "By the time she works out how to get through these, it will be too late."

There was the sound of padlocks being unfastened and bolts being drawn back. A forceful shove sent me sprawling. A thud and a muffled cry told me the same had happened to Madeleine.

Bolts shot back into place behind us and the padlocks were relocked. And then possibly the sweetest voice I have ever heard said, "Don't worry, mesdames, you're safe now. Let us help you."

Someone was untying my bonds and lifting the sack off my head. A man was smiling down at me, a man who looked like a Botticelli angel: serene, slender and boyish, golden curls framing his delicate face. Some people think Leonardo da Vinci is the greatest Italian painter, but it's definitely Botticelli – he is my favourite.

As he helped me to my feet, Madeleine, now also free of her hessian sack, gave a small, gasping sigh, "My Sylvain!"

She pushed me aside and hurled herself into the arms of a figure standing behind the angel.

We were in semi-darkness, in a corridor with flickering candle-light at the far end, but I could see Sylvain well enough. Frankly, he made Serge Gainsbourg look like Robert Redford. I believe the expression in Glasgow would be "a shilpit wee bauchle". But there was no doubting that this was Madeleine's missing husband. They were all over one another like a rash, the most adoring, devoted rash anyone could wish for.

"My love!"

"My life!"

"I thought I had lost you!"

"I thought I had lost you!"

You wouldn't get anyone behaving like that in Morningside. Admittedly, Waitrose is full of couples running up and down the aisles looking for one another, but less adoringly than irritably. However, the romance of the moment got to me. He absolutely wasn't a looker, but he must have something the men of Sans-Saucisse didn't.

The emotion was affecting my eyesight as well. I was seeing double. The Botticelli angel looked as though there were two of him, and right beside him was an elderly, magisterial figure, also duplicated.

"Madame Maque!"

I recognised the voice as that of the mayor, still carefully not wearing out my name.

"Mr Mayor – you're not dead," I said.

"We are none of us dead. At least, not yet." The mayor stepped out of total darkness into semi-darkness. A trick of the light made it look as though he had a black eye. He gestured to the Botticelli angels and the magisterial pair.

"May I present the Dupond Twins, Dupond with a D," he said. "And also the Dupont Twins, Dupont with a T."

The magisterial duo and the brace of Botticelli angels bowed to me.

I inclined my head. "Gentlemen." I followed this up with a questioning glance at the mayor.

He understood me. Indicating the first magisterial Dupond, he said, "Our judge."

"And your teacher," I said, looking at the second magisterial Dupond.

"Indeed, I am," said one of the Botticelli angels.

"I'm the undertaker," said the other angel.

"And cheesemonger," I added.

"And cheesemonger," agreed the second magisterial Dupond.

I was confused. "I thought undertaker and cheesemonger was a single job."

The angelic undertaker and magisterial cheesemonger laughed.

"That would be ridiculous," they chorused.

I looked at the mayor again.

"The Jeans had to double up," he explained, "because there are only four of them. And they needed all five positions for the takeover to work."

This made no sense to me, but everyone else was nodding sagely, so I nodded sagely as well.

Now that I was closer to the mayor, I could see that he did indeed have a black eye. "I take it that the Jeans kidnapped you and put you in here? They beat you up?"

He gingerly touched his eye socket. "They kidnapped me. But

it was Sylvain who beat me up. That time you and I were in here to see the shield, and I mentioned my admiration for…" He nodded in the direction of Madeleine without sighing or saying her name. "It turned out he had overheard me, and was still a bit cross."

"When we were in here, I heard voices in the background and thought it was a radio play," I said. "You said you couldn't hear anything. That wasn't true, was it?"

He shook his head. "It turned out to be Sylvain shouting at me, and the Duponds and the Duponts trying to calm him down. But I didn't know they were there. I just thought it was the fathers, and wanted to get you out before you realised I had lodgers."

"Yes, these fathers," I began. "Who are they exactly? Some sort of village elders?"

"Let me introduce you," the mayor said.

"Let me put my boots on," I said. I pulled the remaining pine needles out of my feet, and went to pick up my DMs. Something brown and furry shot out of the left one. I hoped it was a mouse rather than a rat.

Once I was shod, the mayor led me down the corridor towards the flickering candlelight, which came from round the corner. We were now in a shorter corridor, brightened by several candles stuck on an upturned barrel.

Four men of varying antiquity were sitting round it on the floor, playing cards. They looked up at me incuriously.

"Fathers, this is Madame Maque, a distinguished foreign visitor to our village," said the mayor.

"Not another one," muttered the eldest father. "I don't know why people come here when they can't be bothered to speak the language."

"Madame speaks French perfectly, unlike our other lady visitor," the mayor said hastily.

"Gentlemen," I said, nodding to them. "I believe you're the village elders?"

"No, we're not," snapped the second eldest. "We're the fathers."

"And husbands," said the third eldest.

I wondered if this was a fin de siècle variation on WAGs.

"Ex-husbands," said the fourth eldest.

"We're not ex," said the eldest.

"She thinks we are," said the fourth eldest and cackled.

"And soon we will be, thanks to our lads," said the second eldest morosely. "Jean, are you sure you shuffled these cards properly?"

"Better not disturb their game," whispered the mayor, moving me further down the corridor.

"Sorry, I haven't quite worked out – why are they called the fathers?" I asked.

"We call them that to distinguish them from the sons," said the mayor.

"Yes, I can see that would help," I said. "Who are the sons?"

Even in the gloom, I could see the mayor was astonished by my question. "The Jeans, of course," he said. "They were all named Jean after their respective fathers."

"Right," I said, as though I was following. "And what was all that about ex-husbands?"

"They're not ex-husbands," he said. "They're husbands. There was never a divorce. She thinks they're dead, but they just all ran away. Understandably. The first one was before my time, must have been almost fifty years ago. The second one was before my time as well, about forty years ago. Then the third one, that would be thirty years ago, when I was too young to know anything about it, but I remember the fourth one. When no body was found, people said he must have been torn to death by wild animals."

There was something I needed to clarify. "She?"

"Maman," he said.

If the four fathers were Maman's husbands, then the four sons...

"Oh my God," I said, "she's a 4x4!"

"What?" said the mayor.

"It means she's had four children with four different men. It's an analogy with four-wheel-drive vehicles, where all four wheels get torque from – you've got no idea what I'm talking about, do you? Have you ever seen a car?"

"No," he said, "but I hear they have them in Paris, along with electric street lighting."

"Yes," I said, "yes, they do."

"Speaking of Paris," he said, "come and meet Mademoiselle. We gave her the seat, of course."

He took me round the corner into the last corridor, dimly lit by a couple of candles stuck on the floor. A bearded bloke of about forty was leaning against the wall. He had his eyes closed, and one foot was moving up and down as though he was tapping out some rhythm.

A petite lassie in her mid-twenties, dark-haired and bright-eyed, was sitting on a crate. She jumped up, beaming, at our arrival.

"Madame Maque, this is Mademoiselle–" the mayor began.

"Hello, fit like?" said Mademoiselle.

"Nae bad," I responded automatically, my language skills kicking in as always, before I registered that I'd been addressed in the Doric.

"Are you Mary Garden?" I asked.

"Fairly aat."

The mayor, uncomprehending, went back round the corner to join the French speakers.

Mary Garden might be young, but she was already every inch a star, poised and confident. One thing, however, puzzled me.

"Why are you speaking in the Doric?" I asked. "I thought you left Aberdeen for the States before you were ten."

"Ee kin tak e quine oot o Aiberdeen but ee canna tak Aiberdeen oot o e quine."

How true, I thought. In my own case, you could take the Blainer out of Morningside, but you couldn't take Morningside out of the Blainer.

She was studying me closely. "Wis aat you singin throu ere?"

The moment of truth. She had realised I was the person who had impersonated her.

"It was. What did you think of my singing?"

218

"Nae bad."

The ultimate Aberdonian compliment.

"So, they could have been fooled into thinking I was you?" I asked.

"Nae for a meenit. Tak a look at ye. I'm a wee boukit deemie an ee're a muckle sonsy deem."

The question had been about my singing (which I knew was every bit as good as hers), so I wasn't going to put up with any sizeist comments.

"This is pure muscle," I told her. "Testament to my hours in the gym."

"An yer oors o haein fly cups an funcy pieces."

I was going to protest that at most I had one cup of tea and perhaps two or three Bourbon biscuits at a time, but then I remembered that Bourbons wouldn't be invented for another ten years.

"Just because you're blessed with a fast metabolism," I muttered. And then I thought to ask her how she came to be here. I had got used to her Doric now, and was hearing it as more or less standard English.

"We were waiting where we'd been told for a cairt to pick us up, when a hearse came past. The next thing, we got grabbed and shoved in a coffin."

She saw me glance towards her somnolent toe-tapping accompanist. "Separate coffins. Nae the same one. And then we got dumped in here. I'm going to be having a sharp word with my agent when I get back to Paris."

Her agent was scarcely responsible for her being kidnapped and shoved in a coffin, but was no doubt used to dealing with artistic temperaments.

"How are you finding Paris? Are you enjoying being at the Opéra-Comique?" I asked, remembering she had made her debut there in April.

"It's great. I've got an amazing social life."

I wondered what her social life entailed. Cart Woman had decided it was pretty racy, purely on the basis that she was part of the Paris arts scene. But then, the Paris arts scene was never known for its moderation. Mary Garden was famous for being Debussy's muse. The composer had a reputation for being a bit of a lad, and there was no doubt about it, Mary Garden was very attractive as well as being very talented.

"I hope you don't mind me asking," I said, "but is there anything going on between you and Debussy?"

Her mouth fell open and she clutched her hands to her bosom. I could see why they called her the Sarah Bernhardt of opera. Acting is much more restrained now. It's cinema close-ups that have changed things – big gestures just look ridiculous.

"Michty be here! Niver a bit!" she said.

"Sorry, I didn't mean to imply anything. It's just that he's older than you, and you're at the start of your career. And he's French."

She nodded. "He's fair taken with me, but I tell him I'm married to my music. And I tell him he's married to Lilly Debussy," she said. "Some women like a man with two bows to his fiddle but I'm nae one of them."

It was reassuring that nobody was going to exploit Mary Garden. I felt a bit sorry for her agent.

"They're a at it. Maurice Maeterlinck–"

"Sorry, Maurice Maeterlinck, the playwright? He's been after you as well?"

That really shocked me. He was already in a long-term relationship. We all know about Frenchmen behaving badly, but I had expected better of a Belgian.

"He said he wanted to take a photo of my sole."

"Has he got a foot fetish?"

She tossed her head. "Dinna be daft. Not the bottom of my foot."

"He wanted to photograph your soul, your spiritual self, your emotional nature?"

"Aye, and it turns out you can best see someone's soul when they've nae clothes on."

"Oh, one of these so-called glamour photographs? What did you do?" I asked.

"What do you think I did?"

I got the distinct impression that Maeterlinck had been warned that if he persisted, he would be singing soprano alongside Ms Garden.

"And do you have much trouble with Debussy, with him being a player?" I asked.

"Nae trouble at all. He's a really good player. Pity he never got to play tonight. He's fair upset about it."

She nodded towards her somnolent accompanist.

"That's Debussy?" I gasped.

"Faith aye. Come and I'll introduce you." She prodded her companion, who opened his eyes. They were lovely eyes. Deep pools of longing that you could imagine yourself floating in for aeons. I remembered there was a Mrs Debussy and pulled myself together.

"*Mon cher maître Debussy, permettez-moi de vous présenter une admiratrice,*" said Mary Garden.

Debussy looked at me helplessly. "What's she saying now? She claims she speaks French, but I can't understand a word of it. She's got a really peculiar accent."

"She's got a really peculiar accent whatever language she's speaking," I said. "She was introducing me to you."

And then I heard myself saying, "I'm a huge fan of your work," a slight exaggeration, but we Blainers have good manners instilled in us from an early age. Debussy looked delighted.

I put out my hand to shake his, but he raised it to his lips and kissed my fingertips. I don't normally fancy blokes with beards, but there was something strangely alluring about him, and his eyes were really lovely.

"And may I ask your name, dear lady?" he asked.

"Shona McMonagle."

"Shona McMonagle," he repeated perfectly. "A fine Scottish name. Is your family of Scottish origin?"

Scottish, not English. For a moment, I thought I must have misheard. But my hearing hadn't let me down.

"I *am* Scottish," I said.

"Forgive me, dear lady, I took you for a Parisienne. But I should have known – your charm, your elegance, so much greater than any Frenchwoman's. You could be nothing other than Scottish."

"You've heard of Scotland? Did Mary Garden tell you about it?"

"Dear lady, I heard of Scotland long before I met Mademoiselle Garden. A military gentleman introduced me to the music of your wonderful bagpipes. I felt the country that could produce such divine sounds was my spiritual home. It is my profound sorrow that I was born in Saint-Germain-en-Laye and not in Edinburgh or Glasgow."

He didn't know as much about Scotland as he thought. Being born in Glasgow is definitely a reason for profound sorrow.

"Of course," he said, "our two countries have had an affinity since the thirteenth century through the Old Alliance. Scotland inspires me. You inspire me."

He was gazing at me with those lovely eyes. I felt a little overheated. I decided I had better change the direction of the conversation.

"Mr Debussy–" I began.

"Call me Achille."

"I thought your name was Claude," I said, although I could understand that anyone called Claude would want to be called something else.

"Achille-Claude. But my intimates call me Achille."

I wasn't sure about "intimates".

"Mr Debussy," I said sternly, "may I remind you that you're married?"

He gave a profound sigh. "Ah, it is well that you remind me. For in your presence, any man would forget every other woman, my flaxen-haired Caledonian enchantress."

I was quite startled. Nobody's ever called me flaxen-haired before. But I knew where I'd heard that description.

"Have you written any piano preludes inspired by Scotland?" I asked.

He shook his head thoughtfully. "Not yet. Not yet. That's an excellent suggestion. But I have written a *Marche écossaise* for piano four-hands."

"Now that would have been perfect for me and Madeleine," I burst out. "I wanted to play a Debussy duet, but she insisted on Fauré."

"Don't worry about it," said Debussy. "Fauré and I are good friends."

I remembered that Debussy and Fauré were sufficiently good friends that Debussy would end up with Fauré's bidie-in, and as a result, Debussy's poor wife would shoot herself. I gave him a disapproving frown. He met my gaze with his lovely eyes, and I was startled to find myself prepared to forgive even his future misdemeanours. In confusion, I returned to our original conversation.

"My friend Madeleine's round the corner," I said. "She was my accompanist this evening. She's just got an old Gaveau at home. I think she really enjoyed playing on the Érard."

"She was magnificent," he said. "Not as magnificent as you, of course, my divine songstress, but worthy to support you. Perhaps you could introduce me to her?"

I wasn't that keen, but I couldn't see how to refuse. I went to the corner and called, "Madeleine! Someone wants to meet you."

I was used to the name "Madeleine" being followed by a sigh. This time it was Madeleine's sigh at being disturbed when she was in a clinch with her Sylvain. The pair of them came towards me, Madeleine nestled in the crook of Sylvain's arm, gazing up at him in adoration.

"Madeleine," I said, "this is my friend Achille. Achille-Claude Debussy. He wants to say hello."

Her eyes widened in surprised delight. She disengaged herself from Sylvain and bestowed a dazzling smile on the composer.

"An honour to play your beautiful music," she said. "I bought so much of it when I was in Paris that I could scarcely carry it home."

Behind her, Sylvain was glaring.

"The honour is all mine, to have my music played by such a beautiful and talented lady," said Debussy. "The next time you come to Paris, you must visit me. I would love to have you run your fingers over my Pleyel."

He had scarcely finished speaking when Sylvain grabbed him by the lapels and pinned him to the wall, drawing back his fist.

Debussy covered his face with his hands in a protective gesture.

"Achille!" I bellowed in the prefect's voice that demanded instant obedience. "Drop your hands right now!"

He did, and Sylvain's fist connected with his jaw. He crumpled.

The Dupondts – the combined Duponds and Duponts – and the mayor, hearing the disturbance, rushed round to see what was going on. I knelt down beside Debussy. "That was really stupid," I said. "You must always keep your hands out of harm's way. How could you play if you were injured?"

"I *am* injured," he groaned, experimentally massaging his jaw.

"You'll be fine," I said. "The officer isn't a musician and just misunderstood what you said."

I turned to Sylvain. "When Mr Debussy mentioned his Pleyel, he was referring to his piano," I explained.

Sylvain shot me a contemptuous look. "No, he wasn't."

A Dupondt sniggered.

Madeleine stroked Sylvain's arm appeasingly. "My love, this lady is our guest, and helped me to look for you."

Reluctantly, Sylvain offered me his hand, and I shook it. It was like an electric shock.

"Oh my God," I gasped. "You're the one! I'm tingling all over!"

The next thing, Madeleine sprang at me and started trying to scratch my eyes out.

"Get your filthy hands off my husband!" she screamed.

"Cat fight," announced a Dupondt with some enthusiasm.

I grabbed Madeleine's wrist and got her arm behind her back in a martial arts restraint move, preparatory to immobilising her on the ground, but then Sylvain was on me, yelling, "Get your filthy hands off my wife!"

They were tremendously possessive of one another. I was calculating how to immobilise him without injuring him – I could imagine Miss Blaine wouldn't be happy if I damaged the subject of the mission – when the mayor shouted, "Officer! Stand down!"

They might do some things differently in Sans-Soleil, but at least the mayor was still in charge of the police. Sylvain immediately complied.

I let go of Madeleine, who rushed back to her husband and snuggled up to him.

"If my hands are filthy," I said quietly, "it's because I was recently digging up Officer Sylvain's grave to find out whether he was dead or not."

Madeleine gave Sylvain a quick abashed look, nodding to confirm the truth of what I was saying.

"I was sent here on a mission," I went on. "I wasn't clear what it was until a moment ago. I don't expect you to understand, but when I meet the person I'm supposed to help, I feel a tingling. I'm here to save Sylvain."

It was making sense now. I had tingled from Madeleine because she was Sylvain's other half. I had tingled in the town hall, not because of the time-travelling or because of the louchely attractive mayor, but because Sylvain was close by. Now that it was clear Sylvain was the one I was here to help, all I had to do was complete my mission by getting him out of this prison and back home.

But perhaps that was easier said than done.

"Mr Mayor," I said, "earlier you said nobody was dead *yet*. Did that have any significance beyond the fact that we'll all die eventually?"

"Oh yes," said the mayor. "We were warned that tonight would be the end. All of the merchandise and equipment has been moved out, so my hunch is that they'll set fire to the building with us inside it."

Thirteen

"We have to get out of here," I said.

The mayor shrugged. "Impossible. We've tried. There are too many locks and padlocks on the door, and I built these walls myself. It would take a sledgehammer to get through them."

"Do we have a sledgehammer?" I asked.

"No," he said.

"The front door is open," I said. "Why can't we break into the hall from here and get out that way?"

"The same problem. I made the walls too well. And there's the extra problem of all the mirrors."

Mary Garden looked enquiring.

"Two sides of the hall are covered in mirrors, just like Versailles," I explained. "It's a beautiful venue when the chandeliers are lit. You would have loved playing it."

I started thinking out loud. "If only there was some way of breaking the mirrors, that might weaken the walls, and we could punch and kick our way through."

The mayor gave a wry laugh. "I admire your optimism, Madame Maque, but we can't break the mirrors since they're in there, and we're in here. We must simply accept our fate."

"We have to sing," said Mary Garden.

"That's a great idea," I said. "There's nothing like a wee singsong to raise the spirits during difficult times. Like when they sang 'Abide with Me' on the *Titanic*. I'll divide you into two groups. You lot to my left are group one, you lot to my right are group two. Group one to start, and group two, you come in on my signal. Everyone know the words of 'Cher Fromage'?"

"Dinna be daft," said Mary Garden. "That's nae the song I had in mind."

"You want me to teach them 'The Boddamers Hanged the Monkey-O'?"

"I want you to sing the "Queen of the Nicht" aria from *The Magic Flute*. Do you know it?"

"Of course I know it," I said.

"And can you sing the top F?"

Like Madeleine, she had never heard me perform as a soloist at the school concerts.

"The top F will be no problem," I said. "But I really don't think it's the right song under the circumstances. It's not exactly cheery – 'Death and despair flame about me'. It's bad enough facing immolation without going on about it beforehand."

"And you think 'Abide with Me' is cheery? Just sing, quine," she said tartly, and started up. There seemed to be no stopping her, so I sang along.

We reached top F and, instead of carrying on, she waved her hand at me in a circular motion, indicating that I should stick with the note. It was very diva-like behaviour, but since she actually was a diva, I felt I must go along with it.

We continued with the top F, Mary Garden's voice becoming increasingly strong and piercing. I figured that any note she could sing, I could sing louder, so I upped the ante. I knew that high notes could shatter glass, but now we were singing to break the mirrors.

There was a sudden movement above me. A bat circled over us, its huge wings outstretched. It was squeaking, higher and higher, until even my superb hearing couldn't detect it, and I realised it had gone ultrasonic.

There was another sound now, like the cracking and splintering of a mighty iceberg. It gradually dawned on me that this was the glass in the mini-Hall of Mirrors. Not a moment before time, since I sensed that Mary Garden was about to run out of breath. But she was a trouper – a quick inhalation, and she completed the aria while the din and clatter continued behind us.

Debussy applauded politely when she finished, and she placed her hand on her chest and made a deep theatrical bow.

"That was a great performance," I said. "Such a shame your fans in the Opéra-Comique didn't get to hear it. But now we have work to do."

I put my shoulder to the wall and began to push, signalling the others to join me. As we heaved and shoved, the wall slowly began to give way. But not enough. We were still trapped.

Madeleine was watching me with a mixture of despair and hope. I was here to save Sylvain: I couldn't let him down and I couldn't let her down. But our little band was proving unequal to the task. I needed to enlist more help, but from whom?

There was a low growl beside me, and Mary Garden let out a shriek. "How did that muckle hairy dog get in here?"

"He's not a dog, he's a wolf," I said. "And he happens to be a good friend of mine. Aren't you, boy?"

I scratched him behind the ears. He leaned into the scratching with a contented sigh, then rapidly backed off, his eyes glowing red. I guessed he had remembered that his mama wouldn't approve.

But he was backing up, tensing his hind paws, and I remembered him telling me there was a technique to jumping through windows. He was about to try jumping through a wall.

"Are you sure about this?" I asked. It wasn't exactly Platform 9¾.

The great wolf gave a nod, then leaped at the wall, smashing through it. There was a dreadful howl, like the sound of a terribly injured animal.

"Dracula!" I shouted, shoving my way through the rubble and masonry dust. "Are you OK?"

I could see nothing – the candlelight in our corridor wasn't strong enough to reach in here. I put my hand up to my brow and discovered the head torch had survived all of the rough handling. The elastic must be stretching, since it was no longer giving me a headache.

I switched it on, and light flooded crazily on a ghastly scene, reflected in all the shards of mirror. The great grey wolf lay gasping in the middle of the debris, his flank torn open, and blood gushing out of it.

"A vet!" I shouted. "We need a vet here, right away!"

Dupont the undertaker peered through the hole I had clambered through. "We don't have a vet. The animals either get better, or…" He made a throat-cutting gesture.

I knelt down beside the wolf and gently stroked his head. "You're going to be fine," I said. "You'll be leaping out of here in no time."

He gave a feeble wag of his tail, and tried to lick my hand, but the effort was too great. As I watched, the red light in his eyes flickered and dimmed.

"No!" I cried. "You can't die!"

And then I thought, of course he can't die, he's a vampire – unless that was something else Bram Stoker had got totally wrong. I had thought vampires were self-healing, but the great grey wolf was growing weaker by the second.

As I tried to see how best to help, the animal shape disappeared, and there in front of me was Dracula in human form, or at least apparently human form. Even if he couldn't die, he definitely didn't look well. I didn't know it was possible for anyone to be that pale. Blood continued to pour out of a massive wound in his side. I grabbed his muffler to try to staunch the flow, pressing on it firmly. Dracula gave a faint moan.

The others were beginning to emerge from the corridor, cautiously navigating the wreckage and helping one another avoid the mirrored spikes.

"The English milord!" one of the Duponts said.

Tending to a seriously injured patient, I couldn't shout.

"This man is not English," I whispered, as reprovingly as I could. "And we need to get him to hospital as quickly as possible. Where's the nearest one?"

The Duponts exchanged glances and looked to the mayor to answer. He turned to Sylvain.

"We don't have one," said Sylvain awkwardly. "It's basically the same situation as with the animals."

Dracula's breathing was laboured and his eyes were gradually closing.

"Wake up!" I said urgently. "Stay with me! Come on, you mustn't go to sleep."

With an obvious effort, he kept his eyes open. "Leave me," he whispered. "You must escape."

"He makes a good point," said the mayor.

I turned my gaze and my head torch on the group and saw them shrink back.

"We would still be stuck in that corridor if it weren't for Dracula here," I reminded them. "It was his squeak added to the top Fs that shattered the mirrors in the first place, and he was the one who broke through the wall. We're not leaving without him. Is that clear?"

There was a bit of shuffling, but nobody argued.

I turned back to Dracula. "You're still losing blood," I said. "You need a transfusion." And then I said something I had said many times before, but never in this tone. "Bite me."

"No ... I can't ... vegetarian..."

"Don't give me that," I said. "You told me yourself, you eat wild boar."

"Yes, wild boar," he murmured. "Like hellebore." He was becoming delirious.

"Don't go to sleep," I warned him. "Here." I started to unfasten my high-necked blouse.

"Please ... no ... mustn't..."

"Stop arguing. I'm not talking about your tea, I'm talking about a medical procedure."

"No ... you..." He stretched a shaky hand out towards me.

"It's all right," I said briskly. "I've undertaken a risk assessment." And I had. I foresaw two suboptimal outcomes. The first was that Dracula would inadvertently sever my carotid artery, and I would bleed to death. But at present, that was a possibility, not a certainty. The certainty was that Dracula would bleed to death without a transfusion.

And then there was the possibility that I would turn into one of the undead. Dracula was so adamant that Bram Stoker had got it all wrong that I felt this was unlikely. But what if Stoker was correct? Then Miss Blaine would be happy. She had recruited me for time-travelling missions so that I could help to make the world a better place. If I became one of the undead, I could continue going on missions indefinitely. Although I would probably need some sort of therapy not to bite people the whole time.

I patted Dracula gently on the shoulder. "If it helps you, that's all that matters."

"No … mustn't bite … mustn't take your blood…"

"It's no problem. I'm a regular blood donor. It helps my cardio-vascular system and reduces my risk of heart attack and stroke."

"No…" His voice was getting fainter. "… my mama … shocked…"

"Don't you worry about your mum, she won't know anything about it. What happens in Sans-Soleil stays in Sans-Soleil."

I spoke to the group. "Am I right?"

"Of course," said the mayor. "That's been the village's motto since 1782."

I couldn't help asking what happened in 1782.

"Even now, we don't really talk about it," said the oldest father. "Let's just say there were a number of dangerous liaisons. That marquise, she was a one–"

The other fathers quickly shooshed him and I realised no more information would be forthcoming.

"I'm blood type O positive," I said to Dracula. "Is that OK for you?"

"Anything … anything … all fine…"

His eyes were beginning to close again. I shouldn't have been wasting time on idle gossip. I took an antiseptic wipe out of my reticule and quickly cleaned the side of my neck. I gave him a small shake and when his eyes fluttered open, I leaned over him so that my neck was beside his mouth.

"Go on," I said. "Take a scoof. No more than a pint, though. And please try to avoid severing my carotid artery."

The staff at the Edinburgh blood donor centre are great, but even they were never as good as Dracula. I scarcely felt a thing as his teeth sank into me.

Eventually, in a slightly stronger voice, he said, "Thank you very much. I feel a little better now."

I put a plaster from my reticule over the incisions. I always have a Tunnock's Teacake at the blood donor centre, sometimes two if nobody's looking. It was a shame there weren't any here, but I could have a cup of tea later at Madeleine's.

"Who's next?" I asked. "It's all right, it doesn't hurt."

That elicited no response. I tried again. "This man has lost a great deal of blood. Saving us."

"We're not saved yet," muttered a father.

"Then you'd better hurry up with your donation," I said tartly. "We leave together or not at all."

"Here, I'll take a turn," said Mary Garden. "You needn't look to the men. They always faint at the sight of blood. It's a woman you want."

I should have taken her to task for her sexist attitudes and gross generalisations, but time was of the essence. First Mary Garden, then Madeleine, each antiseptically wiped, bitten and plastered.

"How do you feel now?" I asked Dracula.

"Much improved," he said, attempting to raise himself, and collapsing back on the floor, gasping.

"Come on, lads," I said to the others. "One more. Who's it going to be?"

"Beloved?" said Madeleine. "You are so brave."

"All right," muttered Sylvain. He approached Dracula with obvious reluctance and before contact could be made with his neck, he passed out.

"What did I tell you?" said Mary Garden. "Men are fearties."

Dracula was still too weak to manoeuvre himself into the right position, but I managed to pull Sylvain's arm close to him, and Dracula sank his teeth into Sylvain's wrist. Meanwhile, Mary Garden, who despite her sexism seemed very sensible, held Madeleine back from her beloved until Dracula had taken very nearly an armful.

Once I'd put the plaster on Sylvain's wrist, Madeleine rushed over to him and coaxed him back into consciousness. "My hero," she breathed. "Such courage! You are an example to us all."

Mary Garden and I exchanged an eye roll.

Dracula gave a long, contented sigh. "Thank you. Thank you all. I haven't felt so well for years."

He stood up and stretched experimentally. There was no longer any sign of a wound, or even of blood on his clothes. Being a vampire definitely had its pluses.

"Maybe we can leave now?" said a father quite sarcastically.

I nodded to the mayor, who led us to the front door and opened it. We piled out gratefully into the fresh air, me at the back helping Dracula, who was still limping slightly.

And as we emerged, there was a series of metallic clicking sounds. It took me a few seconds to recognise it as hunting rifles being loaded, four of them.

And then an ancient cracked voice said, "Kill them. Kill them all."

Fourteen

Four hunting rifles were being aimed at us by the fake judge, teacher, policeman, undertaker and cheesemonger.

Behind them was Maman. She scanned our little group, the fathers cowering out of sight at the back, and gave an eldritch screech of rage. "What is the meaning of this, boys?"

The fake judge, teacher, policeman, undertaker and cheesemonger looked shame-faced.

"Sorry, Maman," they muttered.

She grabbed the chubby, young fake judge by the ear and he squealed.

"What did I tell you to do?" she demanded.

"Kill them. Kill them all," he gasped.

"No, you fool, not what I told you to do just now. What did I tell you to do before?"

"Kill the lot of them."

"Exactly. And did you?" She wrenched his ear downwards and he squealed again. "Well?"

The muscular, moustachioed fake teacher intervened, unwisely in my view. "We were busy setting up the business. We forgot."

"I'll give you forgot," she screamed, fetching him a smack round the head. "You had your instructions, and you ignored them. I came here tonight expecting to do away with the Parisian couple, the mayor, Madeleine and the Englishwoman."

I was drawing breath when the mayor turned to me with his finger over his lips.

"And now I find the Dupont twins, the Dupond twins and the

meddlesome policeman, all of whom you assured me were dead."

"No, we never said that," piped up the tall, severe-looking fake police officer. "We just said we'd got rid of them."

"You deliberately disobeyed me?"

"No, not deliberately," said the distinguished middle-aged fake undertaker and cheesemonger. "We had every intention of obeying you, but when it came down to it, we found we're just no good at killing."

"You can start getting good at it right now," said Maman. "There's enough here for you to practise on. Who are all these other people at the back, anyway?" The Dupondts stepped aside to reveal the fathers and she let out another screech. "No! Jean-Visage! Jean-Ferme! Jean-Courage! Jean-Swissure! You should all be burning in hell by now!"

The fathers shrank into a protective huddle.

"Her temper's not improved over the years," one of them muttered.

Maman turned on her sons. "Have you been in touch with your useless, good-for-nothing fathers all this time? Men who haven't even had the decency to be torn to death by wild animals! Ungrateful wretches that you are, you'll break your mother's heart!"

They rushed to reassure her.

"We had no idea," said the muscular, moustachioed fake teacher.

"We found them by accident," said the distinguished, middle-aged fake undertaker and cheesemonger.

"We meant to tell you, but we've been so busy trying to set up the business, we never found the right time," said the tall, severe-looking fake police officer.

"It's all the mayor's doing," said the chubby, young fake judge, and the mayor fell to his knees, pleading for mercy.

But Maman wasn't concerned with him right now – her immediate target was her exes.

"So much for missing, presumed dead," she snorted. "Let there be no more presumption about it. This time, no more mistakes and no more delays. Open fire!"

"I can't kill my father!" said the fake judge.

"Then don't, you fool," said Maman. "Kill your brother's father."

The fake judge took aim.

"Don't kill my father!" protested the fake teacher.

"Useless boys! Work your way up to it. Kill the others first."

"I can't kill Madeleine," said the fake police officer.

They all sighed. "Ah, Madeleine…"

"That's my wife you're sighing about!" shouted Sylvain. "Are you looking for a fat lip?"

They all took a step backwards and shook their heads.

"Morons! Imbeciles! Get on with it," snapped Maman.

Debussy was supposed to live until 1918, and Mary Garden until 1967. What if Maman's boys killed them? It could create a disastrous paradox, altering the course of history, with all sorts of terrible consequences. Morningside Library might never open in 1905, and then I would have to work in another branch, which wouldn't be so convenient.

And while Debussy and Mary Garden might survive, there was no saying the rest of us would. It struck me that it would be very useful if a great grey wolf leaped forward right now, snarling, and scattered our attackers. Even if they shot him, he seemed in such good form after the blood transfusions that I was sure he would recover quickly. But Maman hadn't mentioned the English milord in her headcount. He was nowhere to be seen, nor was there any sign of a wolf or a bat. Dracula had scarpered. This was poor behaviour after all we had done for him.

In his absence, I would have been delighted to see a mob armed with torches and pitchforks descending on Maman and her gang. But the chalets were all in darkness. The villagers had already decided which was the winning side.

"Go on," urged Maman. "Shoot them."

The quartet took aim.

There was one last chance.

I nudged Debussy. "Achille," I whispered, "would you describe yourself as continuing the romantic tradition?"

Despite the seriousness of our situation, he gave a low guffaw. "Scarcely," he whispered back. "I like to think I'm at the cutting edge of the new, not like Fauré and Saint-Saëns. But I know some people class me as a romantic composer, and I put up with it – as long as they don't call me Impressionist."

Under other circumstances, I would have found this really interesting, and got him to say more. But with rifles trained on us, it really wasn't the time to discuss musical styles and categories.

"Right now, I would really like you to be romantic…" I whispered, with a tiny nod in the direction of the *femme fatale* giving the orders.

Credit to him, he was quick on the uptake. "What's her name?"

"Maman."

He stepped forward.

"Shoot him!" Maman ordered.

Since he was neither a father nor Madeleine, all four rifles pointed in his direction.

"Maman," breathed Debussy. I had never heard anything so oedipal in my life.

The effect was instantaneous.

"Don't shoot him!" Maman shrieked.

Debussy approached her as though drawn by magnetism, and when he reached her, she melted into his arms.

"My name is Achille," he murmured. "What do you call yourself?"

"Bérénice-Églantine," she answered. That surprised me. I didn't have her down as a Bérénice-Églantine. Anne-Marie, tops.

"Maman," called the fake undertaker and cheesemonger, "do you want us to shoot the others now?"

Debussy gave Maman a playful tap on the nose. "Of course you don't, my adorable little Bérénice-Églantine. The accompaniment to our love must be beautiful music, not gunfire."

"Oh, Achille," she said, and the next thing, they were snogging.

It was totally embarrassing, right in front of her sons and her exes. And then Maman clutched Debussy's hand and began to lead him away. I was about to try to signal to him to extricate himself when he turned and gave me a wink that definitely meant: "I've pulled."

As we watched them go, the fake policeman said, "She didn't say no."

For a moment, I thought he was talking about Maman's reaction to Debussy. Then I realised he was referring to his brother's question about whether we should be shot.

"She didn't say yes," I said quickly. "If you shoot us, and she didn't want you to, she'll be very cross. But if you don't shoot us, and she wanted you to, you can always shoot us later."

The brothers looked questioningly at one another and then nodded slowly.

"She's right," said the fake judge.

They lowered their rifles, and at that instant, Sylvain and the Dupondts rushed them, wrenched the rifles away from them, and began pinioning their arms with neckerchiefs and belts.

"I didn't bring you up to go around shooting people!" roared a father.

"You ran away. You didn't bring me up at all," said the son querulously, and got a clip round the ear.

"Officer," said the real judge, "arrest these men on suspicion of smuggling, kidnap, assault and attempted murder and bring them to court."

Sylvain saluted. "Immediately, Judge."

It was good to see things working as they should.

Mary Garden went over to the mayor and tugged his sleeve. "Was it you that booked me? It's nae my fault I didn't get to sing. You still have to pay me."

The mayor looked at me helplessly. "What's she saying?"

"She wants her money," I said.

"Tell her agent to invoice me," said the mayor.

Mary Garden, who understood French perfectly well even if nobody understood her, raised an eyebrow. "That'll be right," she said.

"Citizens!" called Sylvain as he and the Dupondts escorted the sons away. "You're needed in the courtroom as witnesses."

The mayor set off with a jaunty smile, clearly thinking that he had avoided paying the performance fee. He would learn about Aberdonians soon enough.

As Mary Garden and I followed on, I asked her, "What about Mr Debussy's fee?"

"What about it?" she asked, and I saw she had perfected the Gallic shrug. "I'm nae his Maman."

The gloom of dawn was breaking over the distant mountains and as we walked through the village to the court, window shutters were pulled open and villagers watched us curiously.

Judge Dupond with a D was already robed and seated behind a long wooden table when Mary Garden and I reached the courtroom, pen, ink and papers in front of him.

The sons were standing in a forlorn little group, flanked by Sylvain. The other Dupondts, the fathers, Madeleine and the mayor had settled themselves on the public benches. Mary Garden and I were just joining them when there was a sudden excited cry from the doorway, "Papa!"

Cart Woman's daughter raced across the courtroom and hurled herself into the judge's arms.

Cart Woman came into the court, followed by hordes of inquisitive villagers, some of whom managed to get seats while the rest were obliged to stand. She nodded to Judge Dupond.

"Husband. Good morning."

He nodded back. "Wife."

"I'm glad to see you alive," she said. "Are you well?"

"Wife, you can see I'm working. I have no time to chat."

She subsided, but she was smiling.

"Papa." Cart Woman's daughter tugged at her father's judicial robes and clambered on to his knee.

"Daughter," he said sternly, "I'm working."

In answer, she wound her arms round his neck. He put up his hand to disengage her, provoking disapproving muttering from the public benches.

"Leave her be. She's not doing any harm," called a villager.

"That little girl has missed you every second of every day," called another.

Cart Woman's daughter looked up at her father. "But I just got on with things," she assured him.

"Good girl," he said, kissing the top of her head.

"Prisoners in the dock, do you have any objection if she stays?" he asked the brothers, who, like everyone else, were surreptitiously wiping away tears at the sight of the touching reunion.

"Absolutely not," said the fake judge.

"It would be a crime to send her away," said the fake teacher.

"And there's far too much crime in this village already," said the fake undertaker and cheesemonger.

"Don't I know it," said Judge Dupond. "Officer, your report."

"Judge." Sylvain saluted and took his place in the witness box. "I recently became aware of unusual activity around the town hall at night, and decided to investigate. For two nights, I kept watch, but I saw nothing untoward."

"That's because we saw you," explained the fake undertaker and cheesemonger, "and we kept away."

"Shut up, you fool!" snapped the fake schoolmaster. "You'll incriminate the lot of us."

Judge Dupond handed the gavel to his daughter, who whacked it down on the bench with enthusiasm.

"Silence in court," he ordered. "Except for the witness. Continue, officer."

"The next day, I found a note had been slipped under the door of the police station, which I construed as a threat, warning me off."

"What did the note say?" asked the judge.

"It said 'Remember you must die.'"

Madeleine jumped up. "You never told me that! You promised

we would never have secrets from one another, and now I find you've been concealing death threats from me!"

"Silence in court!" repeated the judge. "Sit down and be quiet, madame!"

"How dare you talk to my wife like that?" thundered Sylvain. "And may I point out that this is a private conversation?" He turned limpid eyes on Madeleine. "Beloved, I said no secrets apart from police business. The death threat was sent to me in my capacity as a police officer."

"Forgive me, beloved," whispered Madeleine.

"Love means never having to be forgiven," Sylvain assured her.

The judge cleared his throat. "Did you have any idea who sent the note?"

"None. I presumed it was intended to warn me off my investigation. But I know my duty. For a third night, I conducted surveillance of the town hall. I saw movement near the back of the building. As I went to investigate, I was set upon by a number of assailants, and a hessian bag was pulled over my head."

I shuddered in reminiscence.

"I heard a man's voice say, 'I'm disappointed. We sent you a note. I thought you could read.'"

"Did you recognise the voice?" asked the judge.

"I did," said Sylvain.

"Is the individual present?"

"He is," said Sylvain.

"Point him out, if you please."

Sylvain pointed straight at the fake teacher. Madeleine sprang up again and pushed past us, her hands already shaping into claws.

"You dared to threaten my Sylvain?" she shouted at the fake teacher, who was trying to hide behind his half-brothers. She grabbed him by the scruff of the neck.

"I didn't write the note," he protested, his voice high with panic. "It was him!" He indicated the fake undertaker and cheesemonger.

Madeleine grabbed him by the scruff of the neck as well. "You," she said, shaking the fake undertaker and cheesemonger like a rat, "threatened my Sylvain. And you," she said, shaking the fake teacher like another rat, "implied that my Sylvain was illiterate."

It looked very much as though she was about to bang their heads together.

"Get her off me!" squealed the fake undertaker and cheesemonger. "I'll admit everything!"

"So will I," echoed the fake teacher.

"Beloved," called Sylvain.

"Yes, beloved?" Madeleine replied instantly.

"I yearn for you beside me."

"And I for you beside me."

Mary Garden and I shared another eye roll.

Sylvain held out his arms and Madeleine released her two victims and ran to him. They snogged for a while, and everyone looked elsewhere in an embarrassed sort of way. I noticed that Sylvain now had his arm firmly round Madeleine's waist, ensuring that she couldn't rush off and attack anyone else. I was impressed.

"Get on with your admissions," Judge Dupond barked at the younger Jeans.

"Maman was always having a go at us for being useless," said the fake undertaker and cheesemonger.

"She always said we were just like our useless fathers," added the fake teacher.

"That's not fair!" shouted a father.

"Yes, it is. You were totally useless," called a villager to widespread approval. Even the judge nodded.

"So, when we discovered the mayor had an illicit still–" The villagers' mouths dropped open. "–we thought we could take over his business."

"The mayor has a business?" said a villager.

"He's our mayor – shouldn't it be our business?" said another.

"If the mayor has a business, it's definitely our business," said the third. "How long has it been going on, and how much has he made?"

The mayor stood up. "Judge and citizens, I'd just like to point out that my venture was not for personal gain, but for the benefit of our village. How do you think the town hall got built? The Jeans, on the other hand, merely wanted to line their own pockets."

"We may have wanted to, but we didn't manage it," grumbled the fake judge. "We haven't made a brass centime."

"It seemed so easy," complained the fake policeman. "The mayor had a great system, hiding the bottles of brandy in the consignments of cheese that were for export."

Cart Woman turned on the mayor. "I've been working for a smuggling ring? You know my husband's a judge?"

"Of course I do," said the mayor. "Why do you think I never told you?"

"You never told me either," said the other Dupond with a D, the cheesemonger. "I'm not at all happy about my cheese being involved in criminal activities."

"They didn't know," groaned the fake policeman, sinking to his knees. "They didn't know. We could have kept the same system." He began rocking backwards and forwards, keening.

"What the matter with him?" asked the judge.

The fake judge patted his brother's shoulder and addressed his real counterpart. "We thought your good lady and the cheese-monger were getting a cut of the profits. So, we decided to set up our own transport system. The only other vehicle we could think of was the hearse, so we thought we could pretend to be exporting coffins, and put the hooch in the cheese in the coffins."

"Why did you put the hooch in the cheese?" asked the judge. "Why didn't you just put the bottles straight in the coffins?"

The fake policeman smacked the back of the fake teacher's head. "You idiot! Why didn't you think of that? Then we wouldn't have had all the problems trying to make the cheese."

Cart Woman leaned over to me. "Their mother's right. They're completely useless," she whispered.

"And you're right as well – this proves the importance of education," I whispered back.

The magisterial cheesemonger stood up. "Judge, citizens, I

didn't know the full extent of the Jeans' evildoing, but I knew something was amiss. They kidnapped me and forced me to tell them how to make cheese, which I did. Apart from telling them that they needed rennet."

There was prolonged applause from the villagers until Judge Dupond banged his gavel. I didn't like to point out that even though they couldn't make the big truckles without rennet, they could still have made a nice cream cheese.

The mayor stood up. "And I refused to give them the recipe for the eau de vie even though they threatened to kill me."

There was a smattering of applause. The villagers obviously felt more strongly about their cheese than about hooch they hadn't been allowed to sample.

Judge Dupond fixed the Jeans with a judicial stare. "Perhaps you could explain the death threats and the kidnappings?"

They shuffled uneasily, apart from the fake policeman, who was still on his knees.

"We knew Officer Sylvain was on to us," said the fake teacher, with a nervous glance at Madeleine. Sylvain's arm tightened round her waist. "He would obviously approach you as examining magistrate to report his suspicions. We needed to take over the cheese business and the undertaking business, and we needed the school-children as our workforce, so we had to get rid of all five of you."

"Maman wanted us to kill you," the fake judge piped up. "But we weren't very keen on that. Jean here faints at the sight of blood."

"Men," whispered Mary Garden in disgust. I was particularly disgusted to think that they had sent small children to do their bloody crushing.

"We tried to scare you away instead," said the fake undertaker and cheesemonger. "We sent you the notes saying 'Remember you must die'. When none of you went away, we had to kidnap you and hide you, so that Maman would think you were dead. We organised funerals, and used the coffins to store the cheese and hooch the mayor was about to export."

"We threatened the mayor with Maman," added the fake teacher. "We said if he didn't appoint us to the vacant posts, we'd tell Maman he was hiding our fathers, and then she'd kill him."

The courtroom door opened and a slight figure dressed in a double-breasted black frock coat slipped in with a murmur of apology. He joined the crowds who were standing, and when he caught my glance, he mouthed, "I had to go home to let Ermintrude out."

An obvious fib to cover his embarrassment: he was up to his usual trick of avoiding conflict. But I gave him a forgiving smile.

Judge Dupond was speaking: "In my role as examining magistrate, I can verify the accuracy of what you are saying, notably through my own direct experience. I find you guilty of larceny, kidnap, assault, attempted murder and gross incompetence."

I waved my hand to attract the judge's attention.

"Yes?" he barked, peering at me over his spectacles. "What is it?"

"May I approach the bench?" I asked.

"I can see no reason why not, unless your purpose is vandalism, or if the bench has been freshly painted," he said. "But I am currently concerned with conducting a criminal trial rather than answering questions from the general public."

"No, I mean may I speak to you in private," I said.

He peered at me. "Do you have courtroom experience?"

There had been some very flattering reviews for my role as Atticus Finch in the school's dramatisation of *To Kill a Mocking Bird*. I nodded.

He beckoned me forward.

"There are two additional matters to take into account," I told him in an undertone. "First, they stole Count Dracula's coffin and destroyed his bedding."

The judge's brow puckered. "Who's Count Dracula?"

I pointed him out among the crowd.

The judge banged his gavel. "Prisoners in the dock, why did you steal the English milord's coffin and destroy his bedding?"

It was the fake teacher who was nominated to reply. "The workmen who built the milord's castle told everyone at the time about his coffin with wheels. We thought coffins with wheels would be useful for our business, so we took it to copy." His voice tailed away. "But it didn't really work."

"Surprise," said Dupond the cheesemonger. "So, none of you managed to make any cheese, any hooch or any coffins. You really are useless."

"And the bedding?" demanded Dupond the judge.

The brothers exchanged puzzled looks.

"We don't know anything about that," said the fake judge. "We didn't see any bedding."

"Earth," called Dracula. "Did you see any earth?"

"Yes, the coffin was full of it," said the fake teacher. "We tipped it all out."

"That was my bedding," said Dracula, with a catch in his voice.

Judge Dupond made a note.

"And another thing," I said to him quietly, "while you were incarcerated, the fake schoolmaster, and probably his brothers, forced the schoolchildren into an extremely dangerous situation."

The judge looked down at his daughter. "Is this true?"

"It wasn't really dangerous, just hard work," she said.

"Your daughter's being very brave," I said. "She and her little friends were sent out in the forest to crush wild boar."

His daughter giggled. "You say it funny. You make it sound like we were crushing wild boar."

"That's exactly what I'm saying. You were sent out to crush wild boar."

"No, we weren't."

"Yes, you were."

She was laughing now. "The thought of us going into the forest to crush wild boar!"

I could understand her making light of it in order not to upset her father, but it was important that the judge understood the brothers' full culpability.

"I saw your hands," I reminded her. "They were covered in blood. I saw the buckets of blood in the morgue."

The judge looked down at his daughter in horror. She grinned at him.

"It's all right, Papa, we weren't crushing wild boar, we were crushing *wild boar*."

His face cleared. "Ah. Of course. I certainly wouldn't want you anywhere near wild boar. But that's still shocking. You should have been in the classroom, learning, not wasting time in the forest crushing wild boar."

"Hang on a minute," I said. "You accept that they were crushing wild boar?"

He pulled a sheet of paper towards him, took the stopper out of the glass ink bottle, and wrote a couple of words with his dip pen. Then he gave passed the paper to me.

The first word I read was *sangliers*. Wild boar.

The second word was *sangs-liés*. Literally blood links, but I had no idea what it meant, and said so.

"It's the name of our special forest plant," said the judge's daughter.

I remembered the tiny flowers, blood-red, that I had found blossoming throughout the forest.

"Our teacher explained all about them," she went on. "Not the teacher who made us crush the plants; our proper teacher. They're carnivorous, which means they live on insects that are attracted to them, and they attract them by being bright red, and having sugary stuff on their leaves."

It all made sense now. The cute wee flowers were a relative of the sundew plant, which exists on every continent except Antarctica. The children were gathering blood-red nectar for the cheese and brandy production. And Dracula was eating the insect-rich flowers as a source of protein. He really was a vegetarian.

"It seems to me," said Judge Dupond, "that there is an individual who is missing from the dock. Officer, arrest Maman."

Sylvain went off to find this latest culprit, devotedly followed by Madeleine. While we were waiting, there was time for Mary Garden to entertain the gathering with the "Depuis le Jour" aria from Charpentier's opera *Louise*, followed by "The Boddamers Hanged the Monkey-O".

Sylvain returned gripping Maman by the arm, followed by Madeleine and Debussy. They stood before the bench looking for all the world like the bride and groom at a shotgun wedding, flanked by the best man and chief bridesmaid.

"Prisoner in the dock," said Judge Dupond, "We have heard evidence that you are guilty of incitement to murder."

"Yes, but it didn't work, did it?" rasped Maman. "They're useless, these boys, just like their useless fathers."

It wasn't the best defence I'd ever heard, even though the villagers were all nodding agreement.

"What was your purpose?" the judge demanded.

"My purpose? I'll tell you my purpose. First of all, to get those useless boys out from under my feet and into proper jobs. Then, once they'd killed the mayor, to get myself elected in his place and say goodbye to that smoke-filled shack for good."

There was a second's silence, and then the place erupted.

"A woman mayor?"

"A woman? Mayor?"

"How could a woman be mayor?"

"There isn't even a word for a woman mayor."

"There probably is. What about mayoress?"

"That just sounds ridiculous."

"Why shouldn't I be mayor?" shouted Maman. "You think I enjoy spending my life wiping beer spills off tables? I've got a brain, even if my idiot sons and husbands don't."

I couldn't begin to applaud her methods, but I admired her goals.

Judge Dupond put his elbows on the bench and wearily massaged his forehead, his daughter clinging to him to avoid falling off his lap.

"The accused are, by their own admission, guilty," he said. "I shall now consider the disposal."

He continued the massaging.

Beside him, I coughed discreetly. "If I might make some suggestions, judge?"

He turned hopeful eyes on me. "Continue."

I lowered my voice. "There's no point in jailing them. That would be a drain on the public purse, which doesn't have any money in it. And there's only enough room in the cell for Maman."

"And the alternative?"

In a whisper, I outlined my plan. He started taking notes with his dip pen, then put it down. "Just tell them yourself," he said.

"Gentlemen," I said to the Jeans. Courtesy costs nothing. "Judge Dupond hereby sentences you to work as artisanal technicians, your rate of pay to be determined by productivity."

"A proper job?" said the fake policeman in wonder.

"With pay?" said the fake judge.

I nodded. "You will be under the supervision of the operative team." I gestured towards the fathers. "And ultimate responsibility will lie with the chief executive officers." I indicated the mayor and the magisterial cheesemonger. "Cheese and brandy production is to increase with immediate effect."

The mayor looked uneasy. "You know what I'm doing is illegal?"

"Not any more," I said. "You're going to have a properly licensed business. But don't worry about that side of it. It will all be sorted out by Maman when she reaches Paris."

"I'm being sent to the Bastille?" asked Maman, sounding quite proud.

"You're going to Paris as head of the Sans-Soleil syndicate of initiative, in recognition of your having more initiative than your husbands and sons put together," I said. "You will promote Sans-Soleil as a tourist destination, along with its unique local produce, cheese with the brand name *Cramoisi Crémeux* and brandy called *Eau de Vie en Rose*."

The mayor and the magisterial cheesemonger shook hands.

"I don't know how to get to Paris," said Maman, looking at Cart Woman.

"I don't know how to get to Paris either," said Cart Woman.

"Ah, but I do, my sweet little Bérénice-Églantine," said Debussy. "We will travel to Paris together."

Before Mary Garden could say she would be joining them, I changed the subject.

"Monsieur Dupont," I said to the Botticelli schoolmaster, "might your pupils be available to do some sums?"

"It's Sunday," he said. "There are no lessons today."

There was a small wail from the judicial bench. "Please, monsieur! Please, madame! We like doing sums."

The schoolmaster gave Cart Woman's daughter an approving nod. "Go and get your schoolfellows."

The pupils were soon assembled with their slates, squeaking out trigonometry calculations. The wee scone was finished first, and explained it to his slower classmates. Meanwhile, I had sent the villagers to the town hall to pick up the pieces of shattered mirror and bring them to the main square, instructing them to wear gloves to avoid injury

When they returned, I explained that the children had been calculating where to place mirrors on the mountainsides in order to reflect the sunlight into the village.

"It will do wonders for the grass," I said. "And you'll be able to grow all sorts of things yourselves. No need to get produce from other villages."

"Oh, great," grumbled Cart Woman. "Destroy my business some more, why don't you?"

"You're going to be run off your cart wheels with cheese and brandy," I assured her.

The pupils laid down their slates, gloved themselves and picked up pieces of mirror. The mountains loomed all around, craggy and oppressive.

"But how are the kids going to get up there?" objected Cart Woman. "It's too high and too far."

It was true, I hadn't quite worked out all the logistics – but right away a solution presented itself. Dracula touched my arm.

"Perhaps you would allow me to transport them?" he murmured.

I had forgotten Bram Stoker's terrifying description of Dracula crawling head-first down the outside of his castle wall like a lizard. He would be great at negotiating precipitous mountainsides.

But a moment later, I realised I couldn't possibly let him do it.

"It's a very kind offer, but no," I said. "Think of your photoallergic eruption. You'd be exposed to direct sunlight. It's too dangerous. Also, when you're doing your lizard impersonation, the children might fall off."

His expression was pained. "I do not do lizard impersonations, contrary to the misinformation in that … that book. I am suggesting transporting them like this."

Before my eyes, he turned into a massive shaggy-haired wolf. The children were delighted and rushed up to pat him. I settled the wee gloved scone on the wolf's back, complete with a chunk of broken mirror, some nails and twine, and the wolf sped off.

Quicker than I could have imagined, we had a row of children across the mountainside. The wee scone, simply a speck in the distance, turned his piece of mirror until the angle of incidence, at which the sunlight hit it, sent the light bouncing across to Cart Woman's daughter, who had the second piece of mirror. The row of children continued building up the angles of reflection until the village of Sans-Soleil was flooded with sunshine.

The villagers stood open-mouthed, basking.

"Is this what it's like in other places?" asked one.

"Oh yes," said Cart Woman airily. "I've seen sunshine lots of times when I've been out with the cart. It's nice."

There was enthusiastic agreement.

Madeleine, still clinging to Sylvain, murmured, "To have my beloved *and* sunshine – I ask for nothing more in life."

I didn't need to look at Mary Garden to know she was rolling her eyes, as was I.

The great grey wolf, which had returned to wait in the village square while the children organised themselves, transformed itself back into Dracula.

"The mirrors will need readjusting from time to time," he said. "But the children are more than capable of calculating how and when. Let me know when you need me."

"Milord," said the mayor, "in recognition of your service to our community, I bestow on you the freedom of Sans-Soleil."

The villagers broke into applause.

"That's very kind," said Dracula diffidently, "but I wonder if perhaps I could have a little cheese instead?"

"How are you going to cope with all this sunshine?" I asked.

"I have my lovely windowless room," he said. "And if I go outside, I'll take my bed with me and keep the lid closed."

Faintly, from a long way away, came the sound of singing. The sweet, high trilling of children. As they carried out their trigono-metrical exercise, they sang a new verse for their song, of their own invention.

> We like sunshine, we like sunshine,
> We like cheese, we like cheese,
> We like doing sums and we like singing songs with
> Harmonies, harmonies.

A bit of tweaking, and Maman could have a promotional jingle for her Sans-Soleil marketing strategy.

The crowd, led by the mayor and the magisterial cheesemonger, were heading out of the village square. Dracula and I followed them to the kirkyard where we found Sylvain directing an exhu-mation of the other coffins. The smell of decay was horrific, but I now recognised it as cheese rather than anything more sinister.

"Come with me," I said to Dracula, and led him over to a mound of earth. I licked my finger, pressed it on to the earth, and licked it again.

"I thought so," I said in triumph. "Scottish mineral gleys. This is where those villains chucked out your bedding."

Dracula picked up a handful of soil and held it against his face. "Oh, it's so soft," he murmured. "I've missed it so much. I'll have it transported back to the castle, and at last I can get a good night's sleep."

They weren't Scottish mineral gleys at all, but Dracula, happily transforming himself into a wolf to go and collect the children, didn't know that, and the placebo effect can be powerful.

There was a touch on my arm. Mary Garden. She unrolled some papers she had been clutching, and I saw they were my posters.

"These caught my eye as we were on our way to the court," she said with a slight blush. She was definitely well on the way to becoming a real star, noticing anything that had her name on it.

Except it wasn't her name.

"I'm terribly sorry," I said. "I put your name in French because they're not terribly cosmopolitan here."

"I can see that," she said. "Don't worry, all publicity is good publicity."

It was obvious that she came from an age before social media.

"And I'm sorry the posters don't mention Mr Debussy. I had no idea he would be playing the piano."

"Dinna bother about him. He gets enough publicity. These posters are very bonnie – is it all right if I keep them?"

"I'd be honoured," I said.

"I've got a wee pal in Paris, Henry, who's keen on making posters. He'd like to see them."

I almost didn't dare ask the question. "Not Henri Toulouse-Lautrec?"

"That's him – do you know him?"

"No. No, I don't. But I'm sure he wouldn't be interested at all. I wouldn't bother showing him them."

"Dinna be daft, he loves a poster."

I was cringing with embarrassment. I had brazenly nicked his iconic images of Loïe Fuller, La Goulue and Jane Avril. "If he sees them, can you pass on a message? Tell him they're not plagiarism, they're an *hommage*. Can you remember that? It's important to make sure he knows that."

She picked up on my anxiety. "Of course. They're nae plagiarism, they're an *hommage*."

I hoped he wouldn't be too cross. Perhaps there was a way to distract his attention from my posters. I clutched Mary Garden's arm.

"Can you tell him something else? Can you tell him the National Galleries of Scotland are going to put on a big exhibition of his work?" No need to mention it would be over a hundred years from now.

"I'll tell him that too. He'll be richt pleased. He's a richt good laugh and a great cook. He makes a lovely pudding he calls chocolate mayonnaise."

He might be a good cook, but he was rubbish at marketing. "Nobody's going to want to eat something called chocolate mayonnaise," I said. "It sounds totally disgusting. He needs a better name for it than that."

Mary Garden looked thoughtful. "Escoffier invented a pudding for Nellie Melba. Peach Melba, he called it. I could get Henry to call his invention Chocolate Garden. You should see how he makes it, melted chocolate and sugar and butter and egg yolks, and then he puts beaten egg whites in it. You've never eaten anything so tasty. Chocolate Garden would be the perfect name for it."

With sudden clarity, I understood what Toulouse-Lautrec had invented. Mary Garden couldn't be allowed to persuade him to name his confection after her, or it would change the course of history – the history of desserts, at least.

"No," I said. "You don't want it to be called Chocolate Garden."

"Aye, I do," she said.

"No, you don't. You've got your reputation to think of. It would diminish the brand. Poor old Nellie, whenever anyone mentions her, they don't think wonderful lyric soprano, they think Escoffier's puddings."

"They do?" she asked uncertainly.

"Absolutely," I said. "The minute you said Nellie Melba, the first thing I thought of was peaches and ice cream and raspberry sauce."

"I dinna want that," she said. "But you said chocolate mayonnaise sounded disgusting and he needed a better name for it."

"*Mousse au chocolat*," I said. "Tell him to call it that. If he does, I guarantee it will be a success."

"I'll tell him," she agreed.

Four coffins were being opened, to reveal wheels of cheese. Excitedly, the villagers brought out their small change and surrounded the mayor and cheesemonger. Sylvain kept order while Madeleine watched with quiet pride.

I motioned for her to join us.

"When Mary Garden and Debussy get back to Paris, they can send you music to replace the pages you turned into thyme and marjoram," I said.

"*Bien sûr*," said Mary Garden.

Madeleine looked bewildered. "What's she saying?" she asked.

"She's saying she'll be delighted. And I'm sure it won't be long before you're invited to Paris on a concert tour."

Mary Garden nodded enthusiastically.

"Although," I added, "it's probably safer if you avoid Debussy's Pleyel."

"Certainly safer for Debussy when my Sylvain's around," Madeleine said drily. "Excuse me a moment." She went off to join the crowd.

"Debussy's going to dump Maman when he gets to Paris, isn't he?" I asked Mary Garden.

"Aye, but she'll have nae problem finding someone else. There's Fauré, or Maurice Ravel, or if she wants someone closer to her own age, there's Saint-Saëns. Michty, what's wrong with you?"

The abdominal pain was stronger than I remembered.

"I'm fine," I lied, managing to straighten up as Madeleine approached. She was carrying a wheel of cheese.

"Is that for Dracula?" I asked.

"No, the mayor and the cheesemonger have agreed to provide him with cheese for life," said Madeleine.

If vampires lived for ever, it was going to be a costlier deal than they expected.

"This is for you, Madame Maque-Monet-Gueule," Madeleine said, holding out the cheese. "To thank you for saving my Sylvain. And for being my friend. I'm afraid it's only cheese – all the ones containing brandy were snapped up right away."

"That's perfect," I said. "And every time I taste this, Madeleine, it will remind me of you."

I took off my head torch and gave it to her. "You'll need this fascinator for your trips to Paris. They'll be so impressed that you have your own electric light."

Another spasm gripped me.

"So sorry," I gasped. "Got to go."

Cart Woman overheard. Her eyes lit up. "Will I get the cart ready? Are you going all the way to Paris?"

"Much further than that," I managed to say, "but I'm afraid I'm making other arrangements."

I saw her look of disappointment and then she, Madeleine, Mary Garden and the kirkyard disappeared. The temperature plummeted and I felt myself whirling through the decades of the twentieth century, into the twenty-first … and I was back in the library meeting room, clutching the cheese. There before me was the yellow-covered Polygon edition of *The Prime of Miss Jean Brodie*. I hoped the success of my mission had redeemed me in Miss Blaine's eyes.

I unlocked the cupboard on the far wall and shoved the volume in, alongside all the other copies of That Book, hidden well away from the reading public.

I took the cheese to the kitchen, and left it on the counter with a couple of Post-its on it, one saying, "Shona's half" and the other, "Help yourself". I hoped nobody would complain about the smell.

I was about to head downstairs when I caught sight of myself in a mirror. I was wearing my normal work clothes, but my face was still covered in watercolours. Given that librarians are expected to look smart, clean and professional, there could be a question-mark over my stage make-up. I quickly scrubbed it off before anyone saw me.

Coming back down to the main library hall, I passed the CD section. One in particular caught my eye. I went over and picked it up. "*Debussy Preludes*," I read. "Track 8: The Girl with the Flaxen Hair." Written in 1910; inspired, according to the notes, by one of Leconte de Lisle's *Chansons écossaises*. I knew where the true inspiration had come from.

As I passed the fiction section, I scanned the S shelves in case That Book had sneaked in, but all was well. There was Solzhenitsyn, Stevenson ... and along to the right I spotted that other name – Stoker. I surreptitiously removed the volume from the shelf. Another farrago of misinformation and innuendo that many an unwary reader would take as fact.

Far from being turned into the undead by Dracula, I owed him my life. He had saved me from being buried and/or burned alive.

"This is for you, Draculek," I murmured as I hurried back upstairs with it to the cupboard. It was a sizeable hardback and it took me a while to ease it onto the shelf. I was very careful not to damage it or the books on either side of it. I could never harm a book, not even Those Books – it's a librarian thing.

And then I thought: now I've got two books to look out for. I'm going to need a bigger cupboard.

Acknowledgements

A huge thank-you to the kind readers and reviewers who wanted to know What Shona Did Next;

to Sara Hunt and all at Saraband, especially Ali Moore for her meticulous editing, and proofreaders Hamzah Hussain and Grace O'Duffy;

Maggie Topkis and all at Felony & Mayhem;

matchmaker Mary Thomson;

alpha plus reader Iain Matheson;

the supportive and encouraging writing coven: Margaret Ries, Elaine Thomson and Michelle Wards;

Gallic expert Bill Kirton, who embodies the University of Aberdeen's motto, *Initium sapientiae timor domini*, "Fear of one's tutor is the beginning of wisdom";

Mary Johnston (née Mackie), Doric expert and speaker, an gweed freen;

mathemagician Duncan Dicks;

technical advisers Simon Brown, Norma-Ann Coleman, Sue Glover and Lesley Rowe;

Dame Muriel Spark and Bram Stoker;

and Alistair, an affa fine loon.

SHONA McMONAGLE, a Morningside librarian and proud former prefect at the Marcia Blaine School for Girls, is thrilled when entrusted by Marcia Blaine herself to undertake an important mission. Shona isn't entirely clear on the details, but she soon finds herself in 19th-century Russia, and her task appears to be pairing up the beautiful, shy, orphaned heiress Lidia Ivanovna with Sasha, a gorgeous young man of unexplained origins.

But, despite all her accomplishments and good intentions, Shona might well have got the wrong end of the stick about this, her first special assignment for Miss Blaine. As the body count rises, will she discover in time just who the real villain is?

The Author

OLGA WOJTAS was born and brought up in Edinburgh where she attended James Gillespie's High School – the model for Marcia Blaine School for Girls, which appears in Muriel Spark's *The Prime of Miss Jean Brodie*. Like Dame Muriel herself, Olga was encouraged to write by an inspirational English teacher there – in Olga's case, Iona M. Cameron. Unlike her heroine, Olga has a deep respect for Dame Muriel's work and is a member of the Muriel Spark Society. A former Scriever of the Federation of Writers Scotland, Olga won a Scottish Book Trust New Writers Award and has had more than forty short stories published in magazines and anthologies.